Praise for #1 *New York Times* bestselling author

BARBARA FREETHY

The Way Back Home

"Tugs at the heartstrings . . . Freethy's skillful plotting and gift for creating sympathetic characters will ensure that few dry eyes will be left at the end of this story."

—*Publishers Weekly* (starred review)

"[A] touching romance. A spinoff of Freethy's popular 'Angel's Bay' quintet, this satisfying tale will please old fans and garner new ones; a perfect vacation read."

—*Library Journal*

"A heartwarming, passionate contemporary romance that will captivate you from the very beginning and not let go until the very last page."

—*Romance Junkies*

"A sensual and stunning romance."

—*Joyfully Reviewed*

Praise for the Angel's Bay novels

"Heart, community, and characters who will remain with you."
—*New York Times* bestselling author Debbie Macomber

"It is always fun to visit the little town on the bay."

—*RT Book Reviews*

Garden of Secrets

"The relationships among the inhabitants of Angel's Bay . . . are intriguing and make for fascinating, interesting stories. The touch of paranormal . . . is delightful, the romance heartwarming, and the secondary mystery is nicely done."

—*RT Book Reviews* (4 stars)

"A well-rounded and satisfying novel . . . Intriguing suspense, passionate romance, and countless unique characters."

—*Single Titles*

At Hidden Falls

"Freethy updates the lives of continuing characters, adds several memorable new ones, and dusts it all with magic and hope."

—*Library Journal*

"Truly a work of art . . . a very satisfying read."

—*Joyfully Reviewed*

In Shelter Cove

"A compelling story of intrigue, along with a romantic story of love, forgiveness, and faithfulness."

—*Fresh Fiction*

"A good solid romance and a spine-tingling mystery all in a tidy package."

—*A Romance Review*

Also by Barbara Freethy
and Pocket Books

BARBARA FREETHY

The Way Back Home

Pocket Books

New York   London   Toronto   Sydney   New Delhi

Pocket Books
A Division of Simon & Schuster, Inc.
1230 Avenue of the Americas
New York, NY 10020

This book is a work of fiction. Names, characters, places, and incidents either are products of the author's imagination or are used fictitiously. Any resemblance to actual events or locales or persons, living or dead, is entirely coincidental.

This Pocket Books paperback edition November 2021

POCKET and colophon are registered trademarks of Simon & Schuster, Inc.

For information about special discounts for bulk purchases, please contact Simon & Schuster Special Sales at 1-866-506-1949 or business@simonandschuster.com.

The Simon & Schuster Speakers Bureau can bring authors to your live event. For more information or to book an event, contact the Simon & Schuster Speakers Bureau at 1-866-248-3049 or visit our website at www.simonspeakers.com.

Manufactured in the United States of America

10 9 8 7 6 5 4 3 2 1

ISBN 978-1-9821-7907-6
ISBN 978-1-4516-3655-0 (ebook)

To Terry, Kristen, and Logan for their support and encouragement!

Acknowledgments

I would like to thank my writing friends who offered creative brainstorming, business support, and plenty of chocolate! To the ladies that lunch: Bella Andre, Anne Mallory, Carol Culver, Veronica Wolff, Jami Alden, Monica McCarty, Lynn Hanna, Kate Moore, Barbara McMahon, Candice Hern, Diana Dempsey, and Tracy Grant. And thanks also to Christie Ridgway, who always answered the phone when I needed to come up with a new plot twist!

The Way
Back Home

One

We need to buy rafts, hire guides, and update the reservation software, and I have no idea where we're getting the money to do any of that," Alicia Hayden told her father, frustration overwhelming her as she walked across the back deck of Hayden River Adventures. The one-story building, set on the banks of Northern California's Smoky River, was the launchpad for their world-class river-rafting adventures company. Next to the one-room office was the boatyard where they kept their rafting equipment. On the other side of the building, tucked behind the trees, was a dirt parking lot that was empty now. About a hundred yards away and up a grassy incline stood the family home.

In the spring and summer months, they rented rafts and launched day trips off the pier. For more adventurous whitewater experiences, they bused their guests ten miles north for the higher-class guided rapids tours. They'd been in business for more than sixty years, and three generations of Haydens had run the company. But now their business was sinking fast, and Alicia wasn't sure they could save it.

Her father, George Hayden, didn't reply. Leaning heavily on his cane, he'd fixed his gaze on the wide, winding river that ran through the Sierra Nevada mountains. The late-afternoon foggy mist that had given the river its name was a little thicker than usual. While the winter rains had finally tapered off, the late-March air was cold, and luminous clouds shadowed the sun.

As a brisk wind lifted the hair off the back of her neck, Alicia shivered and wrapped her arms around her waist, wishing she'd thrown a jacket over her knit shirt and worn jeans. She'd been hunkered down in the office all afternoon, trying to find a way out of the mess they'd gotten themselves into, but there was no clear path. Rafting season would officially open in two weeks, and they weren't even close to being ready. She needed her father to understand that, but he was living in a world of denial, believing that nothing had changed since the rafting accident six months before, since her brother's death three weeks before. But *everything* had changed. Their world had turned completely upside down in less than a year.

Sadness, anger, and fear ran through her, but she couldn't let her emotions take hold. This was the time for thinking, not feeling. She'd been trying to talk to her dad about the business since her brother's funeral three weeks earlier, and he'd always managed to evade her. But not now, not today.

"Dad," she prodded, stepping up to the railing next to him. "We need to talk about whether or not we can keep on going."

He slowly turned his head. In his early sixties, her father had aged considerably in the last year. But while there was weariness in the weathered lines of his square face and more white than gray in his rapidly thinning hair, he still had some fight in his eyes.

"We've never missed an opening day, and we won't start now, Alicia," he said.

She sighed. "We need more than just a 'can-do' attitude, Dad. We need money and manpower, and we don't have either."

"We'll get the money, and we'll find some guides. We have time."

"Very little."

"We'll figure it out. This is our family business, a business that will one day go to Justin. You don't want to jeopardize your son's future, do you?"

"His future is exactly what I'm worried about. I'm afraid our family business will take every last penny we have and still fail, and then where will we be? I need to make sure I can send Justin to college."

"He's nine years old, Alicia."

"Almost ten, and I should be saving now. I'm a single mother, so it's up to me."

"Being a single mother was your choice," he said with a frown.

She wasn't about to get into that old conversation. "We're getting off track."

"Bill already got us some rafts. We just have to pick them up tomorrow."

Bill ran the local hardware store and was one of her father's best friends, but he was also one of her father's enablers, continuing to tell him that he would be back on the river any day now, when the doctors were saying the opposite.

"Dad, we need to face reality." She drew in a deep breath, then plunged ahead with words that needed to be said. "People have to trust us to keep them safe, and they don't anymore.

They don't want us to reopen. They want us to shut our doors for good."

Her father's face paled. "Once we get back on the river, the trust will come back. We've had one accident in sixty years. It's a damn good record. And it wasn't our fault."

Fault was debatable, but she wasn't going to get into that. "Wild River Tours is breathing down our necks. They're a national company with a sophisticated Web site, and they want our rivers, our runs. How will we compete with corporate money?"

"We'll find a way. I'm not afraid of them. We know the river better than anyone, and we've always made our money on it. The river gives us life."

"And sometimes it takes it away," she reminded him.

It wasn't only her father who had been hurt last year. A local man, twenty-nine-year-old Brian Farr, had lost his life when one of their rafts flipped over, and she'd come close to drowning herself. Another chill ran through her at the memory of those terrifying moments.

"Let's go inside," she said abruptly. "It's getting cold."

"In a minute." He turned his gaze back to the water. "She tested us, that's all, wanted to know if we were worthy."

"We weren't."

"We will be next time." Her father raised his fist to the river. "I'll give you another run for your money. You can't take me down."

Her father often spoke of the river as if it were a woman. Her mother had complained on more than one occasion that George was more married to the river than he was to her. It was probably why she'd left when Alicia was twelve years old; Margaret Hayden just couldn't take coming in second.

Distracted by the sound of barking, Alicia turned her head as Justin, her nine-year-old son, came running up the steps of the back deck, followed by Sadie, their very excited golden retriever.

"Grandpa, look," he said. "I finished Uncle Rob's boat."

Her son held up a model boat that he'd been working on. Her brother had sent Justin the kit a few months earlier. It was a project they'd planned to do together when Rob got out of the Marines. But Rob had been killed in action on the other side of the world six days before he would have completed his service. Just six days, and then he would have been safe. She couldn't get the bitter taste of injustice out of her mouth.

They'd taken one hit after another in the past few months, and she couldn't quite get her feet under her. But she pretended she was coping, because that's what her family needed her to do.

"I did it all by myself," Justin added as he let his grandfather inspect the boat.

With his sandy brown hair, freckled cheeks, and blue eyes beaming with pride, Justin looked a lot like her twin brother. She and Rob had shared blue eyes but not much else. Her hair was golden blond, her skin tanned instead of freckled, and she'd never made it past five foot five, while her brother had topped the family at six foot three. Her heart ached as Rob's smiling face flashed through her mind. Whenever she thought of her brother, she thought of his big toothy grin, his goofy personality. He'd been the bright, shining light of their family, and now everything seemed darker.

"Good job," her father told Justin.

"Can I try her out, Mom?" He turned to her with a plea in his eyes.

"It's getting late. You have homework, and I have dinner to make," she said. "We'll do it tomorrow."

His face fell. "But Mom—"

"Why don't you let him try it out?" her father cut in. "Homework can wait."

It was difficult to face down the two of them, and she was reminded of many other times when her father had gotten Rob or Justin to side against her. It hadn't been easy being the only female in a house full of males. Her dad was a guy's guy, and Rob had been the same. While she'd grown up more tomboy than girlie girl, she was still a woman. Right now, she was a really annoyed, tired, frustrated, overwhelmed woman with a million things on her to-do list.

So why did she hear herself saying "Fine" when what she really wanted to say was no?

Justin led the charge to the edge of the riverbank, her father following far more slowly. As Justin knelt down to launch his boat, she heard the phone ring in the office.

"Go get it," her father said. "I'll watch Justin."

She ran back into the office and grabbed the phone. It was Keith Andrews, the man she'd been seeing for the last few months. Keith and his ten-year-old son, David, had moved to town in September, just in time for the start of the school year. Keith was a history teacher and a soccer coach at the local high school, and David was in Justin's grade. The two boys had become fast friends, and in turn, she and Keith had discovered a connection, too.

Unfortunately, she hadn't been much of a girlfriend in the last few weeks.

"I finally tracked you down," Keith said. "I've been trying your cell phone all day."

"I forgot to charge it. Sorry."

"You do that a lot lately, Alicia."

She *did* do that a lot—maybe because there were very few people she actually wanted to talk to. And the people she wanted to talk to didn't call. "What's up?"

"I heard that it's your birthday on Sunday. Something you neglected to mention. I'd like to take you out to dinner."

Another reason she'd been lazy about recharging her phone. "I appreciate the thought, but I'm not up for celebrating."

"Justin wants you to have a party."

"I know, but the thought of celebrating my birthday without Rob is unthinkable. I'd like to skip the day entirely."

"I understand. Here's another thought. Why don't I take Justin off your hands? The boys have been asking for a sleepover. Sunday night seems perfect."

"Really? It is a school night."

"I'll get them to school, don't worry. I want to do something for you, Alicia. And I can do that."

It would be nice not to have to pretend to be happy in front of her son. "That does sound tempting. Why don't you and David come over for dinner tonight? We'll make plans for the weekend. The Spring Festival starts on Saturday, and I know Justin and David are interested in entering some of the contests." The sound of barking and yelling drew her attention away from the phone. "I've got to go. We'll talk later, okay?"

Hanging up the phone, she walked quickly out of the office, across the deck, and down the stairs. Her father was a few yards away, by an outcropping of rocks. Sadie was barking up a storm, and Justin—

Adrenaline raced through her body. Justin was stretched out on his stomach on a large boulder, trying to snag his runaway boat from the river current.

"Justin, get down!" she yelled, glaring at her father as she ran past him. "Why did you let him go up on the rocks? They're unstable and off-limits."

"He got up there before I could stop him."

She doubted her father had even tried. His favorite line was "Boys should be boys." "Get down, Justin," she commanded. "You know you're not supposed to be up there."

"We have to get the boat!" Justin yelled. "It's Uncle Rob's. We can't lose it!"

She saw the panic on his face and the fear that he would lose the last gift his uncle had given him.

"I'll get it," she said decisively. "You climb down from there right now. And do it carefully."

She kicked off her shoes, rolled up her jeans to her knees, and grabbed the longest stick she could find, then waded into the river. Her heart skipped a beat as the cold water hit her feet, the current swirling around her ankles. She drew in a quick, sharp breath, unexpected fear shocking her into stillness. She knew how to swim. She knew this river like the back of her hand. There was nothing to be afraid of—but she couldn't seem to move.

She could hear Justin yelling at her that the boat was getting away. Sadie barked even louder. Her father was shouting something, but nothing was clear beyond the pounding of her heart. She hadn't been in the river since that day six months earlier, that day she'd gone under again and again and again, struggling to find a foothold, something to grab on to—

A sudden splash next to her brought her head around. A man was wading into the river, heading straight toward Justin's boat. The water was up to his waist by the time he reached the boat. He grabbed it, half walking, half swimming his way back to shore. When he reached her, he grabbed her by the arm, and she was shocked again, this time by the strength of his grip.

Gazing into his dark eyes, her heart skipped another beat. His thick curly brown hair, rough-edged features, strong jaw, dark eyes, and five o'clock shadow were very familiar. *Gabe Ryder.*

She'd been expecting him to come ever since Rob's death. She'd rehearsed over and over the things she wanted to say to him, the questions she wanted to ask. Now that he was here, she couldn't speak.

"Let's go," he said, dragging her toward the shore.

Under his grip, she stumbled onto the bank. As soon as her feet hit solid ground, she yanked her arm away. "What are you doing?" she demanded.

"Saving you," he said.

"I didn't need saving. I was fine."

"You didn't look fine."

Justin came running over, her father and the dog not far behind.

"Is this yours?" Gabe asked, handing Justin the boat.

"You got it," Justin said with reverence. "Thank you."

"Good job," her father said approvingly. "Didn't think Alicia was going to make it out there in time."

"I was just about to go after it," she protested, hating that they'd seen her momentary hesitation. Her dad had always

9

been tough on her, treating her like a son instead of a daughter. Be tough, be strong, don't cry, he'd always told her. Today she hadn't been as strong as she'd needed to be, and it infuriated her. "Where the hell did you come from, anyway?" she demanded.

"Your house," Gabe said. "I rang the bell, but no one answered. I heard voices and the dog barking, so I came down here."

"I mean, why are you here now? The funeral was three weeks ago."

"I'm sorry I missed it," he said. "It was unavoidable."

"Alicia," her father interrupted, a quizzical look in his eyes. "Why don't you introduce us?"

"You've met him before," she snapped. "This is Gabe Ryder, Rob's best friend. The man who was supposed to be watching his back. The man who let Rob get killed."

Gabe paled under his dark tan, but he didn't deny her words. Instead, he turned to her father. "Mr. Hayden, I'm so sorry for your loss."

"I remember you now, of course," her father said with a contemplative nod. "You spent Christmas with us a few years ago. I'm sorry I didn't recognize you."

"Not a problem. It's good to see you again."

"Rob spoke very highly of you," George continued. "I think your name came up in just about every e-mail."

"Rob was a great guy, the best," Gabe said. Turning to Justin, he added, "I don't know if you remember me, Justin. You were a lot shorter when I saw you last."

Justin gave Gabe an uncertain look. "I kind of remember you. How come you let Uncle Rob die if you were his friend?"

10

An awkward silence followed his question. For a moment, Alicia regretted her impulsive comment, but she couldn't take it back. She didn't want to take it back. She did hold Gabe responsible. He'd promised to watch out for her brother.

"I'm sure it wasn't like that," her father cut in. "Come on up to the house, Gabe. We'll throw those wet clothes in the dryer and get you something dry to wear. You can stay for dinner. We'll catch up."

"I don't need clothes or a meal," Gabe said.

Her father waved off Gabe's protest. "Any friend of Rob's is a friend of ours." He gave Alicia a pointed look, then turned to Justin. "Come along, now, Justin. You can help me up the steps."

As her father and Justin started up the hill toward the house, Sadie following close behind, Alicia gave Gabe a long look. He returned her stare with one of his own, his eyes dark and unreadable. She'd never been able to tell what he was thinking, and today was no different.

"So why didn't you come to the funeral?" she finally asked.

"I had to take one of the other men in our unit home. He was injured in the same firefight that took Rob's life. He spent some time in the hospital, and I didn't want to leave him alone there."

"So that guy was injured, and Rob was killed, but you, you're fine." Anger filled her. She'd wanted to scream at someone about the injustice of her brother's death, and Gabe was the perfect target. "How did you escape?"

He swallowed hard. "I don't know, Alicia. Believe me, I wish Rob was here instead of me."

"I don't believe you," she said, shaking her head, tears

burning her eyes. "You promised me you'd watch out for him. You stood right up there, on our porch," she added, pointing toward the house, "and you told me you'd make sure he came home. Remember?"

"I remember everything about that day," he said, his jaw tight, pain in his eyes.

A shiver ran down her spine. Their last conversation had not been solely about Rob.

"And I don't need you to tell me that I failed Rob. I know that," he continued.

She felt a flash of guilt. It wasn't fair to blame Gabe, but she had no one else. The enemy that had taken Rob's life was nameless and faceless. The Marine Corps wouldn't tell her exactly what had happened, only that her brother had been a hero and she should be proud of his service. But that wasn't good enough.

"You need to tell me how Rob died," she said.

Gabe immediately shook his head. "I can't."

"Yes, you can. You have to."

"It's classified."

"I don't care. He's my brother, my twin brother. I should know the truth." Another wave of guilt hit her. "I should have known that he was in trouble. I always had feelings when Rob was in danger. We had that special twin connection, but I didn't sense anything that day. Why didn't I know?"

"We were on the other side of the world."

"That shouldn't have mattered."

He gave her a long look. "Rob wouldn't have wanted you to know what he was going through. Maybe he found a way to block the twin thing."

"You're not going to tell me anything, are you?"

He stared back at her with what looked like regret. "No."

"Then you should go. You've paid your respects. Now you can leave."

"I can't go—not yet. I made a promise to your brother."

"What are you talking about?"

"In the month before he died, Rob talked a lot about coming home and helping you and your father save your business. He was worried about all of you after your rafting accident. He was counting the days until he could get back here. He loved you all a great deal."

Tears blurred her eyes. "I know that. Rob always took duty seriously, even before he went into the Marines."

"He asked me to come in his place, to help you."

She stiffened. "I told you before, I don't need your help."

"Don't you?" His gaze settled on her face, a thoughtful expression in his eyes. "Something happened to you in the river just now. You froze."

"Don't be ridiculous."

"I know what fear looks like, Alicia."

"I'm not afraid of the river. I grew up on it."

"And last year, you almost drowned."

"I never told Rob that."

"Then someone else did. Maybe your father."

"I never told him exactly what happened, and he was too busy fighting for his own life to really understand what I'd gone through." She saw the sudden spark in his eyes that told her she'd revealed too much. "Anyway, I'm fine. My father is getting better, and we're moving on."

"You need help. I made Rob a promise, and I'm going to keep it."

"Consider your promise fulfilled; you saved Justin's boat. Now you can go home."

"I am home." Gabe pulled out a set of keys, very familiar keys.

Her stomach turned over. He had Rob's key ring. "No way," she said, shaking her head. "You are not moving into Rob's house."

"My house. He gave it to me."

She was truly shocked. The property next door had been in the family for generations. "I don't believe you. Rob's house was built by my great-grandfather. Rob wouldn't give it to you."

"I have a letter from him explaining everything."

"No. There's a mistake. If you think I'm letting you move into Rob's house, into his life, you are crazy."

"And if you think I'm going to walk away before I've done what I came to do, then you're the one who's crazy," he said, his gaze hard and unyielding.

"You're not wanted here, Gabe."

"That's not what you said the last time I was here."

She swallowed back a knot of emotion at the memory of that cold winter day, the Christmas tree still up in the living room, the mistletoe hanging over the door, the cozy fire where she and Gabe had kept each other warm. "That was three years ago, one week of madness, and you made it clear when you left that whatever we had was over." Unfortunately, it had taken her a long time to really believe that.

He gazed back at her for a long minute. "I know what I said, Alicia. But that's in the past. I'm here now, and I'm not leaving." He turned and started walking up the hill.

14

"So you're going to save me?" she called out after him.

"Yes," he said, pausing to give her a quick look.

"And who's going to save me from you?"

His chest rose with his swift intake of breath, and then he turned and walked away.

She hated his confident stride, his arrogant attitude, but she couldn't quite hate him even though she wanted to.

Turning her gaze to the river, she drew in long, deep breaths, but they did nothing to slow the rapid beating of her heart. She'd been drawn to Gabe from the first minute she'd seen him, attracted to his dark hair and darker eyes. Her brother had warned her that she should stay away, that Gabe came with far too many rough edges, that he could hurt a woman without even trying. But she'd sensed in Gabe a need to be softened, to be loved, not that he'd ever admitted that need, not that he'd ever let her get close enough to love him. He'd kept her at arm's length, telling her that she was Rob's sister and as far as he was concerned, that made her untouchable, except for one hot, reckless night—a night she'd never forgotten.

She shook off the memory. They were different people now. And she didn't need his help. Well, okay, that wasn't exactly true. Her gaze swept across the yard, noting the rafts in need of repair, the peeling paint on the building, the broken planks on the pier. They did need help, just not Gabe's. He didn't understand their business. It would have been different with Rob. Her brother had known everyone in town. People respected him, adored him. He would have been able to help them get back on their feet. But Gabe . . . What did he know how to do, except fight?

Gabe wiped his hands on a towel as he stared at himself in the bathroom mirror. George had handed him a pair of navy-blue sweats to wear while his jeans were drying and told him he'd have a drink waiting for him when he finished changing. He didn't know why Rob's father was being so welcoming; Alicia's anger was a lot easier to take.

He understood her feelings, and she couldn't possibly blame him more than he blamed himself. Over and over in his mind, he'd relived the minutes of that horrific day. He could still feel the sweltering desert heat, the beads of sweat under his helmet; still hear the screeching of tires, the rocking blast; still see the sudden burst of flame and the shocked look in Rob's eyes as he sank to the ground. Chaos and panic had followed, and so much blood . . .

He splashed some cold water on his face, driving the memory away. In the dark of the night, the images would come back, but he'd be alone then. He wouldn't have to hold it together in front of Alicia or her family. By morning, he'd have his game face back on.

Staring at his face in the mirror, he saw the new scars along his hairline and one across his lower jaw. He felt the ache in his ribs that had been fractured by shrapnel. But none of those pains compared with the loss of his friend. For six years, they'd lived together, worked together, laughed together. That was over now.

Folding the towel over the rack, he told himself to stop stalling. He couldn't hide in the bathroom forever.

He'd known it wouldn't be easy to come here, but he hadn't realized just how difficult it would be, not just because of Rob but also because of Alicia. It had taken him a long time to get past the night they never should have had. For three years, he'd tried not to listen when Rob talked about her, made sure he was somewhere else when Rob and Alicia were video-chatting, and skimmed past photos that had her in them. But he'd never been able to get her out of his head.

And now she was back in glorious color, her golden hair, eyes the color of a morning sky, soft, full lips.

Damn! He needed to get a grip. She might be more beautiful than he remembered, but she was also angrier. She hated him, and that was probably a good thing. He hadn't been the man for her three years ago, and he certainly wasn't that man today. He needed a barrier, and hate was a good one.

After opening the door, he walked down the hall to the family room. The kitchen was just beyond a decorative archway. He could see Alicia busy at the stove. Her movements were efficient but a little jerky, as if she was still pissed off that she had to cook for him. Or maybe she was annoyed because he'd seen her fear. She had looked at the swirling water around her knees as if it were a monster trying to take her down. The accident must have been worse than Rob knew.

"There's your beer," George said, motioning toward the bottle on the coffee table.

"Thanks." He sat down on the couch while George kicked his feet up on the recliner. The local news was on the television. It was a totally normal scene, and yet it felt so strange. He'd spent half his childhood in homeless shelters or sleeping on friends' couches and the next decade in barracks and mess tents, where danger lurked around every corner, where letting down your guard could get you killed. When he'd taken leave, he'd gone to vacation spots with friends. He hadn't spent much time at all in a normal house like this one, waiting for the family dinner. He was completely out of his element.

He'd felt that way the last time he was here, when Rob had forced him to come home with him for Christmas. This room had been decorated to the hilt then, with a huge Christmas tree in the corner, a model train running around under it, Santas and snowmen and sleighs taking up every available shelf, a garland of Christmas cards strung over the fireplace. Rob had joked about how Alicia went Christmas crazy, and he hadn't been lying. It had been the best Christmas of his life. Unfortunately, New Year's hadn't been nearly as good.

"You hungry? Dinner might be a few minutes, but we can get you a snack," George said.

"I'm good."

His gaze moved toward the kitchen. Alicia threw some spaghetti into a pot, and the steam made her blond hair curl. She was thinner than he remembered, more fragile, with a weary set to her shoulders, as if she had the whole world weighing her down.

"Alicia didn't mean what she said earlier," George said abruptly.

Gabe glanced at Alicia's father, who had muted the television. "I understand why she said what she did."

"She misses Rob. We all do. It's hard not to blame someone."

"I miss him, too," he said heavily.

"Alicia and Rob were so close. They knew what the other was going to say before they said it. She felt his death in a way that I can't even imagine. You got any brothers?"

"No, but I considered Rob to be one."

"He felt the same way about you. He talked about you and the other guys in his unit every time he came home. I never understood why he wanted to fight, but I was proud of him. Proud of all of you." George coughed, clearing his throat. "Never thought I'd lose my son." He shook his head, his lips tight, as he struggled for composure. "But he was doing what he wanted to do. I find some peace in that."

A minute or two passed in silence. Then Gabe drew in a breath, deciding that it was time to let George know about his plans. "Rob told me about some of the problems you've had to deal with since your accident. He was very concerned and eager to get home in a way I'd never seen with him before. You were both on his mind a lot. Rob gave me the keys to his house. He asked me to come here and help out with the business or anything else you need. I promised him that I would, and I'd like to keep that promise."

George stared back at him thoughtfully. "Rob knew he was going to die?"

The question took Gabe back to that moment when he and Rob had realized the unimaginable truth. He'd tried to fight reality far longer than Rob had, making up stories about how everything would work out. Rob had let him talk. He'd even offered up a feeble joke, saying that was the best bullshit he'd ever heard from Gabe.

The knot in his throat grew larger at the memory, choking him with a pain he wasn't sure would ever go away. As the seconds ticked by, he realized that George was still waiting for an answer. "Yes," he said, meeting the older man's gaze. "Rob knew he was going to die. He wanted me to make sure you knew how much he loved you."

"You need to tell Alicia that."

"I will . . . when she's in the mood to listen."

"It's been difficult for us to grasp what happened, being so far away and all. It didn't seem real. Rob's body came back in a closed casket. We never saw him."

"You can remember him the way he was."

"That's how I want to remember him. Rob was always laughing, happy, optimistic. Never gave up on anything or anyone." George took a moment, then added, "We could use some help around here. I've been laid up this year and haven't been able to run the business the way I used to. I was counting on Rob to help us get back on our feet. Alicia can't do it by herself. And she has Justin to worry about."

"Then I hope you'll let me help. Of course, I'll be happy to give the house back when I move on. I know it belongs to your family."

"The house belonged to Rob; it was his to do with as he pleased. Maybe you'll decide to stay on. River Rock isn't a bad place to live. Our family settled here almost a hundred years ago, you know."

He had known, and he'd never been able to imagine having roots that went that deep.

"My great-great-grandfather built this house, and my grandfather built Rob's house. My uncle built another house about a mile away that my nephew lives in."

Gabe couldn't help wondering why Alicia didn't have her own place, but that was a question he'd save for another day. As George rattled off more family history, Gabe's attention returned to Alicia. She looked up and caught him staring. She held his gaze for a moment, her beautiful blue eyes begging him to leave. But he couldn't give her what she wanted—not yet, anyway.

Getting to his feet, he told George, "I'm going to see if Alicia needs any help."

As he walked into the kitchen, she frowned. "I wish you'd leave. You're going to make things more difficult."

"That's not my intention."

"It wasn't your intention the last time you came here, either."

"If I hurt you . . ."

"If you hurt me?" she echoed. "Is there really any doubt in your mind?"

"I had to leave, Alicia. I had commitments. You knew that—"

She cut him off with a wave of her hand. "I'm not talking about any of that now."

"You're the one who brought up the past."

"And now I'm done." The doorbell rang, and relief flashed across her face. "That's Keith—my boyfriend," she said, stumbling a little over the word.

"Rob told me about him. He wanted me to check him out."

Her gaze narrowed. "Keith is a great guy. He's a teacher at the high school and a single dad. He's wonderful."

"Maybe I'll think so, too, if you ever let him in," Gabe said as the doorbell rang again.

Two

Gabe followed Alicia to the door, both curious and reluctant to meet the man. He actually didn't know as much about Keith as he'd implied. He'd always cut Rob off whenever Alicia's love life came up; he couldn't stand hearing about her being with another man. Now he was going to have to actually talk to the guy.

Alicia flung open the door, and a tall, lean man in his mid-thirties walked into the room. Keith had light brown hair and friendly hazel-colored eyes. Wearing tan slacks and a button-down shirt, he looked like a man who probably spent more time indoors than out. Next to him was a boy about Justin's age, who immediately ran off to find Justin.

Alicia grabbed Keith's hand. "I'm so glad you could come," she said. "This is Gabe Ryder, one of my brother's friends. Gabe, this is Keith Andrews."

Keith extended his hand with a warm smile. "I've heard a lot about you. Alicia used to read me e-mails from her brother detailing all of your exploits."

"I'm sure Rob exaggerated," he said.

"I wish I'd had a chance to meet him," Keith said. "He sounded like a hell of a guy."

Alicia cleared her throat. "Dinner is almost ready. I hope you're hungry."

"Starving," Keith replied. "I just need to wash my hands. I encountered a leaky gas pump while I was filling up the car."

"Make yourself at home," she said with a wave of her hand. "You know where things are."

As Keith headed down the hall to the bathroom, Gabe said, "So, that's Keith."

"That's him." She folded her arms across her waist. "He's a good guy, reliable, caring, kind, generous."

"I wouldn't want any less for you."

"It doesn't matter what you want. It's my life. I need to get dinner on the table. After that, I hope you'll say good-bye."

She could hope all she wanted, but he had no intention of saying good-bye until he'd done what he'd come to do.

Justin and David dominated the dinner conversation with chatter about school, Boy Scouts, and the upcoming baseball season. Alicia was glad not to have to contribute anything. Ever since Gabe had appeared, she'd felt off balance. She'd been prepared to see him at the funeral, but when he didn't come, she'd thought that was it—she'd never see him again. She wasn't ready to deal with him now.

She darted a sideways glance at him, saw him watching her, and quickly averted her gaze. Gabe had always had a way of looking at her that made her breath catch and her heart beat a little faster. She'd thought she'd put him out of her head years ago. But here in the flesh, he was impossible to ignore. Lifting her gaze, she was relieved to see his attention focused on her father and gave herself a minute to study him more closely.

Gabe was a little taller than Keith, broader in the shoulders, and as fit as a man could be. His hair was longer than the almost-shaved cut he'd had three years ago. Since leaving the Corps, he'd let his hair grow, and she liked the longer look on him. She noted the new scar along his jawline and another one by his chin. They did nothing to mar the rough beauty of his face, the strength of his bones, the power in his dark eyes. Her gaze drifted down across his broad chest. She'd rested her head on that chest, and she knew what lay beneath the T-shirt: flat, muscled abs. The memory made her gut clench.

She'd been attracted to Gabe from the first second she'd seen him. After they'd flirted for three days, their first kiss had been explosive. Gabe had pushed her away, but two days later, they were sleeping together. And then he was gone.

She drew in a quick breath, angry with herself for reliving the past.

Gabe turned his head, and this time, she didn't look away. This was her dinner table; he was the one who should look away first. But Gabe couldn't walk away from a battle, not even one as small as this.

"Mom, are you listening?" Justin interrupted.

She started. Judging by the annoyed look in her son's eyes, he'd been talking to her for a while. "I'm sorry, what?"

"Will you take me to Five Arrows Point for my birthday?"

She shouldn't have been surprised by his question. His tenth birthday was coming up, and going to Five Arrows Point was a rite of passage for the boys in River Rock. Rob had promised Justin that he would take him—another promise unfulfilled.

Her father saw her discomfort and jumped in. "She can't, Justin. She doesn't know where it is."

Actually, she knew exactly where it was, but she wasn't about to share that with her father. Five Arrows Point was sacred male territory.

"Why don't you know?" Justin asked.

"Because girls aren't allowed there," her father answered for her. "It's a place where a boy becomes a man, where in the ancient times braves became warriors."

"Uncle Rob said he was going to take me." Justin's lower lip started to tremble. "On my tenth birthday. He said that's when all the Hayden boys go."

Alicia's heart ached at the sadness in her little boy's eyes. She wanted to make things right, but that was impossible.

"I wish I could take you," her father said with regret. "Give me a few more weeks, Justin, and we'll go there together."

Justin didn't look reassured. To an almost-ten-year-old, her father looked like an old, feeble man who could barely walk down the hall, much less maneuver a raft down the rapids to Five Arrows Point.

"What's the legend?" Gabe asked curiously.

She glanced at her dad. "Do you want to tell it?"

Her father's eyes lit up with enthusiasm. "Before the West was settled, the Native Americans lived by the river. One of their tribal legends is about a sacred place where braves were tested for courage, endurance, and strength, among other things. Along the way, they would collect five special arrowheads, each designating the completion of a challenge."

"What were the challenges?" Keith asked.

"Running the river was one, finding their way through the woods was another, fighting off wild animals, dealing with the cold in the winter and the extreme heat in summer, and climbing a rock wall to get to the top of the canyon," George said in his storytelling voice. "Most of the young men failed in the last climb. Some fell to the river and died. According to legend, ghosts sometimes steer boats away from that fork of the river, keeping the secret for only those who are worthy."

"Did you see any ghosts?" Justin asked, his eyes bright with curiosity.

"No, but your Uncle Rob did. He said the ghost had war paint on his face. I wish I'd seen him, but when I looked, he was gone."

"That sounds cool," Justin said. "I want to go."

"Don't get too excited," Alicia warned, wanting to bring some reality back to the conversation. "The arrowheads are long gone."

"How would you know?" Gabe asked, a small smile playing around the corners of his lips. "I thought you were excluded because you're a girl."

"Almost every guy in town has looked for them, and no one has ever found one."

"One was found about thirty years ago," her father said. "The thing is, Five Arrows Point is on a stretch of river with many different forks winding through the foothills and canyons. No one really knows for sure the exact location. There's a common drop-off point where most people start who don't go there in a boat."

"And every other year or so, some kid gets lost out there,

27

and there's a big search and rescue," Alicia said. "It's a legend that should have ended a long time ago."

"I bet I could find an arrowhead," Justin said confidently.

Her father smiled at Justin. "You'll have your day. Don't worry."

"If my dad were around, he could take me," Justin said, sending her a pointed look.

She sighed. There was nothing she could do about that. Justin's father had left a long time ago. Looking for a distraction, she said, "Who wants ice cream?" After taking orders, she got up from the table and headed into the kitchen.

Keith followed her, bringing along some empty plates. "Are you all right?" he asked quietly. "You seem a little on edge."

"I'm hanging in there. It's been a rough year."

"Is there anything I can do?"

"You're doing it." Keith had been a rock since Rob's death. "I hope you know how much I appreciate your support."

He leaned over and gave her a quick kiss on the lips. "I wish I could do more, but you're a very independent woman."

"Not that independent. You can scoop some ice cream," she said, handing him the half-gallon container of mint chocolate chip.

"Done."

While Keith served dessert, she cleaned up the kitchen. When the boys were done eating, Keith headed home with David to finish a science project, and Justin disappeared into his room, leaving Gabe and her father at the dining-room table. Her dad seemed to enjoy talking to Gabe, and why not? Most everyone else in town had already heard his stories; Gabe was fresh meat.

She went down the hall to her bedroom, shutting the door behind her so that she could no longer hear their voices. Her bedroom had always been her escape, the one room in the house that wasn't dominated by male stuff. She'd gone a little overboard on the half-dozen pillows that decorated her full-sized bed, the frilly curtains at her windows, the scented candles and art photographs that she'd purchased at the local art fair. She'd grown up a tomboy, spending days on the river, camping under the stars, catching fish, throwing footballs with her brother and her friends, but when the day was done, she'd always come home to this sweet, relaxing quiet.

She lit a couple of candles and sat on the bed, trying to find some calm, but she was very aware of Gabe just down the hall. She needed to forget about him. Keith was the man in her life now, and she could count on him. He wouldn't break her heart, and he wouldn't suddenly leave. Justin liked him, too, and Justin and David were as close as brothers. Her son really wanted and needed a father figure in his life, especially now that Rob was gone.

Sighing, she flopped onto her back. She'd never made good choices when it came to men.

She'd met Justin's father, Connor, when she was eighteen years old. She'd been waiting tables at Mullaney's during the summer music festival, and Connor had been the lead singer in a band. She'd fallen for his love songs and gotten pregnant just after her nineteenth birthday. Her father had been disappointed in her, but she'd tried to make it work. She'd moved in with Connor for a year and a half. To his credit, Connor had tried, too, but he was twenty-one years old and a musician. He didn't want to be tied down. Eventually, he'd taken off with his band,

and aside from a few e-mails now and then and the occasional random present showing up for Justin, Connor had been completely absent from her son's life.

She wouldn't make that mistake again. She wouldn't let Justin get attached to someone who wasn't going to stick around.

She got up and tidied her room in an effort to get rid of the restlessness coursing through her body. Soon the room was clean, but she was still on edge.

She went down the hall to check on Justin, who was on the computer with his headphones on. She waved to get his attention. "Fifteen minutes, then bed," she said.

He nodded. "Okay."

The odd expression on his face made her pause. "Is everything all right?"

He hesitated and then said, "Are you sure you don't want me to stay home on your birthday? I don't have to sleep over at David's."

She smiled and walked across the room to give him a big hug. "I love you so much. You know that, right?"

"Yeah."

"And what would make me really happy on my birthday is for you to go to David's and have a great time."

"But you'll be alone."

"I won't be alone. Grandpa will be here."

"He's not very much fun," Justin said with a doubtful look in his eyes.

"Don't worry about me. It's going to be okay."

After closing Justin's door, she returned to the living room. Her father was in his recliner in front of the television, where he spent most of his life these days. He'd always been an active, physical man, and it was difficult to see him so sedentary. But in time, she hoped, that would change.

"Did Gabe leave?" she asked, noting the empty room with relief.

"He went to Rob's house. Apparently, he's moving in there."

She sat down on the edge of the couch. "Gabe can't have Rob's house, Dad. It belongs to the family."

"It surprised me that Rob gave it to him," her father admitted. "But it was his house to do with as he wanted, Alicia."

"I want proof that Rob actually gave him the house."

"Gabe claims he has a letter."

"I'd like to see it."

"Well, you know where Gabe is."

She frowned at her father's uncaring shrug. "Why aren't you more upset? That house has always been in the family."

He took a moment to answer. "Your brother respected Gabe. He told me so many times. And Gabe wants to help us. He said he'll give the house back when he moves on."

"We don't need his help."

"That's not what you told me this afternoon. You said we needed manpower."

"I was talking about the business. Gabe knows nothing about rafting."

"He can learn."

"I don't want him to learn. I want him to leave."

Her father's gaze narrowed. "What's really wrong, Alicia? Do you think Gabe let your brother die? Because I don't believe that's what happened."

"We don't know what happened," she reminded him.

"Maybe you should ask Gabe."

"I already did. He wouldn't tell me."

"So try again." Her father grabbed his cane and slowly got to his feet. "You knew Rob better than anyone. If Rob sent Gabe to us, he had a good reason, and we should honor it."

"We don't need Gabe," she said, feeling a little desperate to get her father to agree with her. The idea of Gabe living next door was too unsettling to contemplate.

"Maybe Rob didn't send Gabe here because we need him but because Gabe needs us."

Rob's cabin was about two hundred yards from the main house through a thicket of trees that provided a wall of privacy. The cabin had a large main room with a stone fireplace and a smallish kitchen and dining room with windows overlooking the river. In the back was a bedroom, and up a narrow spiral staircase was a loft that Rob used for storing camping gear and tools.

Standing in the middle of the living room, Gabe fought an intense desire to run. Everywhere he turned, he could see Rob: sprawled on the large red leather couch in the main room, spinning the old vinyl records that he'd collected since he was a boy, pounding the keys of the dusty piano. He could hear Rob's laugh echoing through the silence and smell the overabundance of cologne that Rob used whenever he had a hot date.

Sweating, he ran the back of his hand across his forehead. It had been three years since he'd been in this cabin. It had suited Rob perfectly, but it wouldn't suit him. He didn't belong in a small town living next door to a woman who hated his guts.

It was just temporary, he told himself. Despite Rob's plea that he take the house and finally make himself a home, he only intended to stay until he made sure that Alicia and her father would be all right. He didn't know where he'd go after that, but it would be far, far away.

As he glanced toward the window, he saw a slender figure moving through the trees, blond hair glinting in the moonlight. His gut tightened as Alicia crossed the lawn. Walking quickly across the room, he threw open the door and met her on the porch, sensing that letting her inside the house could be bad for many reasons.

"Walking over here, I could see the lights on," she said. "And it was the first time in months, and it made me remember . . ." Her voice trailed away. She squared her shoulders, then lifted her chin. "I'm going to need to see some evidence that Rob wanted you to be here. You said you had a letter."

"It's in my bag, in the truck," he said, tipping his head toward the dark gray truck in the driveway.

"So get it."

The distrust in her eyes hurt, but he supposed he couldn't blame her. "Okay."

He walked down the steps and across the grass. Alicia followed at his heels.

As he opened the door, he said, "It didn't look like anyone had been in the house for a while."

"I haven't been in there since we found out Rob was dead," she admitted. "I tried a few times. I walked up the steps, put my hand on the doorknob, even pushed it open, but I couldn't make it across the threshold." Her gaze drifted back toward the house, her voice quieting. "I don't know why it's so hard to go in there. It's not like Rob was there all that much. I used to go in every couple of weeks and dust, air out the place, so it would be ready when he came home. I never imagined that he wouldn't, that the next person I saw inside the house would be you."

"I'm sorry. I know this is hard for you."

"It's hard for me to breathe. Rob was my other half. We came into life together. We shared every birthday. When my mom left, Rob was there. And even when he wasn't physically present, the connection between us was strong, unbreakable; only now it's broken. When I think about all the years to come, and how much he's going to miss . . ." She drew in a shaky breath. "I don't know how I'll make it."

"You'll make it because you have to, and because Rob would want you to be happy."

"He would, and I want that, too, because I have Justin, and he needs a mom who isn't sad all the time."

"Give yourself a break. It's only been a couple of weeks."

"I'm not sure time will make a difference."

He reached into the truck and unzipped a duffel bag on the seat. He pulled out a sealed envelope with her name on it. "Rob wrote this three days before he died."

"Why?" she asked, her fingers tightening around the edges. "Did he think he wasn't going to make it back?"

"Every day was dangerous. Now and then, men in the unit would rewrite wills or write letters to people they loved. It was a way of tying up loose ends so we could focus on what we had to do, knowing that everything was in order if the worst happened."

"But he'd gone on missions before. What was different about this one?"

"I don't know. Maybe it was because we were both getting out soon. The future was on his mind."

"Six days," she said heavily. "Rob was six days short of never being in danger again."

His stomach twisted. "I know."

She looked into his eyes, pleading with him for something he didn't think he could give her.

"Was he in pain?" she asked softly.

Her question was like a knife to the heart. Rob's face flashed through his mind, the pain in his eyes, the blood on his face . . .

Rob would want him to lie to Alicia. Gabe knew that as surely as he knew anything. He tried to think of something that would make her feel better. "Rob wasn't alone, Alicia. I was with him until the last breath."

A tear slid out of the corner of her eye. "I'm glad for that." She wiped the moisture from her cheek and stared down at the letter. "You didn't read this?"

"No. But he told me that he explained about the house in there. If he didn't, then I guess you can kick me out. But I'll still stay in town, and I'll still try to help you."

She looked down at the letter as if it were a bomb about to destroy what was left of her life. The moments ticked by, the silence accentuated by the rush of the river and the song of the crickets. The night was getting darker as clouds slid across the stars and the tall trees threw long shadows on the ground.

A shuffling sound in the woods made him stiffen.

Gabe told himself it was nothing. His nerves had been too tight for weeks. He wasn't in a war zone. There wasn't an enemy behind every tree.

Another snapping of branches.

His heart raced. He needed to get a grip, but his palms were sweating, and he knew instinctively that something was off.

When the crash came, he threw Alicia to the ground, covering her body with his. He was not going to watch another Hayden die.

Three

Alicia gasped for breath, her lungs crushed from the weight of Gabe's body, her mind spinning from his rapid assault. Her head was inches from the tire of his truck, the pebbles from the driveway poking sharply through her shirt.

"Stay down," Gabe ordered in a hushed voice, his dark gaze scanning the grounds.

He was tense, poised to act, and ready to do whatever it took to keep her safe. She knew that without a doubt; she also knew that he was overreacting. If she could just find her breath, she'd tell him so.

Squirming beneath him, she finally got out, "Gabe."

"Don't move. We're in the shadows. They can't see us," he ordered.

"That was just Sadie," she said. "She knocked over the trash cans."

He stared down at her as if he couldn't understand what she was saying. And maybe he couldn't. Because he wasn't there in that moment, she realized. He was somewhere else, somewhere far away, somewhere really dangerous.

"The dog," she added. "Gabe, it's okay."

He drew in a breath, turning his head as Sadie came into view. The dog didn't even see them, her attention distracted by a nice pile of dirt to dig through.

Gabe let out a breath, then looked back at Alicia. He was so close, his lips just inches away from hers, his chest crushing her breasts, his legs entwined with hers. He shifted, the tension in his face easing as he came back to reality . . . and the wariness in his eyes was replaced with desire. She'd seen that look before, and her stomach flipped over.

Three years, and she was suddenly right back where she'd been before—wanting him, needing him, knowing that it was crazy and reckless and not giving a damn.

She didn't know which one of them moved first, but suddenly, his mouth was on hers, his hand supporting her head, his fingers threading through her hair as he kissed her long and hard and deep. The emotions of the past few weeks and the sudden adrenaline rush of the past few moments were a dangerous combination. She didn't want to think anymore. She just wanted to feel something other than sadness or anger. She ran her hands up his back, pulling him closer when he started to move away. She didn't want him to go. She liked his weight on top of her, liked the feel of his hard body pressing her into the ground.

But Gabe finally broke away with a muttered swear and scrambled to his feet. He stared down at her, his breath coming hard and fast, his expression unreadable in the shadowy light. After a tense moment, he held out his hand to her.

She hesitated, then took it, his fingers closing around hers as he helped her to her feet.

"I'm sorry," he said shortly, letting go of her. "That was—that shouldn't have happened."

She put a hand on the side of the truck to brace herself, feeling shaky and unsteady. Drawing in a couple of slow, deep breaths, she brushed the dirt from her jeans, giving herself a moment to regroup.

"Are you okay?" Gabe asked.

"I don't know how to answer that question."

"I shouldn't have kissed you. I wasn't thinking."

"Neither was I." She'd kept her fling with Gabe locked away in a dim, dark part of her memory, but now all of the feelings were back in bright, vivid color. And that wasn't good.

"It won't happen again."

"Not if you leave, it won't."

His jaw tightened. "That's not happening."

"Why did you throw me to the ground?"

He shrugged. "I heard a noise. I reacted."

"Overreacted," she corrected.

"Yeah," he admitted. "I haven't spent a lot of time out of war zones in the last few years. I guess I'm on edge."

Gabe might have survived the mission that had taken Rob's life, but he obviously hadn't come through completely unscathed.

"What's your dog after?" Gabe asked, tipping his head toward Sadie, who was digging fast and furiously under a bush.

"I have no idea. She loves to dig. It's all I can do to keep her out of my vegetable and herb garden."

"Golden retrievers and vegetable gardens," he muttered cryptically. "I feel completely out of my element."

"You said they can't see us. Who were you talking about?"

"No one. Sorry if I hurt you when I threw you on the ground."

"You were protecting me."

"Yeah, from your dog," he said, obviously striving for lightness.

"But you didn't know that." A slash of white on the grass caught her gaze—Rob's letter. She leaned over and picked it up, but she still didn't feel ready to read her brother's final words. "Until we get things sorted out, you can stay. There are clean linens in the hall closet. There's no food, but you can come by for breakfast tomorrow morning. We're up by seven. Justin goes to school at eight."

"Thanks, Alicia."

As she turned to leave, her father's words rang through her head. "You said you came here to help us, but maybe you're the one who needs help, Gabe. I can't imagine what you've been through."

"You don't want to imagine it," he said flatly. "And would you offer me help if I asked?"

"Even if I did offer help, you wouldn't take it. Rob used to tell me that you were the most stubbornly independent person he'd ever met. And from what I've seen, he was right on the money."

Gabe slowly smiled.

"What?"

"He used to say the same thing about you."

Alicia was up before the sun had made it over the trees. She'd spent most of the night thinking about Gabe and Rob and wondering what the hell had happened on the other side of the world. But those answers were going to be difficult to come by, and she needed to concentrate on the present.

After a quick shower, she threw on jeans and a sweater over a tank top, let Sadie out for a morning run, woke up a sleepy Justin, and started the coffeemaker. Her father used to rise with the dawn, but since his accident, she rarely saw him before nine.

While she was waiting for the coffee, she grabbed a basket and headed out back to her garden. She paused on the steps, looking with pride at what she'd created. Along one side of the beautiful garden were rows of herbs: basil, thyme, marjoram, and mint. On the other side, she'd planted tomatoes, squash, onions, carrots, beans, and a variety of lettuces and peppers. In a month, she would have enough produce to sell to the local inns and restaurants. But today she was content to pick a few beautiful tomatoes, some zucchini and spinach. She had just finished when the back door of the house opened and Gabe stepped out.

Her heart skipped a beat at the sight of him. He wore faded jeans and a long-sleeved dark green T-shirt that accentuated his broad chest, the chest that had been crushing her breasts the night before. She drew in a quick breath and ordered herself to get it together. Last night had just been a moment of temporary insanity for both of them.

"This is impressive," Gabe said, glancing around the yard.

A surge of pleasure ran through her. She'd started the garden two years ago, and in the last six months, since the accident, her hobby had become a passion. This was one part of her life that she could control. She could plant and water and make something grow and flourish. She'd needed the creative outlet when the rest of her life had been falling apart.

"It's still a work in progress," she said as she walked over to meet him. "I've just about outgrown this space, and I have my eye on the area behind Rob's cabin. I just need to do some clearing. In the meantime, we have fresh vegetables for breakfast."

"That's not something I get every day."

She nodded. "When Rob used to come home, he craved fresh fruits and vegetables."

Justin stuck his head out through the doorway. "Mom, where's breakfast?"

"It's coming," she said, moving past Gabe. "I thought I'd make a veggie scramble."

"I'll eat anything," Gabe told her, following her into the kitchen.

"Help yourself to some coffee," she said as she set down her vegetables. "Justin, why don't you set the table? And then you can move on to the toast."

"What can I do?" Gabe asked.

"You can sit at the counter."

"You can make the toast if you want," Justin offered.

Gabe grinned. "At least someone in your family is happy to delegate."

She grabbed the bread and passed it across the counter. "Knock yourself out. Justin, do you have all your homework together?" She began dicing tomatoes and onions and whipping up eggs.

"I think so," Justin said.

"Why don't you make sure?"

Justin muttered something under his breath and headed down the hall.

"Your son doesn't appear to be a morning person," Gabe said. "Not like you."

"Guilty," she admitted with a smile. "I love the stillness of dawn, the freshness of a new day, the air clean, the birds chirping. It's a new beginning. Rob liked mornings, too. We were always the first ones up in the house. If my dad didn't have an early-morning river run, he'd sleep till ten, so I was always in charge of breakfast. Rob hated to cook. When he was hungry, he had to eat right that second. He'd grab something out of the fridge and have half of it eaten by the time he got to the table. Or he'd just stand by the refrigerator and inhale something. I used to tell him that he'd never find a girl who'd want to put up with that . . ." Her voice trailed away. Rob would never share a moment like that with a wife. She cleared her throat. "Anyway, Justin takes after his father."

"Where is his father?" Gabe asked.

"I have no idea. Connor doesn't keep in touch."

"Not even with his son?"

"Every now and then, he pops up when he's between gigs."

"Sounds like a great guy."

"Actually, he's a lot of fun. He's just really irresponsible and immature. He wasn't cut out to be a father."

"He should have thought of that before he got you pregnant."

"The condom broke," she said, not wanting Gabe to think she was a complete fool. "It wasn't really anyone's fault. But we were both too young to be parents."

"You managed."

43

"Yes, I did." She cast a quick glance down the hall to make sure that Justin was not within earshot. "And I have never regretted one second of it. I love that kid more than anyone else in this world. Lately, he's been asking a lot of questions about his dad and why he isn't here, and it's not easy to answer him."

"The truth works the best."

"Even when the truth hurts?"

"It's better than a lie."

There was something in his eyes that told her he knew what he was talking about. "I don't think I know much about your family, Gabe."

"My parents are gone. No siblings. Just me." He grabbed two pieces of bread and put them in the toaster. "Do you have any butter?"

She took margarine out of the fridge. "That was succinct."

"You asked. I answered."

"No, you didn't," she said, turning her attention back to the stove.

Gabe didn't comment, and she decided not to push. Getting to know Gabe better wasn't part of the plan. She finished scrambling the eggs while Gabe made the toast and then set everything on the table just as Justin returned.

Gabe brought over the toast and stared down at breakfast in amazement. "This looks incredible," he said. "No wonder Rob put you in charge of breakfast."

"There are too many vegetables," Justin complained as he picked his way around some spinach.

"They're good for you," she told him.

"Uncle Rob said he used to give his vegetables to Bonnie," Justin said.

She smiled at the memory. "Bonnie was our dog when Rob and I were kids," she told Gabe.

"Do you have a dog?" Justin asked Gabe.

"Nope," Gabe answered. "I wanted one when I was about your age, but it didn't work out."

"How come? Wouldn't your parents let you have one?"

"My parents weren't around when I was growing up. I stayed with relatives and friends most of the time."

Alicia sipped her orange juice. That was a longer answer than she'd gotten.

"My dad isn't around, either," Justin volunteered. "He's in a band, and he plays all over the world. He's really good. He sent me a guitar, and he said he's going to teach me how to play it." Justin shot her a look, as if daring her to contradict him.

"Justin, a little less talking, a little more eating," she said. She didn't want to fight with him about his dad. She wanted Connor to keep his promises to Justin, too; it just didn't usually happen that way.

"You never want to talk about Dad," he complained, pushing his plate away. "No wonder he doesn't want to come home."

His harsh words hurt, but she knew it wasn't really her he was mad at.

"I'm done," Justin added.

"Then take your plate to the sink, and go brush your teeth."

"You okay?" Gabe asked as Justin left the room. "He was kind of rough on you."

"His dad's absence is becoming a sore point, and as much as I want to make things right for him, I can't."

"You have a lot on your plate right now. Your dad, Justin, the business. Why so stubborn about taking a little help from me?"

"I have someone else in my life now, someone I can count on." She got to her feet and took their empty plates to the sink. She wasn't aware that Gabe had followed until she turned around and bumped into him. Her pulse leaped at the brief contact. "You move very quietly."

"A well-developed skill. Give me a chance, Alicia."

"To do what?" she asked, very conscious of how close they were standing and that with the sink at her back, she had nowhere to go.

"To prove that you can count on me, too."

"You're just going to leave again. That's what you do. What you're good at."

"It's what I've always had to do," he said. "That's why I got good at it."

"The last time you were here, you didn't even say good-bye, Gabe. You were just gone. You owed me more than that."

Shadows filled his eyes. "This isn't going to be like the last time."

"No, it's not. I have to clean up, take Justin to school, and go check out some rafts. Please move."

He didn't budge. "Not until you agree to take me with you. I promised Rob."

She was fighting a losing battle, and she didn't have enough energy to get into a war with Gabe. She had too many other people to fight. "Fine, you can go into town with me. But right now, you have to get out of my way."

He was making progress, Gabe thought as he got into the car with Alicia and Justin. It was a small step but an important one. She still had her guard walls up, but he'd seen a crack here and there. Not that it was her guard walls he should be worried about; it was his own.

Alicia had been the dream he'd walked away from. When he'd met her three years earlier, he'd been captivated by her sparkle. She was fun, energetic, a whirlwind of laughter and beauty. The fact that she was Rob's sister had kept him in check for a while, but Alicia had been hard to resist. He'd never felt so drawn to a woman, so caught up in lust that he was thinking about her every second of every day. It had scared the shit out of him. Alicia was a single mother. She needed a man who could be a husband and a father, and he hadn't known if he could be either. He still didn't.

"I'll pick you up and take you and David home today," Alicia reminded Justin as she pulled up in front of the school.

"I know. 'Bye, Mom. 'Bye, Gabe."

Justin gave him a casual wave and a smile that reminded him so much of Rob. He turned away from Alicia to catch her watching him. "He's a mini-Rob," he said.

She nodded. "It's bittersweet, isn't it?" Her gaze followed Justin all the way into the school. Then she cleared her throat. "Onward."

As she pulled away from the curb, he said, "There's something I'm curious about. Why did Rob have the house? You have a child. It seems like you're the one who would need the space."

"The house always goes to the oldest male; my great-grandfather instigated that rule. In case you hadn't noticed, the Haydens are big on male traditions."

"That must piss you off."

"On occasion," she said. "But I love my dad, and I adored

Rob, and it was fine that he had the house. It was easier for me to have my dad around when Justin was a baby. He helped out a lot, and I'll always be grateful to him for that. Anyway, Justin was another reason Rob needed his own place, for girls and stuff, you know."

He smiled. "Got it."

As they drew closer to town, he was amazed by how different her world was from the one he'd been living in. They drove by thick, towering redwood trees, open meadows, and farmland. As they neared the town of River Rock, there was a huge banner announcing the upcoming spring music festival strung between two light poles at the entrance to Main Street. While there were a few newly remodeled buildings in the downtown area, the buildings reminded him of some of the Westerns he'd watched as a kid.

"I feel like I've stepped back in time," he murmured.

Alicia gave him a quick smile. "The town was built during the Gold Rush of the eighteen-fifties. The bank over there has photographs of the gold miners and some of the first gold millionaires. The courthouse is also original, although they put on a new roof last year. Oh, and there's Mullaney's," she said, pointing down a side street. "It was one of River Rock's first saloons, and it's the center of a big spring music festival every year. The music scene has really been growing. There are two new clubs on the other side of town by the old mill, with live music near the river. A new housing development is also going up about five miles south of here. We're not as small a town as we used to be." She waved her hand toward Burt's Diner. "I used to work at Burt's in high school."

"I remember. You took me there for chili cheese fries."

Her smile faded. "That's right. I forgot about that. You've seen all this before."

"Not without garlands and Christmas trees and a Santa on every corner. The last time I was here, it was a winter wonderland."

She nodded. "We don't get a lot of snow, but that year we had more than usual. Holidays are big around here. There's not a lot to do, so we celebrate every event we can."

"Do you ever get bored living so far from a big city, Alicia?"

"I've never lived anywhere else. This is home."

"And you've never wanted to live anywhere else?"

She thought for a moment. "I've considered it. I've spent time in Sacramento, San Francisco, made it up to Portland and Seattle, and I must admit I enjoyed the city life. But I was always happy to come back. I never had the kind of wanderlust that Rob had or the opportunity. I was going to go away to school after two years at the community college, but when I got pregnant, my plans changed." She paused. "You've been a lot of places, haven't you?"

"All over the world—wherever the Marine Corps sent me."

"Rob loved the travel, even when the places he was being sent were dangerous."

"Yeah, he loved talking to the locals. Wherever we went, within twenty-four hours, he had a bunch of new friends."

"It's funny that you two became friends. You're so different. Rob was outgoing and never stopped talking, and you're much quieter—darker," she said, shooting him a thoughtful look.

He wasn't surprised by her description. There was a darkness inside him that he couldn't seem to shake. "We were different, but we respected each other."

Alicia pulled into a parking spot in the lot next to the hardware store and shut off the engine. He was about to get out when he realized that she wasn't moving. "What's wrong?"

Her jaw tightened, a steel glint of determination coming into her eyes. "Nothing. I can do this."

Whatever battle she was fighting with herself was clearly a private one, so he got out of the car and waited for her to join him.

Once she got out, she moved quickly through the double doors of Bill's Hardware and up to the counter, where an older man with glasses and gray hair was helping a customer.

As the woman finished her transaction, she gave Alicia a hard look.

"Hello, Mrs. Isler," Alicia said.

The woman gave Alicia an indecipherable "hmph" and walked away.

"Don't mind her," the older man said. "She hasn't been in a good mood in twenty years."

"Bill," Alicia said, "this is Gabe Ryder. He was a friend of Rob's."

"Nice to meet you," Bill said, extending his hand with a warm smile. "I knew Rob from the day he was born. Never met a finer young man. You served with him?"

"For the last six years," Gabe replied.

"So, my dad said the Pioneer rafts were in," Alicia interjected.

"They came in yesterday. I got a good deal for you," Bill said with a nod.

"That's great," she said. "Usually, the good rates only go to the bulk orders."

"A friend of mine hooked me up. He's disgusted with the way the sporting conglomerates are taking over the mom-and-pop shops. He doesn't like dealing with Wild River Tours. He says all they talk about is global domination of the world's rivers. It's about the money for them. They don't love the river the way we do." Bill stroked his jaw. "I heard Chelsea signed on with them, though."

"Yes, she joined up at the end of last year after the accident, and I guess they talked her into coming back."

"Damn shame. She was one of your most popular guides. But you still have Simon, right?"

"I hope so. He's a little hard to track down. He's in South America right now."

"He'll be back. I'll get the rafts for you."

"Thanks."

As Bill disappeared into the back of the store, the front door opened, and a slender woman walked in. She wore black jeans and a white T-shirt under a short gray jacket. Her dark brown hair was short and curly, her eyes dark brown. She stopped abruptly when she saw them.

Alicia stiffened, too. There was about four feet between them, and every inch sizzled with tension.

Finally, Alicia said, "Kelly. You're back."

"Yes, I got in yesterday. My mom is having hip surgery next week."

"I heard that. I hope she'll be all right."

"She'll be fine." Kelly drew in a breath. "Where's Bill?"

"He's in the back, getting our . . ." Alicia's voice trailed away.

Kelly's gaze narrowed. "Getting your what? Rafting equipment? My mother said you're planning to open again."

51

"Yes, we are."

"I can't believe it," Kelly said, shaking her head, anger flashing in her eyes.

"Kelly—" Alicia began.

"No," Kelly said, putting up a firm hand. "I don't want to hear anything you have to say." Turning on her heel, she left the store, letting the door bang behind her.

Alicia put out a hand to the nearby counter, her face white as she stared out the window. "I can't believe she came home."

"Kelly?" Gabe said, a little confused by what had just happened. "Isn't that the name of your best friend?"

She stared at him in bemusement as if she'd forgotten he was there. "Former best friend, yes."

"What did I miss?" he asked, searching her face.

"Kelly's fiancé died on our river trip last year."

Her words shocked him. "I had no idea. Rob didn't tell me that."

"It was a bachelor party for Brian and his friends. Brian and Kelly were supposed to get married three weeks later. I was going to be the maid of honor. We had the dresses, the church was scheduled, the reception was planned. Kelly left town right after Brian's funeral. She wouldn't speak to me. I didn't think I would ever see her again."

"I'm sorry, Alicia."

"She blames me for Brian's death. A lot of people do." She stopped talking as Bill came out of the back room, wheeling a large carton.

"Here you go. The latest and the best in white-water design," Bill said. "Your dad is going to love these rafts."

"Well, I'm not sure my dad is going to be on one of them."

"He'll be out there. No one will be able to stop him. Your father is a force of nature."

"We'll see. He's not in as good a shape as he makes himself out to be."

"I know he's still recovering, and he may not be ready for this season, but your father has the strongest will of anyone I've ever known. When he says he'll be out on the river again, I believe him."

"Wishes don't always come true," she said flatly.

"I'll take this out to the car," Gabe said, grabbing the dolly from Bill.

"Just leave it by the back door," Bill said.

"I'll be right out after I settle up with Bill," Alicia said.

Gabe stowed the box in the back of Alicia's SUV and returned the dolly to the side of the building. As he moved back across the lot, he saw Kelly standing across the street in front of a realty office, and she wasn't alone. She seemed to be having a rather intense conversation with a man. Their focus shifted, however, when Alicia walked out of the hardware store. Alicia saw them, her step faltered for a moment, and then she moved quickly to the car, sliding in behind the wheel.

"Who was that guy with Kelly?" he asked as he got into the car and she started the engine.

"Brian's brother, Russell Farr. He works across the street."

"Was he on the trip?"

"Yes, he was on my father's raft. They were in the lead when they flipped. Russell was the one who pulled my father out of the river. He had no idea that his brother was missing . . ."

"Okay, you're going to have to tell me the story," Gabe said when she fell silent. "I need to know what happened that day."

"Why?"

"So I can help you. Obviously, getting your business up and running isn't just about buying rafts. You've got a huge image problem."

"You think?" she asked sarcastically.

"How many people blame you for the accident?"

"A lot."

"We're going to have to change their minds."

She pulled out of the parking lot. "Maybe we shouldn't try to change their minds."

"Why not? Because you don't want to go back out on the river?"

"Because maybe the accident was my fault."

"Then that's the first thing we have to figure out. Take me someplace where we can talk without being interrupted."

"What makes you think I want to talk to you?"

He shrugged. "You may not want to talk to me, but you need to talk to someone, and I'm here. I won't bullshit you, Alicia. If I think you did something wrong, I'll tell you."

She shot him a dark look. "Fine, but that works both ways, and I'm not going to be the only one doing the talking."

Four

Kelly stared down the street as Alicia's SUV disappeared around the corner. Her stomach was churning, and she felt as if she was about to throw up. Only back in town for twenty-fours hours, and she already wanted to run. She'd known that seeing Alicia again would be tough, but she hadn't expected to feel so shaken.

"You need to stay away from her," Russell said. "You can't let yourself get sucked back into a friendship with her."

"That's not going to happen," she said, turning her attention back to Russell. A thirty-three-year-old real estate broker, Russell had been devastated by his brother's death. It had been his idea to do the river-rafting trip for Brian's bachelor party, and she doubted he'd ever be able to forgive himself for that decision.

"Are you sure about that? You were best friends. She was going to be your maid of honor."

"You don't have to remind me. I knew I'd run into her, but I didn't think it would be so soon. She said she was picking up a raft, probably to replace the one . . ." Her stomach flipped over again, her mind flashing back to the horrible summer day that had changed her life forever. She'd been picking out wedding flowers with her mom when Russell had called, his voice filled with anger, grief, and disbelief. Brian had gone overboard, and no one could find him. For twenty-four hours, she'd held her breath, praying for a miracle, but a miracle hadn't come.

"I can't believe they're going to go out on the river again after everything that happened," Russell said, interrupting her thoughts. "They should be stopped. They're dangerous."

Habit brought defensive words to her lips, but pain kept her from speaking them. Six months ago, she would have been the first one to jump to Alicia's defense. The Haydens had been her second family, especially after her dad passed away. George had been a father figure to her, while her mother had been like a mother to Alicia. There had been times they'd joked about setting up their parents, but they'd never managed to get George or her mother, Lynette, on board. Not surprising, really. George spent more time on the river than he did in town.

"I didn't think George was in any condition to lead river trips," she said. "He must be doing a lot better."

"He still walks with a cane," Russell said.

"You saved his life."

"Not so he could go back out on the river and kill someone else," he said tersely, anger lining his face.

She frowned, realizing that Russell didn't look too good. He'd put on a few pounds around the belly, and his face had that flushed look that usually came when he was drinking too much. His brown hair had also receded, thinning out on the top, too. Brian's death had taken a heavy toll on him.

"You need to let it go, Russ," she said, worried about his overwhelming anger. "Nothing will bring Brian back."

He blew out a breath. "I know. I didn't mean to get into this with you the minute you got back. When is your mom having surgery?"

"Next week."

"I'm sure she's happy to have you back. Everyone misses your food. Nora is a good cook, but she doesn't compare to you."

"Thanks, but Nora taught me everything I knew."

"What's happening with your job in Sacramento?"

"I took some time off." She paused. "I am going back, though. River Rock isn't my home anymore."

"Before you leave, I want to have you over for dinner. My parents would love to see you, and so would Amanda."

"When are you going to put a ring on that girl's finger?"

"I'm getting around to it," he said with a sheepish grin.

"You should do it soon. She's a good one."

"The best—probably too good for me." He leaned over and kissed her on the cheek. "I'm glad you're back. Call me, and we'll set something up."

"I will." As she walked away, she wished she could be happy to be home, but her brief run-in with Alicia had reminded her that this place could never be home again.

Alicia glanced over at Gabe, who had been silent since they'd left the hardware store. She'd needed a minute to regroup, and he'd given it to her. "When Kelly didn't come back for Rob's funeral, I didn't think I'd ever see her again," she said. "She moved to Sacramento and got a job as a chef in a restaurant there. She's an incredible cook. Her mother owns the Blackberry Inn on the other side of town, and Kelly grew up working in the kitchen."

"We need to talk about the accident, Alicia."

"I'm working up to that." She pulled onto a narrow dirt road, driving under towering trees until she came to a grassy landing. She stopped the car and got out. "Come on, I want to show you something."

She led him down a footpath to an old wooden bridge that was about a hundred yards long. Below the bridge, the river splashed through a boulder-filled fork that no one could get a boat through. The bridge had been closed off years ago, too rickety for foot traffic.

"This is nice," Gabe said. "Unless you brought me here so you could push me off."

"For the moment, you're safe." She sat down on the ground and stretched out her legs. She'd thought she could handle the river from this point, but the sound of the water pounding through the rocks put her on edge. It was a different sound from the calm flow that ran in front of her house. This part of the river reminded her of the accident, especially the sharp, jagged rocks.

Her heart began to pound, and she jumped to her feet.

Gabe stood up, too, grabbing her arm. "Alicia?" he asked with concern.

"I shouldn't have brought you here. This isn't a good spot."

"You're safe with me." The strength of his grip and the confidence in his eyes reassured her to some extent but also reminded her that Gabe could be dangerous to her in ways that had nothing to do with the rushing water below.

"Talk to me," he commanded. "Tell me what happened on your last trip down the river."

She pulled loose and backed a few feet away, then sat down on the grass, feeling better a little farther from the edge.

Gabe sat next to her.

"I haven't talked about that day to anyone."

"Not even your brother?"

"I didn't want to tell Rob, because he would have been upset, and he needed to focus on his job so that he could stay safe. My dad was injured. He didn't really know what happened after he went into the water. And Kelly was too distraught about Brian to talk to me. I didn't want to scare Justin, either, so I just kept my thoughts to myself."

"What about Keith?"

"I didn't know Keith then. We met in September, and the accident was in August."

"But still . . ."

She didn't like the question in his eyes. "I will talk to him about it. I just haven't gotten around to it. It hasn't been important."

"Are you serious? You can't even look at the river from way up here, but you think you're going to get out on it in two weeks?"

"I'll be fine. I just need to get my head around the idea."

"You're not fine."

"I will be."

He gave her a doubtful look, then said, "Tell me about that day."

She took a deep breath. "It was a Friday, and the weather was beautiful. We scheduled an all-day trip on a run that had two Class Four and one Class Five rapids. Class Six is the top, basically unrunnable. Class Five is very challenging but doable with skilled guides on board. We'd made the run a couple of times before. There were three rafts with four people and a guide in each raft. My father was on the lead raft, I was on the second, and Simon, one of our most experienced guides, was bringing up the rear. The morning run was great. We broke for lunch along the river, and everyone was laughing, talking, having a wonderful time. In the afternoon, the wind picked up, and the river was running faster. It was higher than normal, but we weren't too concerned. About an hour into the run, things fell apart. We hit what they call the roller-coaster chute, because it goes up and then steeply down. And sometimes it spins you around, which is what happened that day."

She paused, images flashing through her head: the splash of water in her eyes, the speed of the boat increasing, and then the cries from up ahead as her father's boat flipped over. "I saw my dad go into the water. He never *ever* got flipped out. I was stunned, and I didn't react fast enough. Suddenly, we were airborne, too. Almost flying. And then I was in the water."

She could feel the cold, the iron grip of the current tugging her down and away, the sense of futility as she kicked and kicked—

Gabe's hand came down on her thigh. "You're not in the river, Alicia. You're on solid ground."

She turned to him, his gaze anchoring her back in reality. "Russell Farr, Brian's brother, was in the first raft with my dad. He managed to pull him over to some rocks. My dad was unconscious, and he would have died if Russell hadn't gotten to him."

"What about you?"

"I was swept downstream. I could hear shouting. Or maybe it was just the pounding of my heart, the rush of the water; it was so loud. I tried to swim, to grab the boat when I could see it, but it was always just out of reach. I did everything I'd been taught to do, but nothing was working. Finally, I somehow managed to make it to the shore. By then, I was a quarter mile down the river. The raft was even farther away. It was headed the wrong way, straight toward the falls." She cleared her throat, knowing she had to get through to the end. "I didn't think anyone was on it, but later I had the hazy image of someone being dragged down under it. At the time, I didn't know what I was seeing. I looked back, and most of the guys were on the rocks, so I thought everyone had made it to shore. But when we finally managed to regroup, we couldn't find Brian. We couldn't find him anywhere," she whispered. "Now I know he went over the falls with our raft. He must have gotten tangled up in something, I don't know what. He had on a life jacket, but there were a lot of rocks, and one of the other guys said he saw blood in the water."

Gabe's eyes filled with compassion. "Do you want to stop?"

She shook her head. "There's not much else. They didn't find his body until the next day. It was four miles from where we went into the water." She drew in a shaky breath. "He had a gash on his head. It was believed that he got knocked out and then drowned, not that that's a comfort to anyone."

"Maybe it is a comfort. He didn't know what was coming. He didn't feel anything."

"I hope he didn't."

Gabe stared back at her. "It sounds like an accident, Alicia. Why do people blame you? Why do you blame yourself?"

"There were a lot of theories about what happened. Someone suggested that the rafts were underinflated or in poor condition. We weren't the richest rafting company. We didn't have the best equipment. Other people questioned my experience, my father's age, the wisdom of taking that run at all under those river conditions."

"So there was a lot of second-guessing. What do you think?"

"I'm not sure. We found a leak in the raft afterward, but I believe it happened when it was flung against the rocks."

"Sounds reasonable." He gave her a thoughtful look. "You're not telling me something."

She fidgeted, debating how far she wanted to go. "It's just a feeling. Brian was acting a little funny after lunch. A couple of the guys were being a little too loud, too wild. I don't know if the adrenaline rush was making them cocky. But it seemed like they weren't listening very well. They weren't following my instructions like they had been in the morning."

"Were they drinking?"

"Alcohol is forbidden on the trips, but everyone had water bottles. I didn't check them. The guys in the group were friends. I trusted them."

"There must have been an autopsy. It would have showed if there was alcohol in Brian's bloodstream."

"The autopsy didn't happen for more than twenty-four hours. If there was alcohol in his system, it was gone by then. So we'll never know."

"Did you talk to any of the other guys?"

"Are you kidding? No one wanted to talk to me, Gabe. And I

was busy dealing with my dad. He broke his leg in three places and fractured a couple of ribs. He needed a lot of attention. I didn't have time to investigate anything, and I wouldn't have even known where to start. The chief of police from River Rock was on the trip. He investigated. At the end, it was deemed an accident, but there are still people in town who don't believe that."

"The only person who really needs to believe it is you, Alicia."

"I just wish I could remember everything more clearly, but I only saw part of what happened. That's the problem. We were all struggling for survival. No one was watching from above. No one saw the whole thing. We each lived just a part of it."

"So you have the pieces of a puzzle but no way to put them together."

"Exactly. And even if we did put them together, it won't bring Brian back."

"But it might help you get past your fear of the river. Your dad has no idea, does he?"

"No." She hugged her knees to her chest, wrapping her arms around her legs. "At least, he's pretending not to. He's always been of the mind-set that if you get thrown off the horse, or the raft, you get back on. That's the only way to do it—face your fear."

"Do you think he has some fear, too?"

"No, he loves the river. He refers to it as a woman who challenges him and tests him and makes him feel like a big strong man. I guess once my mother left, all he had was the river."

"Why did she leave?"

"That's another long story, and I think I've talked enough. It's your turn."

He stiffened. "I can't tell you what happened to Rob."

"You can't expect me to spill my guts and you say nothing."

"It's an entirely different situation."

"Can you tell me *anything*? Did Rob have any last words?" It was hard to ask the question, and once it was spoken, she wasn't sure she really wanted to know the answer. If Rob had said something important, then that meant he knew he was going to die, and she couldn't stomach the thought that he might have been in pain, might have known what was coming. She jumped to her feet. "Never mind. I don't want to do this now. I have bills to pay and supplies to order and guides to track down."

Gabe stood up. "Alicia. Look at me."

She slowly turned around. "What?"

"Rob wanted you to know that he loved you very much. And I told him that you already knew that."

Her eyes blurred with tears. "You're right. I did." She bit down on her bottom lip. "I want to apologize for what I said when you first arrived. I know you didn't let Rob die. I just wanted to blame someone, and you were there."

"I wasn't the one who was supposed to come back," he said, a hard note in his voice. "I get it, Alicia."

"It's not that I wanted anything bad to happen to you, Gabe. I wanted you both to be safe. And blaming you was unfair. I was doing to you what everyone has been doing to me, blaming me for something I couldn't control. I'm sorry."

"There are things I wish I had done differently."

"Me, too," she agreed. "But sometimes there aren't any second chances."

"You're right."

"So what now?"

"We need to get you back on the river. How about a short trip, just you and me?"

Her pulse leaped at the suggestion. "I—I don't know."

"You wouldn't have to pretend not to be scared with me. We could go at your pace."

"I'll think about it. But if I don't get the business going again, we won't have any river trips to worry about."

"What was Rob going to do to help when he got back?" he asked as she started walking toward the car. "What was going to be his role?"

She stopped by the car. "Rob was going to charm the socks off all the doubters and haters in town. He was going to use that smile of his to bring everyone back into the Hayden camp. Rob was loved by everyone. He would have been able to persuade them to trust us again."

"So you need a front guy?"

"Yes, and no offense, Gabe, but you're not exactly the outgoing, gregarious type."

"I can be charming on occasion."

She gave him a doubtful look. He was sexy as hell, but more in a bad-boy, moody-loner kind of way. "If you want that job, go for it. You certainly can't make anyone hate us more."

"Then that's where I'll start."

"What will you do?" she asked, feeling a bit nervous now that Gabe was taking her up on the challenge.

"Not sure yet. I need to come up with a strategy, identify the key targets, and determine how to neutralize them."

"This isn't a war, Gabe."

He smiled. "You're wrong, Alicia. It's going to be a battle to win back your reputation. Where did you say Kelly was staying?"

"The Blackberry Inn, but I don't want you to talk to her. She doesn't need any more problems. She's still grieving the loss of her fiancé."

"I'm surprised you'd protect her after what she's put you through."

"She was my best friend. I still love her. Leave her alone."

"Fine. Where does all the gossip happen in town?"

"Burt's Diner or Mullaney's Bar and Grill."

"Then drop me off in town. I'll start with those two places."

"How will you get back to the house?"

He grinned. "I'll use my charm."

"Then I hope you like to walk," she grumbled as she got into the car. Gabe might have a killer smile when he chose to use it, but she doubted that he could change anyone's mind.

Kelly walked up the steps to the Blackberry Inn, a beautiful manor house situated on three acres of meadow and forest about five miles from downtown. A small creek ran alongside the property, flowing into the river a half mile away. A big porch sprawled around three sides of the four-story house, and in the back courtyard was a brick patio with comfortable chairs, a fire pit, and a hot tub. The inn offered ten guest bedrooms plus three guest cottages and an attic suite on the top floor where Kelly had lived since she was a teenager. Her mother and her brother had moved into one of the cottages a few years ago, eager to have a little more privacy than could be found in the main house. But she'd loved her attic room too much to move, and she hadn't felt the need for more space. Once she'd started dating Brian, she'd practically moved into his apartment.

As she entered through the front door, the familiar furniture and smells brought back a wave of nostalgia. She'd missed this place. She'd also missed her family and Nora, she thought as she pushed open the door to the big kitchen at the back of the inn. Nora and Kelly's mother, Lynette, had started the inn together fourteen years earlier, right after Kelly's dad died. It was from Nora that she'd learned how to cook. She'd been the sous chef at the inn's restaurant since she was fifteen, finally taking over when Nora fell in love at the ripe age of fifty-seven and decided to travel around the country in an RV with her new husband.

A plump, energetic woman with platinum-blond hair and a friendly smile, Nora greeted her with a big, tight hug. "There you are. I was wondering when I was going to see you. Your mother said she sent you off early to do some errands."

"Yes, I was planning to help you make breakfast, but Mom had other ideas."

"She's stressed out about her surgery and trying not to think about it by making up things for us to do," Nora said. "But we only had a few guests this morning, anyway. We have three couples checking in this afternoon, though, so it will get busier this weekend."

"Good. I'm ready to work."

"So you don't have to think, either," Nora said with a wise smile. "You take after your mother in that regard."

"And because I want to help. I know you didn't really want to come back full-time, and I feel bad that you got thrown into it when I moved to Sacramento."

Nora waved a dismissive hand. "It was fine. That RV was getting too small, anyway. Russell and I were starting to get on each other's nerves, not that I don't still adore the man. I got lucky the second time around."

"You did. And I'm glad that you're okay with being the chef here again, because you know I'm not staying here permanently." She wanted to make that perfectly clear.

"That's what your mother said, but we're both hoping you might change your mind. This is your home. People here love you."

"I can't do it, Nora. I can't walk around town and go to all the places Brian and I went to together. It just reminds me of everything I lost."

"I understand," Nora said with compassion. "But I also know one thing for sure: you can run away from everything and everyone, but you can't run away from yourself."

"I'm not running away. I'm starting over. There's a difference."

"There is a difference. But until you deal with Alicia, you'll never be able to truly start over. You should have come back for Rob's funeral, honey."

She felt a sharp twinge of guilt. "I thought about coming, but there would have been drama, and the Haydens didn't need that." She let out a breath. "I can't believe Rob didn't make it back. He was so close to getting out. He wrote to me just a week before he died."

Nora's gaze sharpened. "Really? I didn't know you were keeping in touch with Rob."

"He wanted me to make peace with Alicia. I told him that wasn't going to happen." She paused. "I saw Alicia in town. She was at the hardware store picking up equipment. I can't believe she's thinking of taking more people out on the river. How can she do that?"

"It's their family business, Kelly. George Hayden isn't going to give up his life's work because of an accident."

"It wasn't an accident. It was carelessness. It was something," she said, still not really sure exactly what had happened, but everyone who'd been out there that day seemed to think the Haydens were responsible in some way.

"Well, Alicia has a boy to raise, and she has to make money somehow."

Her heart softened as she thought about Justin. She was his godmother. She'd been at Alicia's side through the eighteen-hour labor. She'd held Justin when he was only a few minutes old. Until six months ago, she'd been a huge part of his life. "How is Justin?"

"Getting bigger. Looking more like Rob every day. And missing his Aunt Kelly, I'll bet. I doubt he understands why you've disappeared."

"I'm sure Alicia has explained it to him." She sighed. "I don't want to be here, Nora. It's easier when I'm away. I don't have to worry about who I'm going to run into when I walk down the street."

"You can't avoid dealing with Alicia forever. You two need to have it out."

"We can't get past the fact that Brian died on her boat. No amount of talking will change that."

Nora shook her head. "You are one stubborn girl. You two need each other now more than you ever did. You lost your fiancé. She lost her brother. Two very important men in your lives."

"But I wasn't responsible for Rob dying, and she *was* responsible for Brian's death. She was his guide! She was supposed to make sure he was okay."

"White-water rafting is dangerous, Kelly. Brian knew that."

"No, he didn't. He thought it was like a roller-coaster ride. You get on, and you're scared, but you don't think you're going to die." She raised a hand. "I don't want to talk about it anymore. I'm just here to cook for our guests and take care of Mom. As soon as things get back to normal, I'm going back to Sacramento and to my new life. So, what's on the dinner menu?"

"Lamb kebabs with wild rice and fresh asparagus."

"Great." She grabbed an apron out of the cupboard and put it on. She felt better as she got into cooking mode. The kitchen was under her complete and utter control, unlike the rest of her life. But as she pulled out pots and pans and moved between the refrigerator and the stove, she was taken back in time to the last time she'd made dinner there, the night before Brian's accident.

Her bridesmaids had come over to try on their dresses, and she'd made angel-hair pasta with fresh vegetables from Alicia's garden. They'd drunk red wine and talked and laughed.

Pain ripped through her. She wanted to stop hurting. But it wasn't just Brian she'd lost; it was also Alicia. And deep, deep down inside, in the secret place in her heart, she wasn't sure which was more painful. And the guilt of that knowledge made it even worse.

Five

It took Gabe an hour and a half to walk the entire town of River Rock, and he found it more interesting than he'd anticipated. The town had a lot of character and history. But he wasn't there to sightsee. He needed information. The line in front of Burt's Diner was three deep as the lunch crowd descended on the restaurant, so he decided to grab a beer at Mullaney's. The dark interior was filled with flat-screen TVs, big oak tables, and bench seats occupied mostly by men. He stepped up to the bar and ordered a beer and a burger from a twentysomething redheaded bartender named Cassie.

"Coming right up," she said. A moment later, she set down his beer. "You're not from around here."

"How do you know that?"

"Because I know just about everyone in River Rock."

"No, I'm not from around here."

"So, are you passing through?"

"Not sure yet."

"Well, aren't you the man of mystery," she said with a smile.

A sudden light came into her eyes. "Wait a minute. You're from Wild River Tours, aren't you? You didn't get those biceps pushing paper around a desk."

"I didn't get them at Wild River Tours. Isn't that a rafting company?"

"They offer all kinds of extreme sports. I've heard they're expanding into River Rock, hoping to take over the river runs. I sent in a résumé, but no one has called me."

"What kind of job are you looking for?"

"I can handle a raft, and I know the best fishing on the Smoky River. I also rock climb. There are some great cliff walls about fifteen miles from here."

"You sound like you have a lot of talents, so why are you working here?"

"My cousin owns the place. He needed help. I needed money." As she moved down the bar to take another order, Gabe saw Keith approaching the bar.

"I didn't expect to see you here," he said.

"Just picking up my lunch," Keith replied. "We have parent-teacher conferences this week and next, so I called in my order. I need to gather my strength."

"They're tough on you, huh?"

"Some are, usually the ones who are feeling guilty for having no idea what their kid has been doing the last few months. What are you up to today?"

"Just checking out the town." He wanted to dislike Keith for a lot of reasons, most of which had to do with the fact that Alicia liked him, but Keith's nice-guy attitude wasn't making that easy.

"It's good you're here," Keith said, surprising him. "Alicia was really shaken up by Rob's death, and it's difficult for her to talk about him with me because I never met him. And her dad doesn't like to talk about Rob because it's too painful. She's kind of on her own, and I don't think she's handling it as well as she pretends to be."

Gabe nodded, not really sure what to say.

"I just wish she could persuade her dad to give up the business. I wasn't around last year when the accident happened, but it's still fresh in people's minds, especially with the season approaching, and no one seems very happy that the Haydens are planning to go back out on the river."

"You think they should quit?"

"I think Alicia would be just as happy growing vegetables in her garden instead of braving the white water."

He wondered if that were really true. Alicia had to have had a core of fearlessness to run the river all these years. That kind of thrill seeking didn't just vanish. She was afraid now, but burying that fear in a garden wasn't the best idea. She needed to face her fear, to take it down, or it would haunt her for the rest of her life.

"She has to find a way to stand up to her father, which won't be easy," Keith continued. "George loves the river. Never seen a man so passionate about anything. I don't understand it."

"I admire his sense of purpose. He knows what he wants, and he goes after it."

"Sometimes at the expense of his family. Alicia has lost a lot of friends. I worry about her and Justin, too. David says the kids at school say mean things to him."

Gabe frowned, hating the thought of little Justin getting bullied because of what sounded to him like an accident. Another reason he needed to find out what had really happened.

Keith paid for his lunch, then said, "I'll see you around, Gabe."

"I'm sure you will," he replied as Keith walked away.

"You're friends with Keith?" Cassie asked curiously.

"We met last night."

"And he called you Gabe?"

"Yes. Gabe Ryder."

Surprise flashed in her eyes. "You're Gabe Ryder, Rob's best friend. I was wondering why you didn't come to the funeral. He used to talk about you all the time when he was home."

"Unfortunately, I couldn't make it to the service."

"We all miss Rob so much," she said, her eyes a little too bright. "He used to sit just where you're sitting and shoot the breeze with me. What a good guy."

"He really was."

"I'll get you your burger," she said.

While he was waiting for his food, he glanced around the room, noting a familiar face at one of the booths. It was the man he'd seen with Kelly earlier, Brian's brother. He was seated with another guy about his age, and he was talking a lot, gesturing every now and then. Gabe wondered if he was always pissed off, or if there was something about this day that was annoying him, because he'd seemed just as aggressive with Kelly earlier. Maybe it was anger at losing his brother that made him seem so intense.

Gabe could understand that. He'd been living with that

inner rage, that sense of injustice, since Rob had died. But he couldn't give in to his emotions. He had to hold it together for Rob's sake and for Alicia's.

How he was going to help them, he had no idea. Maybe Alicia would be happier giving up the business. Would saving it help her or just keep her chained to a company that had become a huge weight around her shoulders?

Rob had always spoken about the business with fondness. Then again, Rob had rarely worked the river; he'd just enjoyed it. And when he'd been home, Rob had been treated very well. Gabe had seen that firsthand when he'd come home with Rob that Christmas. George and Alicia had catered to him like he was a visiting king. And Rob had lapped it up.

He'd lapped it up, too, he thought somewhat guiltily. He'd never had a family to come home to, no one who was worrying about whether he would make it out alive. He'd enjoyed their attention, especially Alicia's. God, she was pretty, he thought with a sigh. A little bit battered by life now, but she still had a light in her eyes. Keith was a lucky guy.

"Hey, Cass, where's our beer?" Russ bellowed as he came up to the bar. His step was unsteady, his tie slightly askew, his button-down shirt creeping out of his slacks.

"I'm getting them," Cassie called back. "You're drinking a lot for lunch, aren't you, Russ?"

"I'm thirsty," he said. He caught Gabe staring and gave him a belligerent look. "I saw you before with Alicia."

"He's Rob's friend," Cassie cut in.

"Yeah, well, you can give Alicia a message for me. Stay the hell off the river, or she'll be sorry."

Gabe got to his feet, happy to top the other man by about three inches. "Let me give *you* a message. You threaten her again, and *you'll* be sorry."

"She deserves to be threatened. That bitch is a goddamned murderer."

The rage that had been simmering for weeks exploded, and Gabe smashed his fist into Russell's face. The other guy stumbled but then came back swinging. His first shot missed, but the second connected with the right side of Gabe's jaw. He was about to hit back when someone grabbed his arm. Russ's friend did the same to Russ.

"That's enough," Russ's friend said. "This isn't going to solve anything."

Gabe shook his arm away from the large man who'd grabbed it.

"You should go," the guy told him. "Now."

He hesitated a second, then headed toward the door. Shit! So much for his campaign to win over the town. He'd wanted to help Alicia, but he'd just made things worse.

Alicia spent most of the day in the office doing paperwork, updating their Web site, leaving messages for river guides, and ordering supplies. Despite being busy, she couldn't keep her mind off Gabe, wondering where he was, what he was doing. Checking her watch, she saw that it was almost two, and he'd been gone for hours.

After a few more minutes of restless work, she got up and headed out the door. She went up the hill and across the grass, cutting through the thicket of trees that separated the two properties. Gabe's truck was parked where it had been the night before, and as she approached the steps, she saw movement inside. He was back.

She didn't bother to knock, just turned the knob and walked in. Gabe was standing by the sink with a towel pressed to his face, a scowl on his lips.

"What happened to you?"

"Nothing," he ground out.

"It doesn't look like nothing."

"I walked into a tree branch."

She walked over to him and pulled the towel away from his face. His right eye was swelling. "You walked into someone's fist."

"It's not a big deal."

"Are you kidding me? You got into a fight. Did you hit someone, too?"

"He deserved it." There was not a speck of remorse in Gabe's dark eyes.

"You were supposed to charm the people in town."

"Yeah, well, this one was a lost cause."

"Who was it?"

"Brian's brother. The one who was with Kelly earlier."

"Russell?" she asked with a sinking heart. "You fought Russ? Why?"

"He was drunk."

"That's crazy. He's a real estate broker. It's the middle of the day."

"He was drunk," Gabe repeated. "And angry."

She gave him a long look, reading between his very short lines. "He said something about me."

"He was an asshole."

"You need ice," she said, opening the fridge. She took the towel from Gabe, grabbed a few cubes, rolled them up, and handed it back to him. "Tell me what he said."

"He doesn't want you to reopen your business," he said, pressing the ice pack against his face with a wince.

"Well, that's nothing new. He lost his brother."

"That doesn't mean he has the right to threaten you."

"He threatened me?"

"He won't be doing that again," Gabe replied.

She frowned. "I appreciate the defense, but fighting with Russ isn't going to help."

"You can't let him bully you."

"I'm not going to let him bully me." She paused. "How did you get back here?"

"Some trucker gave me a ride down the highway. I walked the rest of the way. What are you staring at?" he asked, shifting the ice on his face.

"You. Most of the time, you're so controlled. I can see the tension in your body, your face, as if you're afraid to relax, but then other times you're . . . completely different." She ran her tongue across her suddenly dry lips, remembering how passionate he'd been with her, how completely out of control they'd both been.

Desire glittered in his eyes, as if his mind was taking the same walk down memory lane.

A knock at the door startled them both.

"I'll get it," she said. She was surprised to see Cassie on the porch with a brown paper bag in her hands. "Hi, Cassie."

"Oh, hey, Alicia. I didn't know you were here," Cassie said, glancing past her to Gabe. "I brought you your lunch, Gabe.

You didn't get to eat it earlier. Actually, I had the cook make you up another burger," she added, sliding around Alicia.

"That was nice of you," Gabe said, taking the bag from her hands.

"I was so impressed at how you stood up to Russell," she added, her gaze filled with admiration. "He was way out of line."

Alicia felt an unexpected twinge of jealousy at Cassie's flirtatious smile.

"I could have handled it better," Gabe said.

"I think you handled it perfectly." Cassie looked at Alicia. "You should have seen him take on Russell. Rob would have been proud. Anyway, I have to get back to work, but if you need someone to show you around town, you know where to find me."

"I might take you up on that," he said.

"I'm counting on it," Cassie replied. "'Bye, Alicia."

"'Bye," she muttered, shutting the door behind Cassie. "Well, it looks like you managed to charm someone after all."

Kelly was in the checkout line at the market when she heard about the fight at Mullaney's. She hadn't met Gabe Ryder when he'd come home with Rob one Christmas, but she'd certainly heard a lot about him, both from Rob and from Alicia. Gabe had broken her best friend's heart. She'd never seen Alicia so destroyed. It had taken her months to get over him.

Gabe must have been the guy with her in the hardware store. She'd been so shocked to see Alicia that she hadn't paid him much attention until they'd walked out together and gotten into her car. They'd certainly looked friendly enough.

This was the problem with coming home. She had only been back in town a few days, and she was already getting caught up in gossip.

After paying for her groceries, she put them in the car, closed the door, and headed to Russ's office. Russ had always had a short fuse, but he was a good guy at heart, and he was still struggling with Brian's death. She needed to make sure he was all right.

Opening the front door to his office, she saw no one in reception, so she walked down the hall. Russ sat in the chair behind his desk, holding an ice pack to his face. His brown hair was tangled, his right eye was swollen, and there was blood on his white shirt. He couldn't have looked less like a successful real estate broker than he did right now.

Jared Donovan, a longtime friend of the Farr brothers, sat in one of the chairs in front of the desk. He had sandy blond hair and hazel eyes and wore his usual worn jeans and a long-sleeved T-shirt. He'd tilted the chair back on two legs, his boots resting on the desk. He set it down with a clatter when he saw her, his eyes a bit wary.

Seeing Jared only made her blood pressure rise. She'd known him since she was in kindergarten, and he always annoyed her.

"What happened, Russ?" she asked, moving into the room. "I heard you got into a fight."

"Some friend of Alicia's took a swing at me," he ground out.

"Why?"

Russ shrugged. "I don't know."

She looked to Jared for answers.

"We had a few too many beers at lunch," he said.

"Yet *you* seem fine." She turned back to Russell, not understanding his behavior. "You don't drink when you're at work."

"Well, I felt like it today. It wasn't a big deal. It was over before it started."

"It shouldn't have started at all. You run a business in this town, Russ. You can't be getting into bar fights. Everyone is talking about you."

"He hit me first."

"For no reason?" she asked doubtfully.

"I might have said something about Alicia staying off the river," Russ grumbled.

She let out a sigh and sat down on the edge of an empty chair. "This isn't going to work, Russ. We have to find a way to move on."

"It's easier for you," he said. "You don't live here anymore. I have to look at that damn river every day. And it's not like I can move somewhere else. I have a girlfriend here and my parents, my grandparents."

"Fighting isn't the answer."

"Actually, it felt pretty good to hit that guy."

"That guy was Rob Hayden's best friend, and he's a military veteran. He's won all kinds of medals for bravery and honor."

"I held my own," Russ said with annoyance. "He wasn't so tough."

She could see she wasn't going to get anywhere with Russ, so she got to her feet. "I'm going to head back to the inn. I'm glad you're all right."

"I'll walk out with you, Kelly," Jared said, following her out of the office. As they reached the sidewalk, he asked, "Where is your car?"

"At the market. I was buying some food when I heard about the fight." She paused. "You have to talk to Russ, Jared. He's out of control. The anger is coming off of him in huge black waves, and I'm afraid it's going to eat him up inside. The Farrs already lost one son because of that accident; I don't want them to lose another."

"There's nothing I can say. Believe me, I've tried. Russ was better for a while, but with rafting season coming up, he's been on edge again."

"I understand that, but I don't want to get caught up in a fight between Russ and Alicia."

"Good luck avoiding that."

She frowned at his sarcasm. Jared had been a thorn in her side most of her life. "You have such a lazy-ass attitude," she snapped.

His eyes widened. "Me? What did I do?"

"Nothing. That's the problem. You *never* do anything. You don't want to get in the middle, be involved, or say anything. You're neutral. You're Switzerland."

"What do you want me to say?"

"Something," she said in frustration. "You can't always be uninvolved. Russ is your friend, and you let him get in a fight."

"He did that on his own. And I don't want to take sides. I like Alicia, and I was close to Rob. But Brian was my friend, and Russ is, too. It's just a bad situation," he added, running his hand through his hair. "I'm sorry if I disappoint you."

"Well, that's nothing new."

"Ouch. What part of our history are you referring to?"

"Let's see. There are so many situations to choose from." She put her hands on her hips. "How about when Ricky Gaines put a frog down my shirt and you just laughed while I screamed?"

"That was in fourth grade!"

"Or when that slut you used to hook up with called me a bitch and you stood there and said nothing?"

"You *were* being a bitch, Kelly. And we were fifteen years old."

She drew in a sharp breath. It was both shocking and refreshing to have someone talk to her without choosing their words carefully, worried that she was going to faint or cry. "I was not being a bitch. You guys were making out in front of my locker. I couldn't get my books because you had your tongue down her throat."

"Yeah, and you were jealous," he said with a grin.

"In your dreams." She started walking down the street, but he fell into step alongside her.

"So what else did I do to piss you off?" he asked. "We might as well clear the air; you're on quite a roll."

"I said before, it's not what you do; it's what you don't do. You don't stand up for people. Or even for yourself, for that matter. You want to fight fires, but what are you doing? You're working in your dad's auto shop."

"He named his company Donovan and Sons. What was I supposed to do, leave him without a son?"

"That's just an excuse."

He grabbed her arm, halting her progress. "I know you're still grieving for Brian—"

"This has nothing to do with Brian. You've always been a pain in the ass."

"And you've always thought you were too good for me. The little princess in the manor."

She was shocked at the accusation. "That's not true. My family certainly isn't rich."

"You acted like they were."

"Really? You think I'm a snob?"

He stared down at her. "No, I don't think that," he said slowly. "We're not going to do this, Kelly. There's no point."

"See, you're backing down again. Why don't you just stay and fight for once?"

"I don't want to fight with you, even though you seem to be up for it. But we both know I'm not the one you're really angry at."

"At the moment, you *are* the one I'm mad at," she said, blowing out a breath. "Fine, whatever. I have to go."

"What's on the menu at the inn tonight?"

"Lamb. Why?" she asked, suspicious at the abrupt change in subject.

"You owe me a meal."

She shook her head. "I don't think so."

"You have a short memory. I built you that bookcase, remember? You said you'd make me a meal one night."

"That was almost a year ago."

"Is there a time limit on your promises?"

"Well, it's not going to happen tonight."

"Why not?"

"Because you make me mad," she said, her stomach churning with her words. "I don't need any more trouble, and every time you're around, trouble follows."

Six

Alicia sat in her car outside Justin's school, still thinking about Gabe's fight with Russell. Deep down, she was flattered that he'd stood up for her. It had been a while since anyone had done that. But her practical side told her the fight would only make things worse.

Pushing that thought aside, she smiled as Justin came out of school with his friends. He was doing well, better than expected. Rob had been a father figure to him in many ways, despite his absences. But kids were resilient, and Justin was bouncing back.

He opened the car door, David on his heels. David seemed to grow an inch every time she saw him, stretching out his thin body, making him a little awkward. He was a good kid, a little more serious than Justin, with not as much of a mischievous glint in his eye. He was a great influence on her son, as was Keith. Their arrival in town had certainly changed one part of her life in a good way.

"We need to catch some frogs, Mom," Justin announced.

"The annual frog-jumping contest is tomorrow afternoon, and David and I want to enter."

"Didn't Keith say he'd take you tomorrow morning?"

"He just found out he has to work," David interjected. "He has to ref a soccer game for the school."

"Oh." Maybe that's why she had two missed calls from him. There were a dozen other things she needed to do right now, none of which involved catching frogs, but she didn't want to disappoint Justin. And maybe an afternoon away from work and problems was just what she needed. "I guess we're catching some frogs then."

"We need Uncle Rob's lucky net," Justin said.

"Okay. We'll get a snack at home, and then we'll start looking for some jumpers."

Thirty minutes later, the boys had finished granola bars and apples and were eager to start their hunt. First stop was Rob's cabin. Alicia drew in a deep breath as she mounted the stairs, something she seemed to need to do every time she was about to come face-to-face with Gabe.

Instead of walking in, she decided to knock. Gabe opened the door a moment later. He must have just gotten out of the shower, because he was barefoot, his brown hair was damp, and there were beads of water lingering on his forehead. His eye was more swollen than before, and the skin around his cheekbone was bruised. She felt an irresistible, ridiculous pull of attraction. Knowing that he'd gotten those bruises defending her was incredibly hot, and she felt her cheeks warm under his gaze.

"Sorry to bother you," she said, trying to tear her gaze away from his broad chest and up to his face. "I need to get something out of Rob's laundry room."

"Come on in."

"Wow, your eye is turning black," Justin said, a note of awe in his voice. "Did you get in a fight?"

"I had a disagreement with someone," Gabe replied.

"Did you beat him up?" Justin asked.

Alicia sighed at the look of adoration in her son's eyes. Justin seemed to be drawn to men who exhibited larger-than-life qualities. She didn't want him to admire someone who used his fists to solve problems. She'd rather have him looking up to Keith, who used his intellect and his communication skills. "Fighting is not the way to solve your problems," she said. "Talking is better."

Justin gave her a doubtful look and then turned to Gabe. "Who did you fight?"

"No one important. And your mom is right; fighting should always be the last option. I made a mistake today. So, what brings you all here?"

"We need Uncle Rob's lucky net," Justin answered. "David and I are in the frog-jumping contest tomorrow, and we need to catch some frogs."

Alicia smiled at the look of amazement that crossed Gabe's face.

"Seriously?" he asked.

"Yes," she said. "River Rock sometimes seems like it's right out of a Mark Twain novel. It's part of its charm. The annual frog-jumping contest is part of the spring festival, which starts tomorrow."

"I saw the signs in town," Gabe said. "Where do you get the frogs?"

"There are a couple of good ponds around town. I think the net is in Rob's laundry room."

"Have at it."

As she left the room, she heard Gabe talking to Justin and David. Justin, as usual, had a million questions, and Gabe handled them well. That shouldn't have surprised her. Rob had always told her that Gabe was a great leader.

After retrieving the buckets and nets, she returned to the living room. She noted one of Rob's favorite books open on the coffee table. "Were you reading?" she asked Gabe. "Rob loved that book. He was a Civil War buff."

"I know. He used to talk about it all the time."

"He read it to me, too," Justin volunteered.

"I guess you're making yourself at home," she said, not sure how she felt about that. She had yet to read Rob's letter, but she didn't really think it would deny Gabe's story. It was just like Rob to send Gabe here. But she couldn't let herself get used to depending on him, because he wouldn't be here permanently. He'd already told her that he was only staying until they got back on their feet.

"I haven't touched much else," Gabe said quietly, catching her eye. "But if you want help going through the clothes or whatever . . ."

"I don't want to talk about that now," she said quickly. "We have frogs to catch."

"Can you come with us?" Justin asked eagerly.

"I'm sure Gabe isn't interested in catching frogs," she said.

He met her challenging gaze with a smile. "I've never done it before. Sounds like fun."

"It's not. It's wet, and it's dirty."

He smiled. "I don't mind wet or dirty."

She frowned, seeing the sexy sparkle in his eyes. Acutely

aware of the two ten-year-old boys in hearing distance, she said, "Suit yourself," and handed him the buckets.

They piled into her car and drove to a swampy area about a mile away. The low-lying land around the pond was undeveloped, since the area often flooded during storms. Large, thick trees hung over the pond, and the water flowed around hundreds of small, slippery rocks. The water was only a foot or two deep, perfect for wading.

"Rob and I used to have a lot of luck here," she said as they got out of the car.

"So, this isn't your first time?" Gabe asked.

"Not by a long shot. I've been catching frogs since I was six years old. I even won the frog-jumping contest when I was eleven."

"You won, Mom?" Justin asked in surprise. "But you're a girl."

"Girls can win contests." Her father's chauvinistic attitude was already rubbing off on her son. "Girls can do anything boys can do."

Gabe smiled. "I agree. Some of the finest marines I worked with were women."

"There are girl marines?" Justin asked, even more astonished by that thought.

She tousled her son's hair. "That's right, kid."

"I'm going to be a marine when I get older," Justin announced. "David is, too, aren't you?"

David didn't look quite as convinced as Justin, but he backed up his friend with a nod.

Alicia had no intention of letting Justin follow in her brother's footsteps, but that was a discussion for another time. She walked over to the edge of the pond, kicked off her shoes, and rolled up her jeans to the knees while the others followed suit.

"The frogs have to be four inches in length from head to toe," she told Gabe.

"Did you bring a ruler?" he teased.

"Just eyeball it."

The boys quickly stepped their way across the rocks as she looked into the grassy part of the pond nearer to shore. She could hear the sound of the frogs, but catching one wasn't quite as easy as it looked. They were slippery little suckers and very quick.

After several attempts, Gabe managed to grab one, turning to her with a triumphant smile. "Got a big one for you."

She laughed at his boyish pride. The boys and the frogs had brought out a playful side of him that she hadn't expected.

He tossed the frog into the bucket. She was just about to tell him to cover the bucket when the frog jumped out and back into the pond.

He stared at the escapee in bewilderment. "What the hell?"

She grinned. "You have to put the lid on."

"I'm going to get him back," he said with determination.

"You should try, because he's obviously a good jumper."

Watching Gabe try to recapture his prey was very entertaining, especially when his foot slipped off a rock and he landed in a foot of murky water. The boys called out tips to Gabe, and all three males suddenly zeroed in on one poor frog.

After getting her own frog with a lot less drama, Alicia sat down on the bank. Justin and David had lost interest in Gabe's efforts and now seemed just as entertained by skimming rocks off the surface of the water. But Gabe didn't give up. He went after his escaped prey like the ruthless warrior he was, determination etched on every line of his face, and in the end, he caught him, landing him in the bucket and sealing it with a satisfied smile.

He sat down next to her, a warm burn of sun on his cheeks, a light in his eyes. She couldn't help smiling back at him. "You like to win, don't you?"

"Losing is not an option."

She considered that. "I used to think that way—never quit, never give up—but it's exhausting sometimes."

"You just need to regroup, accept a little help. Stop being so stubbornly independent, and—"

"I get it," she said dryly, holding up a hand. "But I let you help this morning, and look what happened—you came back with a black eye."

"That was not my finest moment."

"I don't think I thanked you for defending me."

"Anytime," he said, giving her a warm smile. For a moment, there was nothing between them but silence and the chirping of the frogs. "They have their own song, don't they?" he said.

"A loud one," she agreed.

"This place has a rhythm to it—the frogs, the water, the wind through the trees. It's nice. Sometimes I wonder why Rob ever left."

"Too slow, too quiet. Rob wanted a more exciting life. Last time you were here, you said you couldn't imagine living in a place like this."

"I said a lot of stupid things back then, Alicia. You made my head spin. You made me question my choices. And I didn't handle it well."

She was surprised at his candor. "Really? I did that? In one week?"

"It shocked the hell out of me, too," he said, meeting her gaze. After a moment, he turned away, gazing out at the pond.

"What were you going to do, Gabe, before Rob died? Before you decided to come here and save us? What was your plan for when you were out of the service?"

His jaw stiffened, his profile turning hard. "I had an offer to work for a private security company."

"What does that mean, exactly?"

"The group takes on jobs that the military isn't equipped to handle."

"Well, that's nice and vague. Are you a mercenary?"

"I will be getting paid," he said with a short smile that no longer reached his eyes. "But I wouldn't call it that."

"But it's still war games for you." She didn't know why she was disappointed. "Sounds like it's right up your alley."

"I thought about doing something else, but I've been a marine my entire adult life. I don't have a lot of other skills."

"I'm sure that's not true." She paused. "You've never really told me what happened to your parents. Are they dead or just absent?"

"My mother is dead. She OD'd when I was eight." He stared out at the pond. "But she wasn't really around much before that. Every once in a while, she'd go to rehab, get cleaned up, promise never to do it again, and then a week later, she'd be crazy high. My father wasn't any better. He worked as a trucker, and he got hooked on amphetamines to keep him awake. Then he just used because he couldn't stop. I wasn't planned, just another mistake in their mistake-filled lives. After my mom died, I lived with an aunt for a while. Then she got married, and her new husband didn't want me around. I spent time off and on with my dad, but he could barely keep himself together. And one day, he just took off. I got stuck in some teen foster-care homes, and that was that."

"You never saw him again?"

"Once, after I graduated from high school. I was working at a burger joint before I enlisted, and he showed up, asking me if I had any money. That's the last I saw of him. When I turned eighteen, I joined the Corps. I knew they'd give me three meals a day and a roof over my head, or at least a tent."

No wonder he was so guarded, so dark; he'd never felt the unconditional love of a parent for a child. Her heart ached for him, but she knew that the last thing he wanted was her pity. And she didn't pity him; she admired him for enduring and triumphing.

"I wasn't being noble or patriotic," he added. "I just wanted something stable."

"I can understand that. You had it rough."

"Some people shouldn't have kids."

"That's true. My mom took off when I was twelve, and I never forgave her for that. After I had Justin, I saw how difficult motherhood could be, but I couldn't imagine ever walking out on my child. I adored Justin from the second he was born. I didn't know what the hell I was doing; sometimes I still don't. But I try my best." She paused. "I just worry that I'm not enough for Justin. He needs a dad. And Connor will never be the kind of father that Justin deserves."

He picked a blade of grass and twisted his fingers around it. "Is that why you're involved with Keith? Because he's good dad material?"

"Keith is a good father, but that's not the only reason."

"He makes you hot."

"I don't want to talk about Keith with you," she said, feeling more than a little uncomfortable.

"Fine with me."

"What about you? No woman in your life?" she asked, deciding it was time to turn the tables.

"Nope. I like to travel light."

"That's what you said the last time you were here, right before you left."

His gaze settled on her face. "I wasn't prepared for you, Alicia. I didn't expect what happened to happen."

"I didn't, either. You were like a tornado. You came in and took over my life, and then you were gone just as quickly. It hurt."

His eyes darkened. "It hurt me, too."

She shook her head. "I'm not going to feel sorry for you. It was your decision to end it. I wasn't asking you to quit the Marines. I just wanted to know if there was the possibility of a future together."

"You were looking for a husband and a man who would be a father to Justin, and I couldn't be good in either role. I wasn't that guy then, and I'm not now."

"You're not? Or you don't want to be?"

"I don't know how to be a family man. And I wouldn't want to screw up some kid's life the way my parents screwed up mine."

"That's a cop-out. Just because you share someone's genes doesn't mean you'll be just like them. I'm not like my mother. I'm not going to quit on my kid. And I can't imagine that you would ever do that, either."

Justin and David came back with their bucket of frogs, and

Gabe looked relieved at the interruption. In truth, she was a little relieved, too. Their conversation had gotten too heavy, too personal.

"Can we practice getting the frogs to jump?" Justin asked.

"Let's do that back at the house," she said, getting to her feet. She rolled down her jeans and slipped on her shoes.

"I'll text my dad," David said, taking out his phone. "He said he'd meet us."

"Good," she said, not liking the sudden spark in Gabe's eyes. She didn't need him analyzing her relationship with Keith. It was none of his business. "Stay out of it," she muttered as they walked to the car.

"What are you talking about?"

"You know what I'm talking about," she said, glancing around to make sure Justin and David were out of earshot. "Don't try to mess up my relationship with Keith."

"I'm not planning to do that."

"Good. Because he's a great guy."

"That's what you keep saying, and I'm starting to wonder who you're trying to convince—me or yourself."

Gabe felt restless. It was nine o'clock at night, and he didn't know what the hell to do with himself. After the frog-collecting expedition, he'd left Alicia and the boys with Keith and gone into town. He picked up some food at the market, made himself some spaghetti, read the newspaper, and looked through some of Rob's things, wondering how he could make himself a little more help-ful to the Hayden family. So far, he hadn't come up with an an-swer. Maybe it was time to take a closer look at the business.

He left the house and walked across the grass and through

the trees. He could see Alicia, Keith, George, and the boys gathered around the dining-room table. It looked like they were playing some sort of board game. The windows were open, and the sound of family laughter washed over him, making him feel even more restless. That kind of scene was what he'd always wanted and never had.

Turning away from the house, he headed down to the office of Hayden River Adventures. As he climbed the stairs to the deck, he was surprised to see a flicker of light coming from the yard. A flashlight? His senses went on high alert. Who the hell would be wandering around the yard with a flashlight at this time of night?

He moved closer, staying as quiet as he could, keeping to the shadows, and then he slipped through the back gate, which had been left ajar. A dark figure was leaning over a box that appeared to be filled with oars.

Creeping up behind him, Gabe grabbed the man's arm, whirled him around, and shoved him up against the side of the building. The flashlight fell with a clatter as the man gasped in alarm.

"Who the hell are you?" Gabe demanded. "And what are you doing here?"

The man squirmed under his grasp, his face in the shadows. "I'm Kenny Barber, and I work here. I'm one of the guides."

"Why are you out here with a flashlight?"

"I was looking for a backpack I left here. Let me go."

Gabe gave him a long look, grabbed the flashlight off the ground, and turned it on the man's face, then took a step back. The guy was early twenties, scruffy beard, hooded sweatshirt, dark jeans. "You got any ID?"

"Are you a cop?"

"No, but I can get one. Right now, you're trespassing."

"You're the one who's trespassing," the guy said, reaching into his pocket. He pulled out a billfold and opened it up, revealing his driver's license.

Gabe stepped forward. *Kenny Barber, age twenty-five, River Rock, California.* He lowered the flashlight. "Do the Haydens know you're down here?"

"I didn't want to bother them."

"You're going to have to come up with a better story." Something was off about Kenny Barber, and he wasn't about to let him go without finding out what that was.

"Why should I? Who are you?"

"Gabe Ryder, friend of the family."

Awareness registered in Kenny's eyes. "Rob's friend. Dude, I'm so sorry about what happened to him. Rob talked about you all the time. Look, I've been working for the Haydens for the last four years. I left some of my personal equipment here, and I came to get it."

"In the dark, without telling anyone?"

Kenny shifted his feet. "Okay, here's the deal. I like George and Alicia. They've been like family to me, but the accident last year destroyed the business. I need to work, and I need to move on."

"Why not just tell them that?"

"George doesn't take no for an answer. And with Rob's death, I didn't want to talk to Alicia. But I will," he added quickly. "I'll come back in the morning."

"Who are you going to work for?" Gabe asked.

"Wild River Tours. They're looking for guides, and I'm one of the best."

"You must know the Haydens need you."

"Even if I stayed on, it wouldn't help. They're not going to have any customers. Their name has been trashed up and down the river."

"If you're one of the best guides, then you must have people who'd have faith in you. Why not bring those customers in and show them that this company is still worthy? What happened last year was an accident, right?"

"That's what they said. I wasn't on that trip. I feel bad about deserting them, but I have to look out for myself. Wild River Tours is paying double. They're grabbing all of the good guides, too. The Haydens are done, whether they accept it or not."

"I'll let Alicia know you were here," he said.

Kenny took off without his flashlight, so Gabe put it to good use. There were a couple of kayaks in the yard, a box of oars, an old bicycle, and two big walk-in storage lockers with locks on them. He wondered what Kenny had been looking for. He couldn't quite buy the idea that Kenny would choose nine o'clock on a Friday night to collect some personal belongings.

Flipping off the flashlight, he headed toward the Hayden house, pausing under the trees as he saw David come out of the house, going toward the car while Keith and Alicia paused on the porch.

His gut twisted inside as he watched Keith put his arms around Alicia. He said something, and she smiled; then she lifted her face to his.

It was a quick kiss, but it still burned him.

Alicia waited on the porch as Keith got into the car and pulled out of the drive. As she turned to go inside, he called her name.

"What are you doing here?" she asked in surprise.

"I walked down to the boathouse and saw a guy with a flashlight. He said his name was Kenny Barber and he'd come to collect something he'd left there."

"Kenny is one of our guides. I've been calling him for the last three weeks, and he hasn't returned my calls."

"He told me he signed up with Wild River Tours."

Disappointment filled her eyes. "I was hoping he was just out of town."

"Why would he be messing around behind your building at nine o'clock at night?"

"I have no idea." Her gaze narrowed. "But you obviously have a theory."

"More of a gut instinct. He was up to something."

"I don't know. Kenny has worked for us for four years. He's like family."

"Sometimes family turns on you."

"I don't want to be that cynical. Maybe you're overreacting, like you did last night when Sadie knocked over the trash cans. If Kenny said he left something in the yard, he probably did."

"He didn't have anything in his hands when he left."

"I'll call him tomorrow. What were you doing down there, anyway?"

"I was taking a walk. How was your night with the boyfriend?"

"Good. We played Monopoly. A hot Friday night in River Rock."

"About as hot as that kiss you gave him."

She crossed her arms in front of her chest. "You *were* spying on me."

"I didn't want to interrupt—not that there was much to interrupt."

"David was in the car," she said defensively.

"That's the only reason you gave him a peck?"

"I'm not going to discuss how I kiss with you."

"You don't have to, because I know how you kiss when you want someone. It sure as hell wasn't like that."

"I care for Keith. And he's good for me and Justin. So leave it alone, Gabe. Just leave it all alone."

She returned to the house, the front door banging behind her.

He let out a breath. He *should* leave it alone. But somehow he didn't think that would be possible.

Seven

 L ong time no see," Alicia said as Gabe appeared on her doorstep just after eight-thirty on Saturday morning. She didn't like the way he'd questioned her relationship with Keith the night before, the way he'd critiqued their kiss. They had plenty of passion; they just didn't have very much alone time in which to express it. "What do you want?" she asked shortly.

He gave a hopeful sniff. "Do I smell breakfast?"

"When Rob gave you his house, it didn't include meals."

"Gabe," her father said, coming up behind her. "Good to see you. Are you going to the festival with us?"

"I wouldn't miss it," Gabe said with a cheerful smile. "I'm just going to go home and have some cold cereal, and then I'll be back."

"Don't be ridiculous. Alicia has enough food for an army here, don't you, honey?"

"Of course, plenty for everyone. I wouldn't want you to have to eat cold cereal."

Gabe gave her a teasing wink as he passed by.

She shook her head. Gabe had a lot of weapons in his arsenal, and right now he was being charming and playful, which was pretty irresistible. But she didn't intend to let him know that.

In the kitchen, she busied herself with the food while the guys talked about the festival. As usual, Justin and her dad kept the conversation going, so neither she nor Gabe had to say much. After they were done eating, they headed out to the festival. She insisted on taking two cars so that if someone wanted to leave early, they'd have the option. She also didn't want to tie herself to Gabe for the day. Keith was going to be at the festival, too. And she wanted to spend time with him.

A carnival had been set up at the fairgrounds on the outskirts of town. There were the usual game booths and rides, including a Ferris wheel and a small roller coaster. In addition, there were unique River Rock events such as the frog-jumping and log-rolling contests. Musical performers would keep the crowds entertained, and food booths had been set up, with every local restaurant owner participating.

As she got out of the car, the first of the day's music acts was warming up on the bandstand. The familiar sight made her think of another day just like this one when she'd watched Connor play from a blanket on the grass. At eighteen, she'd been a sucker for his love songs. That night, they'd made love by the river. It hadn't been nearly as romantic as she'd imagined it would be. The grass had been wet and cold and uncomfortable, and they'd both been a little drunk, a little too caught up in some springtime magic and a lot of teenage lust.

"Mom?" Justin's impatient voice brought her back to the present. "Are you coming?"

She looked away from the bandstand, away from the past. "Yes," she said, moving around the car as her father and Gabe joined them. Within minutes, her father saw some friends and quickly disappeared, leaving her with Justin and Gabe.

Justin seemed to have a good case of hero worship, and she couldn't really blame him. Gabe had a presence that couldn't be denied. Walking by his side through the carnival, she couldn't help noticing the attention they were drawing, and for the first time in a long time, she didn't think anyone was really looking at her. It was Gabe they were curious about. He was a ruggedly attractive man who walked with a sense of purpose, of command. Gabe was a born leader, and it was clear that more than a few ladies in town wanted to follow. But for the moment, Gabe seemed more interested in winning Justin a prize.

"Which one do you want to play?" Gabe asked Justin.

"The biggest prizes are over there." Justin pointed to the shooting booth.

Gabe gave her a questioning look. "How do you feel about that?"

"It's your money."

"All right," he said, pulling out a dollar bill and setting it down on the counter. As soon as he picked up the gun, he went from man to marine. It might have been only a carnival game, but Gabe aimed and fired with absolute precision, hitting the bull's-eye six times in a row.

The carnival hawker, a young tattooed guy, was as blown away as Justin. "Man, this game is rigged, and you still got 'em all," he muttered.

"That was so cool," Justin said, his eyes wide and impressed. "Can you teach me how to shoot like that?"

"Why don't you pick out your prize?" Gabe said, setting down the gun.

"Not bad," Alicia commented.

"I wasn't sure how you felt about guns."

"I grew up with a father and a brother who used to take me to the shooting range."

"That explains why Rob was so good."

"As good as you?"

He shrugged. "Perhaps. I've always had a good eye." He cleared his throat, a spark coming into his eyes as he said, "I bet Keith couldn't do that."

"He's pretty athletic," she said. "But it wouldn't be an even playing field, considering how much training you've had. If you want to impress me, you're going to have to win at something you haven't spent the last decade perfecting."

"Name your game."

She looked around. "Water-balloon toss?"

He smiled. "Did I mention that I've handled grenades?"

"Okay, forget that. How about tossing a baseball into a bucket?"

"I was the star pitcher on our unit's baseball team."

"Really? Rob let you be the star?"

Gabe's smile broadened. "Rob was the catcher, so he liked to think it was his calling of the pitches that won us games."

"I didn't know you guys played baseball."

"Sometimes it was a makeshift game in the middle of the desert, a little taste of America's favorite pastime when we were far, far away. Soccer was big, too. A lot of the local kids would bring by soccer balls and kick 'em around."

"So anything with a ball is probably out," she mused. "Well, we still have the frog-jumping contest."

"When is that?"

"This afternoon." She gazed up at the darkening sky. Clouds had been blowing in all morning, and it was getting downright cold. "Hope the weather holds." She drew the edges of her jacket closer together. "It doesn't really feel like spring at the moment."

"Alicia!"

She smiled at the woman jogging toward her. Jordan arrived as she always did, in a whirlwind of smile and hugs.

"When did you get back?" Alicia asked.

"Yesterday. Paris was amazing. And Italy was over the moon. I'm still giddy."

A tall, willowy strawberry-blonde with lightly freckled skin and beautiful green eyes, Jordan was an artist who'd recently met and married the man of her dreams, who'd promptly taken her off to Paris to fulfill more of her dreams.

"You look happy."

"How could I not be? Philip treated me like a queen." Jordan gave Gabe a quick, curious look. "Sorry to interrupt. Have we met?"

"Gabe Ryder," he said, extending his hand.

"Oh, of course," she said, shaking his hand. "We met when you were here before. You probably don't remember me. I was waiting tables at Mullaney's back then. I'm Jordan Wilms."

"It's nice to see you again. And I do remember you. The painter, right?"

"Very good. I recently got married," she said, shamelessly showing off her ring. "Philip runs the Cantor Deli on Main Street."

"Congratulations."

"Thank you. So, what are you two doing?" Jordan asked.

"Actually, I'm going to get something to drink," Gabe said. "Do you ladies want anything?"

"No, thanks," Alicia said, and Jordan shook her head.

Before Gabe could take off, Justin came running over with a glittery sword in his hands and an excited grin on his face. "Look what Gabe won for me, Aunt Jordan."

"Very impressive," Jordan said. "How did he do that?"

"He shot the bull's-eye six times in a row."

Gabe cleared his throat. "I got lucky. You thirsty, Justin? I'm getting a drink."

"I want to get a snow cone," Justin said. "Can I, Mom?"

"Sure. But don't swing that sword at anyone."

She was surprised to see Justin slip his hand into Gabe's as they walked away. The sight made her heart turn over.

"That's sweet," Jordan commented, following her gaze. "Looks like Justin has a new friend. What about you?"

"I don't know how I feel about him," she admitted.

"When did he come back?"

"Two days ago. He just showed up and announced that he was moving into Rob's house. He claims Rob gave it to him."

"Seriously? His house? Did he offer any proof?"

"He had a letter from Rob. He gave it to me, but I haven't had the guts to open it yet. It would be hard to see Rob's handwriting, especially on something he wrote fairly recently."

Jordan's gaze filled with compassion and concern. "How are you handling his being here?"

"It's fine," she said awkwardly.

Jordan gave her a knowing look. "Come on, Alicia. I was

here three years ago when you cried your eyes out for a solid week. He broke your heart."

"Well, I'm not in love with him anymore."

"Are you sure? He's still damn hot."

She dragged her gaze away from Justin and Gabe, who had gotten in line by the snow-cone machine. "He dumped me, Jordan. I'm not putting myself in that position again."

"I bet there are *some* positions you'd like," Jordan said with a mischievous twinkle in her eyes.

"You have sex on the brain."

"Well, I *did* just get back from my honeymoon."

"Was it everything you hoped it would be?"

"And more. I'm so happy, Alicia. I never imagined that Philip had such a romantic side, but he was incredible." She laughed as she blinked away a happy tear. "Anyway, as much as I loved Europe, I'm happy to be home. The month passed quickly, but it was still a long time to be gone. I'm so inspired by everything I saw, I'm itching to paint again. I have an offer from a gallery in San Francisco to show some of my work in their summer sidewalk art show, so I have a lot to get done."

"I'm glad things are falling into place for you," Alicia said. "You've worked hard, and you deserve it."

"And what about you? How's your dad?"

"Getting better."

"When I left, you were still debating if you were going to reopen the business."

"We're trying to make it happen, but there's a lot of resentment around town, and I'm having trouble getting some of our guides back."

"I heard that Kenny Barber is going to Wild River Tours. Phil said he stopped into the deli the other day and told him they made him a great offer."

"I wish he would have told me that instead of ignoring my calls." She also wondered again what he'd been doing at her boathouse the night before.

"He probably just wants to avoid an awkward situation. Speaking of awkward, Philip was approached by Wild River Tours to do box lunches and dinners for their overnight trips. I told him to turn it down."

"You didn't have to do that."

"Honey, you and I have been friends most of our lives. I'm not turning my back on you."

"Thanks," she said with a smile, touched by Jordan's loyalty. "I appreciate it, but if Phil can make some money off Wild River Tours, then he should do it."

"I just don't like the way they're trying to take over your runs."

"We don't own the river."

"No, but your reputation was impeccable for sixty years, and it's time people stopped blaming you for what was an accident."

"I hope they will. Not just for the sake of the business but because it's been hard coming into town and not knowing who's trying to avoid me."

Jordan frowned. "I thought things might have gotten better since the funeral. My parents said there was a good turnout."

"Yes, there was, but not many people came back to the house. Just a few friends."

"I should have been there."

"No, I didn't want you to come back," she said with a definitive shake of her head. Jordan had already left on her honeymoon when they'd gotten the news of Rob's death. "There was nothing you could do. And Rob was so excited when he heard you were finally going to see real art; he wouldn't have wanted you to miss that."

"I miss him already," Jordan said. "It doesn't feel real."

"Not to me, either, but it felt a little more real when Gabe moved into his place. It's weird looking out my window and seeing the lights on in Rob's house, knowing it's not my brother there."

"I can't believe Gabe is going to live in River Rock. I thought one of the reasons you two broke up was that he wasn't cut out for life in a small town."

"It was hardly a breakup," she corrected. "More of a one-night stand."

"We need to get together and have a long talk. What are you doing for your birthday tomorrow night?"

"Absolutely nothing, and don't try to talk me into anything," she said firmly. "I don't want to celebrate. I just want to get through the day."

"I don't want you to be alone on your birthday."

"It's what I want, really."

Jordan frowned. "Fine. We'll go to dinner one night next week and catch up. It will be like old times."

"Not exactly old times," she said with a sigh. "Kelly is back. She came home for her mom's surgery. I ran into her yesterday, and it was a very brief, very uncomfortable thirty seconds."

"I was hoping you two might be able to work things out."

"I wish we could," Alicia said, feeling the pain of lost

friendship deep in her heart. "But Kelly blames me for Brian's death. I can't change her mind, and I'm not going to try."

"I might try. The three of us were best friends for years. I don't want to be torn between you two."

"You don't have to be. You can be her friend, and you can be mine."

"This is a small town. That would be weird."

"I don't think she's planning on staying." Alicia paused as Keith and David walked toward them. Keith's boyish smile lightened her heart. One of the things she liked most about him was that he wasn't part of any of her past drama. Meeting him had made her feel like she could start over. And their relationship was good. She needed to make sure she didn't mess it up.

"Jordan," he said. "Good to see you. How was the honeymoon?"

"Very beautiful and romantic," Jordan replied.

"I'll bet. Where's Phil?"

"The deli has a booth over there," she said, waving toward the food court. "He's selling sandwiches."

"I'll have to get one later."

"Where's Justin?" David interrupted.

"He's over at the snow-cone machine," Alicia said. Gabe and Justin were sitting on the top of a picnic table, and she could see Justin talking a mile a minute.

"I want one, too," David said.

"That sounds good to me." Keith smiled. "You want anything, Alicia?"

What she didn't want was for Keith and Gabe to get better acquainted, but she could hardly tell him that. "I'm fine, thanks. You two go ahead."

"Well, well," Jordan muttered.

"Don't," she warned.

"Gabe and Keith are friends?"

"They both had dinner at my house the other night. I made it clear to Gabe that Keith and I are involved."

"Are you involved with Keith?" Jordan asked. "You didn't seem so sure when I left."

"Keith has been very supportive, and Justin and David are like brothers already. They adore each other."

"You can't be with Keith just because Justin and David are friends."

"It's not just because of that, but it's also not a bad thing. Justin needs a father figure, and Keith is a great dad."

"No argument there. But I want you to have a man you really want, not just a man who's good for your kid."

She shook her head. "I haven't made very good choices in the past, Jordan. Connor was a disaster, and my fling with Gabe wasn't my best idea, either. Maybe Keith is exactly the kind of man I should be with."

"You and Connor were kids when you got together, and I'm not so sure Gabe was a big mistake. Maybe it was just bad timing."

"I thought you liked Keith."

"I do. He's a wonderful guy, and if you love him, then I'm all for it."

"But . . ." Alicia prodded.

"But I have been your confidante through every crush you've ever had, and I've never heard you talk about Keith the way you talked about any one of the other men who've passed through your life."

"That's exactly it," she said. "They all passed through my life. They didn't stick, and I need someone to stick, especially now." She straightened. "Anyway, this is a carnival, and we're supposed to be having fun. So, maybe we should get a snow cone."

"You go ahead. I'm going to help Phil sell sandwiches." She shivered as the wind picked up. "It doesn't feel much like spring today."

"Storm coming in tonight, I heard. They're anticipating a couple of inches of rain by tomorrow night."

"The river is already high," Jordan said.

"Yeah," Alicia said with a sigh. "And it looks like it's going to get higher."

Gabe watched Alicia brush the hair away from her face as she and Jordan continued what appeared to be a fairly serious conversation. It was clear that at least one person in town had not turned her back on Alicia.

"Justin is very impressed with your shooting skills," Keith said with a friendly smile as he and David brought their snow cones over to the picnic table.

Gabe tipped his head, feeling a little uncomfortable with Justin's adoration. Justin's smile reminded him so much of Rob. He'd seen Rob look at him with that same confidence, but he'd let Rob down, and if he stayed too long in River Rock, he'd probably let Justin down, too.

"Have you ever shot a gun?" Justin asked Keith.

Keith shook his head. "Only a water gun, buddy. Usually at one of my sisters."

Justin and David giggled at that.

"Do you have any siblings?" Keith asked him.

"Nope, only child."

"Sometimes I wished I was. I have three sisters and a younger brother."

"Big family."

"Yeah, my parents liked a lot of kids around. Half the neighborhood had dinner at my house. Good times."

Gabe certainly didn't have any happy childhood stories to share.

"Is it time for the frog-jumping contest?" Justin asked.

"About a half hour more to go. Why don't you two get the frogs out of the car?" Keith suggested, handing his keys to David. "You can practice, get warmed up."

As the boys left, Keith gave him another easy smile. "How long do you think you'll be staying in River Rock?"

"Not sure yet."

"It's a great place if you're into small towns."

"Alicia tells me you moved here a couple of months ago," Gabe said, deciding that this was the perfect opportunity to follow up on one of Rob's other requests: *Make sure this guy she's seeing is good enough for her.*

Keith nodded as he chewed on some ice. "Yeah, we moved here in September. I teach history and coach soccer and track at the high school."

"Where were you living before?"

"We were in San Francisco, but David and I were both tired of the city. When I saw the job here, I decided to take it."

"It's not too quiet around here for you?"

"I like the peace, the calm. The pace is just right."

Peaceful and *calm* were also perfect words to describe Keith.

He didn't seem to get too worked up about anything. Gabe had never felt relaxed, not once in his entire life. He was always trying to get somewhere, beat somebody, win something. What would it feel like just to be happy in the moment? He couldn't imagine things ever being that good. Even when his luck seemed to change for the better, he was always preparing for the other shoe to drop.

"My wife was actually the one who wanted to move here," Keith said. "She had the idea right after David was born. A friend of hers grew up here, and she used to spend summers on the river. She had great memories of this place. We came here once for a long weekend, and we picked out a few houses to check out the next summer. She wanted David to grow up in a place where he had room to run and where everyone knew their neighbors." His expression grew sad. "But then she was diagnosed with cancer, and we never made it back. She died four years ago."

"I'm sorry," Gabe said, realizing that he'd misjudged Keith, thinking the guy had never had a hard day in his life.

"Thanks. Anyway, last year, I decided to make her dream a reality, and I'm glad I did. David was having a rough time at school in the city, and it was hard for him to make friends, but he and Justin just clicked from the first day they met. I like teaching in a place where the kids aren't quite so tough. Not that there aren't challenges, but it's nothing like the public schools in a big city."

"No, it's not. I grew up in a tough neighborhood in San Diego. I can't imagine what it would be like to go to school here."

"It's a little old-fashioned," Keith said with a grin. "Frog-jumping contests and all. But at least here, David will have a childhood."

"And maybe you and Alicia . . ." Gabe suggested.

Keith nodded, a hopeful smile on his face. "Maybe. She's a little gun-shy after what happened with Justin's father, and Rob's death really shook her up. She was counting on his help to get the business going or to talk her father into quitting."

"I don't see that happening."

"It should," Keith said. "Like I said yesterday, she needs to move away from that business."

He was surprised at the sudden forcefulness of Keith's words. The guy seemed so chill and easygoing, but there was an unusual intensity to his expression now.

"It's dangerous on the river," Keith continued. "A man died, and George almost lost his life. You'd think Alicia would realize that it was time to hang it up. I know George is putting pressure on her, but he's delusional to think he's going to be up to guiding a raft through treacherous rapids in a couple of weeks." He gave Gabe a serious look. "I'm hoping you can talk to them about quitting."

"I don't think they'd listen to me."

"You have an objective perspective, and they both know how much Rob respected your opinion."

"I can't give them an objective opinion yet. I'd like to know more about what happened last year, but so far, I haven't found anyone to talk to."

"I heard you and Russell Farr got into it at Mullaney's yesterday."

"He was drunk. He said some nasty things about Alicia and her father."

"Russell Farr is just one of many people who want to see the Haydens close their doors. I hate the things I hear about Alicia and her dad. It's tough to take. And I don't see how she's going to change public opinion. She just needs to quit and move on. What else can she do?" he added with a fatalistic shrug.

"She can fight to save her business." Keith's attitude was beginning to annoy him.

Keith shrugged. "I suppose a military man would choose that course of action."

A lot of men would.

"I just don't think she has anything left to hang on to, and she's not happy. She doesn't want to go back out on the water. She's just doing it for her father. In fact, she was always just doing it for him. She said she never made a conscious decision to go into the business; it was just expected, especially after Rob joined the Marines. She had to carry on for the family name."

Gabe wondered if that was completely true. Alicia had been riding the white water since she was a teenager. Three years ago, she'd shown nothing but excitement when she talked to him about the river. Family loyalty aside, a part of Alicia loved the water. Maybe Keith didn't know Alicia as well as he thought.

He turned his head as another man approached. The guy was in his late thirties, sunburned, with white-blond hair, stylish sunglasses, and a button-down plaid shirt over some gray slacks.

"Keith," he said, extending his hand. "Good to see you."

"Mitchell," Keith replied after shaking his hand. "This is Gabe Ryder. Mitchell Robbins."

"New in town?" Mitchell asked.

He wondered if he had a stamp on his forehead. "You got it."

"You look like you do sports."

"Some."

Mitchell pulled out a card. "I'm with Wild River Tours. We specialize in extreme adventures: river rafting, rock climbing, snowboarding, aerial skiing. You name it, we do it."

So this was Alicia's competitor. "Thanks," Gabe said, slipping the card into his pocket.

"Did you get those soccer nets I dropped off at the school?" Mitchell asked Keith. "I hope they were the right size."

"Perfect. We set them up on the practice field. Thanks for doing that."

"Anytime. Let me know if I can do anything else for you."

As Mitchell left, Gabe gave Keith a thoughtful look. "Isn't that Alicia's competitor?"

"One of them," Keith said with a careless shrug. "He's a good guy despite the sales pitch. He's gotten the high school a few deals on sporting equipment. It's really making a difference."

"Alicia thinks he's trying to drive her out of business. Does she know the two of you are friends?"

"I'm not trying to hide it, but my dealings with Mitchell don't have anything to do with Alicia."

Before Gabe could continue the conversation, the boys returned with Alicia and the bucket of frogs. Alicia made a point of standing next to Keith, sliding her arm around his waist, her expression a little defiant when it met Gabe's.

"How's Jordan?" Keith asked.

"Bursting with joy," Alicia replied. "What are you guys talking about?"

"Not much," Keith replied. "I think it's time to get over to the frog-jumping area." He tossed his empty snow-cone wrapper into the trash. "Let's get the boys signed up."

"Sounds good," she said.

Gabe followed the group over to a wide, grassy area where the frogs would be competing, feeling very much like a fifth wheel. Keith and Alicia and the boys looked like a family, and he looked like someone who didn't belong.

What else was new, he thought grimly. He was crazy to think he'd fit in there any better than he'd fit in anywhere else.

Alicia turned to him as Keith took David and Justin over to register. "You okay?"

"Fine," he said shortly, digging his hands into his pockets. "Did you know that Keith and the Wild River Tours guy are friends?"

"I know Mitchell donated something to the school. He's been very generous all over town. He has lots of corporate money behind him, and he likes to throw it around."

He gave her a thoughtful look. "You don't like it, though, do you?"

"There's nothing to dislike. Keith is a friendly guy, and to be fair, so is Mitchell."

"Yeah, but Keith is your boyfriend. Mitchell is your enemy. Those two should not be friends."

"It's not that black-and-white, Gabe. Keith doesn't see Mitchell as my enemy."

"He should. And you can't tell me you don't see it that way."

"If you're trying to make me doubt Keith, you're not going to succeed. He's not plotting against me. He's a nice guy."

"Maybe a little too nice."

She gave him a suspicious look. "What does that mean? You don't think I deserve someone nice?"

"You deserve someone who stands up for you, who'd fight to the death for you. Is that Keith?" He moved closer until she was just inches away. He could feel her sudden tension, and everything else around them faded away. He forgot what he was going to say. All he could think about was her soft pink lips and how much he wanted to kiss them.

Her hand came up to his chest. "Gabe, don't."

"Don't what?"

She stared up at him. "Make me want you again. It's not fair."

He swallowed hard as she walked away. The sway of her hips called to him to follow, but he had to resist. He didn't want to want her again, either.

The only problem was . . . he already did.

Eight

Alicia tried to pay attention to the frog-jumping contest but was still shaken by their almost-kiss. It was ridiculous. Gabe should not be able to get to her that way. She'd learned her lesson three years ago. She needed to focus on Keith.

After David and Justin collected the second- and fourth-place ribbons, respectively, they splurged on cheeseburgers and French fries, followed by ice cream sundaes. The conversation was light and easy, the way it always was when the four of them were together. This was what she wanted her life to be, she told herself again. But she still couldn't stop looking for Gabe in the crowd. Had he gone home, or was he still hanging around town somewhere? Maybe he'd gone back to Mullaney's to flirt with Cassie. *She* certainly wouldn't turn away from Gabe's kiss.

"Alicia?" She came back to reality as Keith gave her a questioning look.

"Sorry. What?"

"I'm taking the boys back to my house. Is that okay with you?"

"Sure, if you don't mind."

"Justin is easy to have around," he said with a smile.

"Okay. I'll look for my dad and see if he's ready to go home."

"It's good that he's having fun in town today," Keith said. "Maybe he'll realize that he can have a life that doesn't involve the river."

"I doubt that, but I appreciate your optimism. It's one thing I like about you."

He smiled back. "I hope there's more than one thing you like about me." He leaned over to kiss her, and she let her lips linger against his, trying to chase Gabe completely out of her head. But Keith wasn't one for public displays of affection, and he quickly turned back to the boys.

"You guys ready to go?" he asked.

"Be good," she told Justin.

"I will, Mom. Do you know where Gabe went? I want to show him my ribbon."

"You can show it to him later. I'm sure he'll be very impressed."

After Keith and the boys left, she headed toward the beer garden, where her father and Bill were sharing a pitcher. Her father's ruddy complexion was glowing, his eyes lit up with more energy than she'd seen in a long time. He probably needed to get out of the house more. Maybe Keith was right; perhaps her father's obsession with the river would diminish if he had something else to do.

"I heard from Simon," her father said with a smile. "He'll be back next week, and he's ready to be our head guide."

Simon Hunt was a fantastic river guide, and she was hugely relieved to know that he hadn't gone to Wild River Tours. "What did you say to convince him?"

"I told him we'd give him a raise."

Her heart sank. "And how are we going to do that, exactly?"

"I'll take a little less. We'll find a way. With Simon on board, we can open for reservations."

So much for thinking her father was going to be distracted from his goal of getting back on the water. "Are you ready to go home?"

"Bill said he's going to make me one of his famous steaks."

"I'll make you one, too, Alicia," Bill said. "Doris is out of town visiting her mother, so I have the run of the house."

"Then I think I'll leave you two on your own. Besides, I'm stuffed."

"Alicia, this is good news," her father said, as if he wasn't getting quite the reaction he'd hoped for.

"I'm glad Simon is coming back, but that's only going to solve one part of the problem."

"You can go a long way, taking one step at a time."

She tipped her head. "True. I'll see you later tonight."

As Alicia walked back through the carnival, drops began to fall from the sky, and some of the booths started shutting down. At least the storm had held off for most of the festival. The rain began to come down harder, so she cut through the old barn on her way to the parking lot. Loud voices made her pause.

"I'm done. That's it," a man said. "Just leave me alone."

A guy came around the corner so fast he almost knocked her over. He grabbed her arm to steady her, and she found herself looking into the eyes of Kelly's younger brother, Ian. At twenty, he had grown up and filled out. She couldn't remember when she'd last seen him—he'd been back and forth between college and home the last three years.

"Alicia," he said in shock. "What are you doing in here?"

"Taking a shortcut. It's raining outside."

"Oh." He flung a quick look over his shoulder. "I gotta go."

He was gone before she could say another word. As she continued through the barn, she wondered whom he'd been talking to, but she didn't come across anyone else. Walking through the large double doors, she exited into the parking lot, which was almost empty.

A quick dash in the rain, and she was inside the car, a little wet and feeling oddly unsettled by her encounter with Ian. She'd known Ian since he was a baby. Nine years younger than Kelly, Ian had been a "happy surprise" for Kelly's parents, and Kelly had loved having a little brother to mother. Alicia had been right there with her. They'd taken Ian everywhere with them—until they got to high school, when having a little kid around wasn't quite so appealing.

But today Ian had looked at her through cold, dark eyes, as if he didn't remember all the times she'd read stories to him or taken him out on the river. He'd looked as if he hated her. The enemy camp grew larger each day.

With a sigh, she started the car and pulled out of the lot. The rain grew heavier as she got out of town, streaming down so hard she had the windshield wipers going triple time. She slowed down as she turned off the main highway to cut through the back roads. When she put her foot back on the gas, nothing happened. The car began to sputter and kick, shuddering to a stop as she managed to get it over to the side of the road. She stared at the gas gauge in astonishment. Empty? She'd filled it up two days ago and hadn't driven more than fifteen miles since then. She should have a full tank.

She tried turning the key again, thinking the fuel indicator was stuck, but nothing happened. Grabbing her cell phone, she called Keith to come out and pick her up. But there was no reception. She moved the phone around but couldn't pick up a signal, which wasn't all that surprising since the signal out there was always weak.

She debated her options. She was on a side road. It might be a long while before anyone came by to help her, especially in the rain. And it was going to be dark soon, not to mention cold, she thought with a shiver. Walking to get help or until she found a cell signal seemed like the best option.

Looking around the car, she was thankful to see a jacket in the backseat. She grabbed it, stuffing her wallet and cell phone into one pocket. Then she got out and began to jog down the road. There was no signal to be found, and even worse, there was a good chance that the people at the closest house would slam the door in her face.

Kelly tossed some salt and pepper into her beef stew and inhaled the fragrance with a satisfied smile. She'd decided on the stew earlier, and now that the weather had changed, it was the perfect choice. The restaurant would probably be slow with the festival in town, maybe only the guests staying at the inn, but they would be well fed.

She looked up as the back door opened and Ian walked in, rain dripping off his hair and clothes. His brown hair had gotten longer since she'd last seen him, and his shoulders seemed broader. He was no longer her little brother, towering over her at six feet two inches. "You got wet," she said, stating the obvious. But lately, she and Ian seemed to be having trouble communicating. They'd only talked a couple of times since she'd moved to Sacramento, and since she'd come back, he'd made himself scarce.

"It's pouring out there." He took off his jacket and hung it on a hook on the closed-in porch next to the kitchen.

"Where have you been? Mom was looking for you earlier."

He scowled at her as he reached into the refrigerator and grabbed a beer. "I get enough third degree from Mom; I don't need it from you, too."

"I was just asking. And you need to put that beer down. You're not twenty-one yet."

He gave her an incredulous look. "Are you fucking kidding me? I've been drinking since I was fifteen."

"Well, you can't drink here, Ian. This isn't just your home, it's a business, and we have a liquor license to protect. So put the beer down."

Instead of doing as she asked, he raised the beer to his lips and chugged every last drop. When it was empty, he burped and set the empty bottle down. "Happy?"

"Hardly. What's wrong with you?"

"Me? Everything is wrong with me, Kelly. You're the perfect child, and I'm the screwup. Haven't you heard?"

She'd known he was having trouble at school and that he was on academic probation; she just didn't know why. "You're a smart guy. Why don't you just stop screwing up?"

"Yeah, I'll do that," he said sarcastically, banging through the door into the dining room.

Nora came in a second later. "What's wrong with your brother? He just about ran me over."

"I was hoping you could tell me."

"Well, I don't know anything for sure, but I've heard that he was gambling again at the Indian casino."

Her heart sank. Ian had gotten into trouble with online poker betting when he was in high school, and she thought he'd realized the danger of gambling after she and her mom had spent five thousand dollars bailing him out. "Does Mom know?"

"Your mother spoils him rotten. She only sees the best in him. You should know that by now."

True. Her mother was always an optimist when it came to family. "I guess I can't really be mad at her for that, since she usually only sees the best in me, too, and I don't always deserve it."

Nora smiled. "How's that stew coming?"

"Simmering nicely."

"I'm going to run home for a bit. I'll be back before the rush—if there is one. With the festival going, I expect it will be a slow night." Nora grabbed an umbrella from the back porch and opened the door.

It *was* pouring outside. Kelly hadn't realized the storm had gotten so bad. "Are you sure you don't want to wait a few minutes?"

"I promised Harry I'd get him his dinner early tonight. I'll be fine. I don't have far to go, and it's only water."

"Be careful you don't slip on the pavement. One hip replacement is all I can handle."

Kelly shut the door behind Nora and returned to the warm stove to give her pot another stir. The night's menu was simple and easy. She'd already made a house salad and a Caesar.

Vegetables were ready to cook, and there were several loaves of bread ready to be browned in the oven. Nora had made some lemon tarts and triple-chocolate-chip cookies earlier, so dessert was covered. They didn't offer a huge menu, but the food was always first-rate, and their clientele was often a mix of tourists and locals.

She had to admit that it was nice to cook in her own kitchen again. In Sacramento, she worked in a busy restaurant with a head chef and two other sous chefs. The menu was large and rather bland, with not a lot of room for creativity, but it was a job and a new life, and she'd made some friends there. But there was no place like home, she thought with a smile as she gazed around the country kitchen.

A moment later, a knock came at the door. When she opened it, she found Alicia on the step, and she was soaking wet.

Kelly's heart stopped, and a tiny part of her wanted to slam the door shut.

"My car broke down," Alicia said between chattering lips. "Phone isn't getting reception. Can I use yours?"

"All right." She stepped back as Alicia came into the room. "You're soaked. How far did you walk?"

"About a mile. For a minute there, I didn't think you were going to let me in."

Kelly stared into the wary blue eyes of the woman who had once been her very best friend and knew that one thing hadn't changed: they could still read each other like a book. "You need to dry off. You can use my bathroom. I still have the attic room."

"Just the phone is fine."

"Don't be stupid, Alicia. You'll get sick."

"And you would care?" Alicia asked doubtfully.

"Well, Justin needs you to be healthy. And besides that, you'll drip all over our floors. Go on upstairs and dry off. There's a bathrobe hanging on the back of the bathroom door."

"Thanks," Alicia said as she left the room.

Kelly sank down onto a stool by the counter, suddenly weak in the knees. Just like the day before, she was ill prepared to deal with Alicia. There were so many things to be said and yet so many things that shouldn't be said.

She could just let Alicia dry off on her own, use the phone, and get someone to pick her up. She didn't have to get any further involved. She could hide out in the kitchen. No doubt Alicia would be happy to avoid her, too.

But five quiet, tense minutes later, she was on her feet, moving up the stairs. She entered the attic room just as Alicia was coming out of the bathroom in the pink floral bathrobe, squeezing her hair dry with a cherry-colored towel.

The sight shook Kelly to the core, taking her straight back to her teenage years, when she and Alicia had spent every second together. They'd been as close as sisters, sharing clothes and gossip, doing homework, watching television, sewing prom dresses, and painting posters for the school fund-raisers. They'd danced around the room, perfecting their sexiest moves. They'd laughed at late-night slasher movies, and they'd cried together when one of them was going through a breakup.

She'd been the first one Alicia had turned to when she found out she was pregnant. She'd held Alicia's hand during labor, changed Justin's first diaper, and held hands with Alicia as they watched Justin go to his first day of kindergarten.

And Alicia had been there for her, too. She'd sat with her all night when her dad died and had scoured five miles of countryside when her cat went missing. Alicia was the first one she'd told when Brian had asked her to marry him. Every event of her life had been shared with Alicia, and she'd known Alicia as well as she'd known herself. She'd thought she could count on her to always be there, until six months ago . . .

Her stomach turned over, and her heart actually ached with the memories.

Alicia wrapped the towel around her head turban-style. Her face was devoid of makeup, her blue eyes filled with uncertainty, sadness, maybe a wistful yearning.

"You don't want me here," Alicia said, not making it a question. "I knew it was a mistake to come upstairs, but I was really cold."

Alicia was always cold. She was the first one to shiver when the sun went down, the first one to go looking for a blanket at a summer barbecue, and she'd moan through the winter months that she just couldn't get warm. Kelly used to think it was Alicia's mother's leaving that had left Alicia so cold. It was as if she needed someone to wrap her up in their arms until she finally got warm. Unfortunately, the men she'd chosen for that job had fallen short, first Connor, then Gabe. Which reminded her . . .

"What were you doing with Gabe Ryder yesterday?"

A warm pink spread across Alicia's cheeks. "Oh, he just showed up the other day. Rob apparently gave him his house."

"Why would he do that?"

"I don't know. Gabe made some promise to Rob about looking out for us."

"Now he wants to look after you?"

"Yeah, crazy, huh?" Alicia sat on a chair by the desk. "When he left three years ago, he made it clear that he wasn't coming back."

"But you're with someone else now, right? My mom said you were involved with a teacher."

Alicia nodded. "Keith Andrews. He teaches at the high school. His son, David, is in Justin's class, and Keith is a single parent, too. His wife died a few years ago. Justin and David are really close."

"He sounds perfect," she said.

Alicia gave her a hesitant look. "Do you want to talk, Kelly? Really talk?"

Kelly hesitated. "A part of me does, and another part doesn't." Swallowing hard, she sat down on the edge of the bed, twisting her fingers in the material of her apron. "I'm sorry about Rob."

Alicia's lips tightened. "It was so unfair. He was going to be home for good in just six days. All those years I worried about him, and it was coming to an end. And then I'm out in the garden one day, and I see these two guys in uniform get out of their car and start walking toward the house. Even though I knew what was coming, I couldn't believe it was happening."

Kelly felt a wave of compassion as she looked at the pain in Alicia's eyes. She knew how much Alicia loved her twin brother, how tight they were, and she was sorrier than she could say, because she knew what it meant to lose someone you loved.

"I loved Rob, too," she said. "He wrote to me about a week before he died."

"I didn't know you were keeping in touch."

"I was avoiding his e-mails, but for some reason, I opened that one."

"What did he say?"

"That he couldn't wait to get home." She wasn't about to tell Alicia the other things he'd said, his plea that she find a way to make up with his sister. "How's Justin?" she asked, changing the subject.

"He's sad about Rob, but he's bouncing back. I don't think it feels real to him. Rob was gone so much; he was used to him being away. But there are moments when he realizes the truth, and he just bursts into tears. I think about all the things that Rob is going to miss, and the relationship I wanted Justin to have with his uncle is gone now."

Silence descended between them.

"I wanted to come back for the funeral, Alicia, but I thought there might be too much drama if I did, and I didn't want to complicate things."

"Was that the real reason, Kell? Or do you just hate me too much?"

Alicia's blunt words shouldn't have taken her by surprise. Her best friend had never been one to beat around the bush. Her directness was one of her best traits. Which was why it had driven her crazy that Alicia wouldn't take responsibility for what had happened to Brian. She prided herself on honesty, but when it came to that truth, Alicia couldn't tell it.

"I just don't understand," she said, "why you couldn't own up to what happened."

"What do *you* think happened, Kelly? Because it's obviously different from what I know," Alicia said, her voice laced with frustration.

She drew in a breath. "I think you got distracted when your father flipped his boat. You took your eyes off the water, off the guys in your raft, and that lack of concentration was the reason your raft flipped over." She paused. "Russell also believes that the rafts were underinflated, and that's why they flipped. I know they found a small tear after the accident."

"That could have been caused when the raft hit the rocks."

"I know you were short on money. You were cutting corners."

"Not those kinds of corners. I was careful. I did all the checks, and so did my dad. How can you doubt that, Kelly? You've been out on the river with us. You know we don't take chances."

"That's not true. Your dad takes more and more chances every year. He likes to show people a thrilling time, and he was feeling the heat from Wild River Tours. He wanted to impress the guys that day."

"My father didn't do anything wrong. It was an accident, a terrible, tragic accident. Unless you can prove to me otherwise, I don't know what to say."

"I don't have to prove it to you. You need to prove it to me. I've heard stories from everyone who was there."

"Most of whom were in the water, myself included," Alicia pointed out. "We were struggling to survive. It was impossible to see or hear anything but the rushing water."

Kelly wished they hadn't started this conversation, because the idea of Brian drowning was so hard to bear. "You're making excuses. You have been for months."

Alicia stared back at her. "I am so unbelievably sorry for what happened, Kelly, and I have asked myself a million times if I could have done something differently. I have gone over and over that day in my mind."

"And now you want to go back out there and relive that? It's all over town that you're opening the business again. The Farrs are out of their minds about it."

"It's not my first choice, but it's our livelihood."

"Maybe you should find a new way to make money."

"You think that would be easy to do in this small town?"

"You could leave, go somewhere else. I did."

"And take Justin away from the only home he's ever known? And my father wouldn't leave. He's going to die by that river. You know that, Kelly. You know him. You know *me*."

She did. Their families had been connected for years. But that didn't mean she didn't see George's flaws, and his competitiveness was well known.

"Well, I guess you'll do what you have to do," she said finally.

"What about you, Kell? What are you doing? Are you happy in Sacramento?"

"I'm not sure *happy* is the word, but it's a good change. I'm glad to be away from the memories. I don't see Brian around every corner. I don't run into the Farrs—or you."

Alicia sucked in a quick breath. "I hate what's happened."

"Me, too."

"I wish you'd come back. I know your family misses you."

"My mom does, but I don't know about Ian. He thinks I'm a pain in the ass, and maybe I am. I've always worried about him, and it's hard to stop."

"I saw him earlier at the carnival. He was in the barn having an argument with someone. I didn't see who it was."

Kelly didn't like the sound of that. "What was he saying?" Maybe that's why her brother had been so pissed off when he'd entered the inn.

"Something about he was done, and he wanted to be left alone."

"I hope he's not gambling again. He promised my mother he would never go near another poker game, but Nora said she heard he was up at the Indian casino last week."

"I thought he was away at school."

"He took a quarter off, because his grades were horrible and he needed to regroup. I guess you haven't seen him around town."

"I don't go into town that much, and when I do, I try to leave as quickly as possible. You're not the only one who hates me, Kell."

She resisted the urge to say that she didn't hate Alicia, because she felt so conflicted. "I have some clothes you can put on. I don't think your things will be dry for a while." She reached into her dresser drawers and pulled out some leggings and a sweater. "Will these work?"

Alicia smiled as she took the red sweater. "I remember this—your lucky sweater. You wore it once to get Dan Wiggins to kiss you and the other time to try to get Larry Cader to ask you to prom. Are you sure you want to lend it to me?"

"As I recall, it wasn't that lucky. Dan Wiggins's kiss was disgusting, and Larry disappeared halfway through the prom to make out with that slutty Marla Hodgkins."

"Which I could never understand. Marla wasn't even pretty."

"Yeah, but she was way more fun than I was." Kelly stiffened, realizing she was letting down her guard. She had to be loyal to Brian, to the Farrs. "Get dressed and make your call. Where is your car, anyway?"

"Spring Road. It's the weirdest thing. I filled up two days ago, but the gas gauge said it was empty."

"Maybe you have a leak."

"Maybe." Alicia got to her feet. "Thanks, Kelly."

"For what?"

"Opening the door."

"What else could I do?" she asked helplessly.

"Slam it in my face."

"That wouldn't have been polite."

"I miss you, Kelly. I've needed you more in the last year than any other year of my life. And you weren't there."

The moisture in Alicia's gaze made Kelly's own eyes tear up. "I needed you, too, Alicia, but Brian was my fiancé. And when I agreed to marry him, I made a promise to stand by him. Even though we never said our vows, I felt them in my heart. And I can't be friends with the person who . . ." She couldn't get the words out. "You should go."

"I wish it didn't have to be this way."

"But it is," Kelly said as she left the room.

Nine

Alicia put on the clothes Kelly had given her, feeling a bittersweet emotion as she pulled the familiar red sweater over her head. Being in Kelly's room had brought back a lot of good memories. It was hard to believe that their friendship could be over. She'd never imagined that anything could tear them apart. But Kelly was resolute, determined to blame her and her father for Brian's death, and they were never going to be able to get past that. She needed to stop hoping that they could.

She grabbed her wet clothes out of the bathroom and headed toward the door, pausing to look at the photograph on the desk. It had been taken at their high school graduation, and they were wearing their caps and gowns, beaming at the camera. Three best friends, she thought sadly, tracing the faces with her finger: Kelly, Jordan, and her.

But no more. Those days were gone.

With a sigh, she set down the photo and went downstairs.

The living room was beautiful and warm, with big picture windows and oversized sofas and reading chairs, the lamps casting a cozy glow against the dark day outside. There wasn't anyone around. Perhaps the guests were still in town sitting out the storm, although it appeared that the rain had stopped.

She pulled out her phone and called Keith, but it went to voice-mail. He was probably busy with the boys. She debated her options. Her father was having dinner with Bill, and he couldn't drive, anyway. Jordan was with her new husband. Who else could come rescue her?

Gabe. He'd put his number in her phone earlier, but she really didn't want to call him. Still, what option did she have? She didn't want to spend any more time at the inn, where it was clear she wasn't wanted.

He answered on the first ring. "Alicia," he said.

"Hi. My car broke down. I was wondering if you could pick me up."

"Of course. Where are you?"

"The Blackberry Inn, four-ten Blackberry Lane. I can give you directions."

"I've got GPS. I'll see you in a few minutes."

"Thanks." As she ended the call, the front door opened, and a man walked in, shaking raindrops off his yellow slicker.

Jared Donovan. She stiffened. Jared had been in her father's boat the day of the accident. He was good friends with the Farrs and with Kelly. At one time, he'd been a friend of hers, but since the accident, they'd had little contact. She had seen him at Rob's memorial service, but like so many others, he hadn't come back to the house.

"Alicia," he said. "I wasn't sure you'd come here."

"Because it's enemy territory?" she asked dryly.

He tipped his head in acknowledgment. "I guess it feels that way."

"My car broke down."

"I saw it on the road. I had just finished jumping a battery on Elmwood Lane. I figured you were walking, but I wasn't sure you'd come here."

"It was raining pretty hard."

He nodded. "What's wrong with the car?"

"My gas gauge says empty, but I filled it on Thursday, and I haven't driven more than thirty miles since then. I don't know what happened. It just died on me."

"Well, I've got some gas in the truck. Let's check it out."

"Really? Kelly won't like it."

"Does she know you're here?"

"Oh, yeah. These are her clothes. But after a very tense, awkward conversation, she disappeared into the kitchen. She always hid out there."

Jared shook his head. "The two of you fighting just doesn't seem right."

"I know. I wish we could get past the accident, but I don't know how."

The kitchen door opened, and Kelly moved through the archway between the living room and the dining room. Kelly gave Jared a hard look. "What are you doing here?"

Alicia was surprised at the animosity in Kelly's voice.

"I saw Alicia's car on the side of the road a few blocks over and thought I might be able to help."

"Seems like you should be at the car, then, and not here."

"We were just leaving," Alicia said.

"Then go," Kelly said. "We're opening for dinner soon, and I don't need you two here."

Alicia moved quickly to the front door and went out onto the porch. Jared said he'd be out in a minute. A part of her really wanted to eavesdrop, but that old adage about people never hearing good about themselves while eavesdropping would probably come true.

"What were you two talking about, Jared?" Kelly demanded.

"We were talking about how this sucks—the way things are between you and her, between all of us."

"The rest of us are fine. And I can't believe you went looking for her after you saw her car on the road."

"I don't hate Alicia. Sorry if that goes against the party line, but that's the way it is. And I can't believe you're mad that I would try to help someone who's in trouble. Didn't you just criticize me the other day for not getting involved?"

She sighed. "I'm overreacting."

"You think?"

"Why did you guys have to go rafting that day? Why couldn't you have just gone to a bar and hired some strippers like everyone else does?"

"Russell wanted to have an adventure. And Brian did, too." He paused. "Brian was having a great time on that trip. Maybe too good of a time."

"What does that mean?"

He hesitated. "Nothing. Forget I said anything."

"That's not going to be possible, so just tell me what you're getting at."

He drew in a long, deep breath. "Brian and a couple of the other guys took a hike during lunch. They were gone for a while."

"So?"

"You should talk to Marco and John. They were with Brian. And they were all really happy when they got back."

She was trying to read between the lines, but he wasn't making it easy. "Are you saying something happened at lunchtime?"

"This is a bad idea."

"Just say it, whatever it is."

"I wondered if they drank or smoked or took something."

She stared at him in shock. "Why would you think that?"

"Just a gut feeling from the way they acted when they came back."

"You never said that before."

"Well, the autopsy didn't show anything in Brian's bloodstream, so I figured I was wrong."

"Exactly. You *are* wrong. I can't believe you're trying to blame the accident on Brian."

"I wasn't doing that. But you asked."

"You should go, Jared."

As he walked out the door, she drew in a shaky breath. He was right; he never should have said anything. Because now she wasn't going to be able to think about anything else. The autopsy had come back clean, so he was wrong. Brian was a responsible man. He knew that drinking was prohibited on the trip, and he didn't do drugs. She was *not* going to let Jared's doubts become her own.

Alicia was standing on the half-circle drive when Gabe pulled up in his Jeep at about the same time Jared came out of the house. Jared looked pissed off, and she wondered what on earth had gone on between him and Kelly.

Gabe gave her a nod as he got out of his truck. "You called a tow truck?"

"No, Jared saw my car and thought I might be here looking for some help. Jared, this is Gabe Ryder. Gabe, Jared Donovan." The two men gave each other a brief assessing nod. "Jared has some gas in the truck that I can use."

"You ran out of gas?"

"I filled up two days ago, but the gauge said empty."

"We'll check it out," Jared said. "Why don't you two follow me?"

"Thanks for coming," she said to Gabe as she got into the passenger seat. "I hope I didn't interrupt anything. Where were you?"

"At Mullaney's."

"Talking to Cassie?"

He gave her a smile. "She was there."

"She's a pretty girl."

"That she is."

She didn't like his ready agreement. "Are you interested in her?"

"Do you care?" he countered, a sparkle in his eye.

"Of course not. You can do whatever you want with whoever you want."

"Exactly."

A moment of silence passed, and then she couldn't help adding, "But seriously, Cassie? She's not the smartest girl in town."

"She's friendly and welcoming."

"Among other things," she muttered.

"You're jealous."

"I am not."

"You're lying."

"Fine, it bothers me a little. The last time you were here, it was you and me. It's weird to see you with someone else."

"How do you think I feel seeing you with Keith?"

"Probably happy, because now you don't have to worry about me throwing myself at you again."

"Do you ever throw yourself at Keith? The two of you don't seem very passionate."

"You've only seen us in public," she said defensively. "And I don't rush into things the way I used to. I learned my lesson with you."

"And I don't take small-town girls to bed anymore. I learned my lesson with you," he said with a hint of sarcasm.

A minute later, they pulled up behind the tow truck. Jared was already crawling under the car with a flashlight when they got out.

"What do you see?"

"Nothing good," Jared said as he scooted back out from under the car, concern in his eyes.

"Do I have a leak?"

"You have more than a leak, Alicia. Your fuel line was cut."

A shiver ran down her spine.

"Someone did this deliberately?" Gabe asked, his body stiffening beside her.

"The line was sliced, but not all the way through. Someone gave you a slow leak. Whoever did it knew what they were doing."

"Why? Why would someone do that?" she asked.

Jared got to his feet. "Could be teens, vandalism."

"Or someone who wants to send you a message," Gabe said.

She liked Jared's theory better, but she couldn't discount Gabe's words. "If someone wanted me to run out of gas, what's the message?"

"Stay off the river," Gabe said. "Come on, Alicia. That's all anyone is talking about in town."

She looked at Jared. "Do you agree?"

He shifted his feet. "I'd hate to think someone would do this to you for that reason."

"But you *do* think it. So what do I do?"

"I can tow the car to our garage and fix the line."

"Thanks. I guess I should talk to the police, too."

"I'll drive you into town," Gabe said.

She walked with Gabe back to his truck. They watched in silence while Jared hooked the car to his tow truck, and then they followed him into town.

"Are you all right?" Gabe asked.

"Not even close. What if Justin had been in the car? What if it had been night? What if someone had been following too close when the car slowed and stopped? How could someone do this to me? I grew up in this town. I don't get it."

"We're going to find out who did this."

"I doubt that. My car was sitting in the carnival parking lot all day. Anyone could have done it. There were literally hundreds of people around. It was the perfect opportunity."

"It's a long shot, but we should make a police report anyway." He paused. "It's funny that that guy with the tow truck just happened to show up."

She frowned. "What are you saying?"

"Just that he was right on the spot. You didn't even have to call him."

"He said he had just jumped a battery nearby, and he recognized my car. I grew up with Jared. His family owns the auto shop."

"Was he friends with Brian?"

"Yes. He was on the rafting trip."

"Interesting."

"It's not interesting," she said hotly. "I don't believe Jared cut my gas line and then waited around to rescue me."

"It would be one way to ensure that you got the message without really putting you in danger."

"It was probably kids," she said, even though her gut instinct told her that the act had been deliberate and personal. "I don't want to go to the police, Gabe. I just want to go home."

"You need to report this."

"The chief of police was also on the trip," she said. "Do you really think he's going to care?"

"We'll make him care." He reached over and put his hand over hers. "Your battle is my battle, babe. This is something I know how to do. Let me do it."

His gaze burned into her. And for the life of her, she couldn't say no. "Okay. Do it."

Ronnie D'Amico was young for a chief of police, in his mid-thirties, having gotten the job after his father retired. Like so many other organizations and businesses in River Rock, the police department was a family affair. Gabe pulled up in front of the two-story building near the county courthouse and shut off the engine.

"What else do I need to know before we go inside?" he asked.

"Like what?"

"Like what did Ronnie think happened out on the river? If he's a cop, he must have done some investigating."

"Ronnie was on the third raft with Simon. They were at least two hundred yards behind us, and the river was narrow and twisting along that stretch. They didn't see my father's raft overturn. Simon told me that he caught a glimpse of my raft going airborne, and when they came around the bend, they saw a lot of people in the water. Simon managed to pull the raft over to the side and avoid the worst of the rapids. Then they tried to get people out of the water."

Alicia was telling the story as matter-of-factly as she could, but her fingers were twisting together, and there was a sheen of sweat on her forehead.

"Hang in there," he said. "Anyone else from the police department on the trip?"

"Ronnie's cousin, Ernie. He was also in the third raft."

"So, no cops actually saw what happened or experienced it?"

"No, but Ronnie said in retrospect that the river was too high, running too fast, and that we should have called the trip off. It was a popular theory after the accident."

"Was it too high?"

"It was high," she admitted. "We had a lot of rain that winter and spring. The runoff was the highest it had been in years. But we weren't the only company running the river that week. Wild River Tours had gone out the day before."

"Well, that's interesting. It proves that other companies weren't staying away."

"I guess. But they weren't on the river that day, and I've heard rumors that Mitchell said they called off a trip because of what they'd seen the day before."

"But they didn't communicate any information to you?"

"We're competitors, not friends."

He nodded, the picture becoming a little clearer in his mind.

"My father likes to run the river when it's high and fast." Alicia turned to meet his gaze. "He loves the challenge of it. And he thought 'the boys,' as he called them, would like it, too. And they did. They were having a great time, until that minute when everyone ended up in the water."

"How many times have you ended up in the river?" he asked.

"A half-dozen times in the last ten years."

"So you knew what to do."

"Theoretically. But once you're in the river, the current has a mind of its own."

"Where is Simon?"

"Well, according to my dad, he's coming back to town next week, and he's planning to work for us again."

"That's good news, right?"

"Yeah, but I'm not feeling too excited about anything right now. Shall we go inside?"

"Sure."

They walked into the police station and asked to speak with the chief. Unfortunately, he was at the festival along with most of the staff. They were forced to give their report to a young officer named Michael Tarry, who jotted down notes and told them he'd pass the information along.

"That was a waste of time," Alicia said as they left.

Gabe felt much the same way. "At least there's a report on file, just in case something else happens."

Her face paled. "You think something else is going to happen?"

"I hope not."

"But that's what you think?" she asked as they got into the truck.

"Yes. Last night, Kenny Barber was walking around your boatyard with a flashlight, and he had no business being there. He might be a former employee, but now he's working for your competitor. Today your fuel line is cut. Someone wants to make sure that you don't go back on the river. Where does Kenny live?"

"An apartment building a few blocks from here."

"Great. I'll take you home, and then I'm going to pay him a visit."

"If you're paying him a visit, I'm going, too. This is my problem, Gabe."

"He could be dangerous."

"Kenny is just a young guy who likes to ride the white water, and I've known him since he was eighteen years old. I can't blame him for finding a better gig than the one I have to offer, and if he said he was looking for something he left behind, then I have no reason not to believe him." She blew out a breath of frustration. "I hate this. I used to be able to trust people, trust my instincts. Maybe you're blowing this out of proportion, Gabe."

"I don't think I'm overreacting," he said carefully. "Last night, you talked me into believing that Kenny had a reason to be wandering around your yard in the dark. But with the car incident, I think you need to be on alert." He turned the key in the ignition. "Promise me one thing. Until we know what we're dealing with, don't underestimate anyone. Don't think because someone was a friend that they still are. A man is dead. And it's possible that someone wants revenge."

"And they waited six months to go for it?"

"Maybe the idea of you going back out on the river pushed them to act now."

She pressed a hand to her temple. "I have a headache."

"I'm getting one, too," he said dryly.

She gave him a weak smile. "Bet you're sorry you made that promise to Rob now."

"No. Now I understand why Rob wanted me to make the promise. I think he knew you were dealing with more than you realized."

"And you don't think cutting the gas line is the end?"

"No, Alicia. I think it's the beginning."

Ten

Kenny Barber lived on the second floor of a run-down apartment building near the liquor store. His girlfriend, a skinny blonde who looked barely out of her teens, opened the door wearing tight jeans and a tank top. Kenny was sitting on the couch of the small apartment, strumming a guitar, a couple of empty beer bottles on the coffee table in front of him. When he saw them in the doorway, he jumped to his feet, and Alicia saw something flash through his eyes that looked a lot like guilt.

"Kenny," she said, pushing her way past Gabe and the girlfriend. "Why were you in our yard last night? What were you looking for?"

"I—I thought I left a backpack there, but I didn't see it."

"Maybe you should have looked in the daylight," she said pointedly.

"Yeah, I just kind of thought about it last night and figured it was worth a quick look. I didn't think you'd care, Alicia. I didn't want to bother you."

"I haven't seen any backpacks lying around."

"I guess I left it somewhere else, then."

She didn't like the way Kenny couldn't quite look her in the eye. They'd spent a lot of hours on the river together, and she'd thought they were a lot closer than this awkward conversation. It probably didn't help to have Gabe giving him suspicious looks or his girlfriend looking at them with a worried expression on her face, but that was beside the point.

"Kenny, what's going on?" she asked directly. "Did you sign on to be a river guide with Wild River Tours?"

He gave her an apologetic look. "I'm sorry, Alicia, but they're giving me a lot more money. Plus, I didn't even know if you and your dad would make it back onto the river. He's still using a cane."

"It would be easier for us to make it back onto the river if our guides didn't keep deserting us."

"I didn't know what else to do, Alicia."

"Well, the first thing you should have done was return my phone calls and be honest with me. The second thing you need to do now is tell me why you were on my property last night in the dark with a flashlight."

"I swear, I was just looking for my backpack. I've looked everywhere else, and I thought it might be there. I didn't come during the day because I didn't want to run into you. I didn't know how to tell you I was leaving."

She gave him a long, searching look, wanting to believe him, but Gabe's warning was fresh in her mind. "Okay, here's another question: Do you know someone who would cut the fuel line on my car?"

Shock flashed through Kenny's eyes. "What are you talking about?"

"What she just said," Gabe said, stepping forward, his powerful stance making Kenny take a step backward. "Someone made sure she ran out of gas today. Any ideas who would do that?"

"It wasn't me. I wouldn't even know how to do that. You gotta believe me, Alicia."

"I'd like to believe you, Kenny, but you're acting really secretive."

"It wasn't me. And no offense, but a lot of people don't like you anymore."

"Why don't you give us a name or two of people who could do something like that?" Gabe suggested.

Kenny looked from Gabe to her. "Russell Farr, his friends, Brian's friends. Go down the list of who was on the trip last year."

"What about someone who wasn't on the trip?" Alicia asked, not liking the way Gabe had taken over, although he was definitely intimidating Kenny. "You know a lot of people in town. You must hear things."

"Just tell them, Kenny," the girlfriend suddenly said.

"Joanie, shut up."

Joanie moved around Gabe to stand next to Kenny. "There's a rumor going around town that anyone who can stop you from going back on the river can make some nice cash," she said.

Alicia looked at the girl in shock. "Where did you hear that?"

"I work at Mullaney's, and some guys from Wild River Tours were in one day. They were drinking and laughing and making it all seem like a joke, but some people think they were serious. And money has been tight for a lot of people around here the last few years."

Alicia looked back at Kenny for confirmation. "Is that true?"

"It was a joke."

"You think it's funny for someone to threaten me? To threaten my family?" she challenged, feeling angry and worried.

"No, I didn't think it was funny. I'm sorry, Alicia. You don't deserve this," Kenny said. "I know the accident wasn't your fault. It was just an accident."

"Then why doesn't anyone else believe that?"

"Maybe you could tell some of your friends that you think it was an accident," Gabe suggested. "You might have some sway."

"I've tried, but they all think I'm being loyal to Alicia because I was working for her."

"But you're not working for her anymore, so you could try again."

"I will. I promise," he said. "And, Alicia, I hope you do get back out there. You were one of the best, and so was your dad."

"You should have talked to me, Kenny. We were more than employer-employee, we were friends." She turned to Gabe. "Let's go."

They were at the door when Kenny called out, "Alicia, wait."

"What?" she asked.

He looked at his girlfriend as if for confirmation and then back at her. "Ian Palmer."

Her stomach tightened. "What about him?"

"He's been looking for a way to make some quick cash to pay off a bookie. Not saying he did it, but since you asked . . ."

A wave of nausea ran through her. She'd been a big sister to Ian for most of her life. Would he really do something like this to her? She walked back to Gabe's truck, completely shaken. As she fastened her seatbelt, she remembered Kelly telling her that she was worried about Ian gambling again. Apparently, her worry was justified.

Gabe glanced at her as he started the engine. "You want to tell me about Ian Palmer?"

"He's Kelly's little brother. I considered him to be my brother, too, but since the accident, we haven't spoken."

"Kenny might have just thrown Ian's name out there to get the heat off of him."

"I don't know what to think, Gabe."

"Then let's go home—sort things out. You look like you've been through the wringer."

She looked awful, Alicia realized as she stared at her reflection in the bathroom of Rob's cabin. Her towel-dried hair was tangled, her face was pale, and Kelly's sweater was big on her. Reaching into the drawer, she found a comb and ran it through her hair.

When she returned to the living room, she was surprised to see Gabe at the stove stirring something in a pot. "You're cooking? I thought you didn't know how."

"I bought some cans of soup at the store earlier. And I make an excellent grilled cheese. What do you say?"

"Sold." Glancing at the clock, she realized how late it was. She'd left the carnival at about three, and it was now after eight. "I should check in with Justin."

"Is he with Keith?"

"Yes. Keith has a huge play structure in his backyard. It's a two-story house with ladders and windows and little rooms. It's very cool for two boys with big imaginations."

"I always wanted a tree house, but shockingly enough, they didn't have those in the big city or in any of the shelters I stayed at."

"It must be strange to grow up in a big city—traffic, sirens, tons of people. I don't think I'd like it."

"What about art museums, five-star restaurants, theaters? They don't appeal to you?"

"They do, but I can always visit those and then come home." She perched on a stool in front of the counter where he was cooking. "I need to go through this place and figure out what to do with Rob's stuff." She paused. "Maybe you'll want some of it."

"Maybe. But you should figure out what you want to keep, and then I'll help you get rid of the rest. I didn't see a lot of clothes in the closet, but I'd be happy to take what's there to a donation site. There must be one in town."

"There is, and we should do that. I've been putting it off. I was almost afraid to come in here. I don't know why. It's silly."

"It's not silly. You're grieving."

She drew in a breath. "I thought it would be more difficult to have you here, but in a strange way, it feels better seeing you over here than seeing the house empty and silent."

"Did you ever read Rob's letter?"

"Not yet. But I believe you. Rob had his reasons for wanting you to come here, and I'm going to respect them." She looked around the room at the things her brother had accumulated in his short life. Most of what he had in the way of furniture was old or used. Rob was so rarely at home that he'd never put much effort into getting beyond the basics. There were probably no more than three things in the whole place that mattered to him.

"The records," she said abruptly, her gaze landing on the crate filled with old vinyl records and the ancient stereo that Rob played them on. "You should take them. They meant a lot to Rob. He loved old music."

"Then maybe you should keep them, to remind you of him."

"Maybe. But you'll definitely take the baseball cards."

"Rob had baseball cards?"

She nodded, smiling at the new interest in his expression. "Some pretty rare ones, too, I think. He started collecting them when he was seven. They're on the shelf in the bedroom closet. One of them could be valuable."

"I'll take a look later."

"And you should take his guitar."

"You don't think Justin might want it?"

She shook her head. "Justin has a guitar from his dad, and frankly, the last thing I want to do is encourage him to become a musician. That probably seems wrong, but I don't like the lifestyle. I don't want that for my kid."

"Understandable, but Justin is going to have some interest in what his father does. It's only natural."

She watched as he slathered bread with butter and placed it in the middle of a large frying pan. "Is a lot of butter the secret to your masterpiece?" she asked teasingly.

"Two kinds of cheese—that's the secret," he said with a grin.

"Is this your comfort food?"

"Yeah. Couldn't always afford the second slice of cheese, though."

"I'm sorry you had such a rough childhood. Will you tell me a little more?"

"There's nothing else to say. I grew up, got out, and didn't look back."

"Not ever?" she couldn't help asking. "You never look back on your life and wonder if you should have done something differently?"

He gazed at her, all trace of amusement gone now. "We're not talking about my childhood anymore, are we?"

"I just wondered if you had any regrets, Gabe."

"More than I can count, but regret doesn't get you anywhere. You have to move forward. It's the only way out."

"That's the second time you've used the word out. You're always looking for an escape route, aren't you?"

"I've learned the hard way that it's important to have an exit strategy in place."

"What was your exit strategy with me?"

"I didn't have one, because I wasn't planning on getting involved with you."

"But you saw me, and you couldn't keep your hands off me," she teased.

His expression lightened. "I think it was the other way around."

She smiled. "Guilty. I found you irresistible. I wanted to be with you from the first second you arrived in town. But you were Rob's best friend, and Rob warned me not to mess around with you, so I tried to play it cool. That obviously didn't work."

He shrugged. "I don't know what to say."

"You could say you felt the same way about me."

He flipped one sandwich over and then the next before replying. "I felt the same way about you."

"You could use your own words," she said pointedly.

"Yours were good enough." He gave her a grin. "Rob warned me to stay away from you, too."

"So, my brother didn't want us to get together three years ago, but then he decided to leave his house to you so we'd end up right next door to each other. What the hell was he thinking?"

Gabe stared at her for a moment. "I never told him what happened between us. Did you?"

She shook her head. "No. He left with you, and I didn't talk to him again for a few days. By then, I had decided it was better left unsaid. I didn't want Rob to beat you up."

"You were protecting me?"

"And myself. I didn't feel like a lecture on what an idiot I'd been." She drew in a breath. "How are those sandwiches coming along?"

"Almost ready," he said, giving them another flip. "I picked up some beer while I was in town. Do you want one?"

"I'd love one."

He pulled a bottle out of the fridge, popped the cap, and handed it to her, then dished up the soup and sandwiches. "Why don't we take these over to the couch?"

"Great idea." She took her food to the coffee table and sat down on the big leather couch. They ate in companionable silence. It had been a long time since someone had made her a meal. In fact, she couldn't remember when that had last happened. Probably before the accident, when Kelly used to invite her over to the inn.

"What are you thinking about?" Gabe asked.

"What do you mean?"

"You sighed like you had the weight of the world on your shoulders. Is my sandwich that bad?"

"No, it's delicious. I was just thinking about Kelly. She was the chef at the Blackberry Inn, and she is an amazing cook. Far better than me. She can take three ingredients and turn them into an award-winning dish." She paused. "Today was the first day I really talked to her since right after the accident."

"How did it go?"

"In some ways, better than expected; in other ways, worse. She's still angry and thinks I'm not taking responsibility for my actions. Her hatred hurts so much more than the others, because we were so close. I knew everything about her, all her secrets, her hopes, every last thing. I even knew she was a little nervous about marrying Brian, that she was concerned that he was too much for her."

"In what way?"

"He had a big personality, very outgoing, life of the party. Everyone loved him. He was a photographer. He had his own studio in town, and he was always busy. He was quite the talker. Sometimes I think he talked Kelly into marrying him."

"What's Kelly like?"

"She's friendly and sweet, super generous, the biggest heart ever. She's intense and driven but not in the same bold, colorful way that Brian was. They were opposites, but they made a good pair."

"Did you have doubts about them getting together?"

"A few. But I liked Brian. And I liked seeing Kelly happy. She wanted a husband and a family, and she was ready to settle down. She would make an awesome mother. You should have seen her with Justin." She felt another wave of sadness at another broken relationship. "He misses her a lot. I don't think he knows what's happened; he just thinks Kelly moved away."

"Brian and Kelly both grew up here?"

"Yes, but Brian was three years older than Kelly, so they didn't look at each other in a romantic way until about two years ago." She took another swig of her beer and popped the last bite of sandwich into her mouth. The warm, cheesy, buttery taste was quite comforting. "That was good."

"Not exactly gourmet."

"Sometimes simple is the best. I tend to make my life far too complicated. I bet you don't do that. You're much more straightforward and analytical, the kind of guy who always takes the shortest route between point A and point B."

"Why does that sound like an insult?" he said, wiping his mouth with a napkin.

"It was actually a compliment. I'm impulsive, which can lead to a bad decision, and then I make another bad decision to make up for the first one."

He grinned. "You want to get more specific?"

"Well, getting pregnant at nineteen was pretty stupid. Moving in with Connor and pretending we could be a family was another bad idea. I wasted too many years trying to get that to work. In reality, we were far better off apart. We make better friends than lovers."

"Maybe you and Keith will be both—friends and lovers,"

he said, taking a long drink of his beer as he propped his legs on the coffee table.

She didn't want to talk about Keith with Gabe sitting so close, his nearness sending little shivers of awareness down her spine. "Maybe." She got up from the couch and moved across the room to Rob's record collection. "We need some music." She flipped through the rack. "What decade would you like?"

"You pick."

The records that Rob had acquired over the years were from their parents, their grandparents, garage sales, and flea markets. She'd teased him about his collection, saying that he was living in the dark ages. To which he'd replied, "Sometimes I need an escape to a simpler time and place." Well, *she* needed that escape now.

"This one," she said with a nostalgic smile as she pulled a record off the rack. She pressed it against her chest as she looked at Gabe. "My mom and dad used to have big parties when Rob and I were really little, when they were still in love. We used to sneak into the room and hide behind the couch and listen to their talk. Everyone in town would be there. They'd drink wine, and they'd laugh and dance. This was my father's favorite song. He'd put it on, hold out his hand to my mom, and then he'd twirl her around the room. Sometimes they even kissed. I thought it was so romantic. I wanted that kind of love. At the time, I didn't know it wouldn't last."

She pulled out the old record player, blew some dust away from the needle, and put on the record. A moment later, a scratchy but beautiful melody took her back about twenty years.

"'Moon River,'" Gabe said with a laugh. "How appropriate."

She laughed. "Would my dad have chosen anything else? It makes you feel like you're in another time, doesn't it?" She swayed with the music, lost in thought, only to be brought back to awareness when Gabe got up from the couch and held out his hand to her, in much the same way that her father had done with her mother.

She should not have taken his hand. It was a very bad idea, but when his fingers curled around hers, she went willingly into his arms. She put her arm around his neck as he pulled her against his chest, so close she could have sworn she heard his heart beating—or maybe that was hers.

"Relax," he murmured. "It's just a dance."

She tried to relax, but that was easier said than done. Closing her eyes, she breathed deeply, trying to remember the past, watching her mom and dad dance, feeling loved and protected and happy. But the present was much more compelling. The man holding her in his arms was very, very real. His chest was solid, muscular. His body had power, strength. He was holding her tenderly, but it wouldn't take much to turn that gentleness into passion.

She had to resist. Gabe was the wrong man for her. He'd told her that. She'd told herself that. They were in complete agreement.

But she could feel his muscles tensing. His lips brushed the top of her head. His arms tightened around her. Oh, God—she wanted to kiss him, wanted to lift her gaze to his, to cover his mouth with her own. Her heart began to pound faster as temptation filled every breath. She'd told Gabe that she was too impulsive, that she made bad decisions, and she could sense another one coming on.

She raised her head so she could look at him.

His dark eyes met hers, and she saw the desire there. She licked her lips. He uttered a small, sensual groan, his body hardening against hers. His fingers gripped her waist like he never intended to let her go, and then he breathed her name. "Alicia."

She opened her mouth to say something, but no words came out. Gabe's gaze dropped to her mouth. And then, suddenly, they were kissing, long, deep, soulful kisses that shook her to her core, that made it hard to breathe, that made everything fade away but his touch, his taste. She was at passion's mercy. Every yearning thought she'd ever had about him kept her going back for more and more.

Then a shrill, screeching noise broke through the romantic haze in her brain, too loud to ignore. Gabe jerked away from her, breathing hard, his eyes as dazed and confused as she felt. It took her a moment to realize that the record was stuck on the word river, playing it over and over and over again.

Gabe turned to the stereo and pulled up the arm. Quiet filled the room. Tense, unnerving silence. He drew in a long breath and then let it out as he turned back to look at her. "I'm—"

"Don't apologize," she said quickly. "Don't tell me you're sorry."

He stared back at her, his expression a mix of anger, regret, and a little frustration, which pretty much mirrored everything she was feeling.

"What do you want me to say?" he asked.

"Don't say anything. It was a kiss, and it's over."

"It was a hell of a lot more than a kiss, Alicia."

She met his gaze. "We can't do this. I can't do this," she corrected. "I'm with Keith." What kind of a woman was she, making out with another man when she was supposed to be exclusive with Keith? At least, she thought they were exclusive. They hadn't actually defined their relationship, but they certainly hadn't been seeing other people.

"You don't love Keith," Gabe said.

"Yes, I do," she replied defensively. "This was just a moment of temporary insanity."

"You still want me."

"And you want me. But where does that get us? You're not a small-town guy. You're not cut out to be a husband and a father. Isn't that what you told me before? Has that changed?" His hesitation was one beat too long. "That's what I thought," she said. "Thanks for dinner."

She walked across the room and threw open the front door. When she hit the porch, she saw smoke, and her pulse leaped in terror at the flicker of flames through the trees. "Oh, my God, the house is on fire!"

Eleven

Alicia, wait!" Gabe yelled, but she ignored him as she ran across the yard.

The flames were getting bigger, the smoke thicker. What if her father was home? What if Keith had dropped Justin off? Fear lent wings to her feet. But as she made it through the thick line of trees, she realized that it wasn't the house that was on fire; it was the office building and the boatyard by the pier.

"Call nine-one-one," Gabe told her, grabbing her arm.

She battled against his grip. "Let me go."

"We need help. Make the call. Is there a hose somewhere?"

She waved toward the side of the yard as she pulled out her phone and called for help. Gabe had found the hose, so she ran to get the fire extinguisher from the kitchen.

As she entered the house, she stumbled over a barking and excited Sadie. "It's okay," she told the dog, then yelled for her father and Justin, but no one answered. She grabbed the fire extinguisher from the kitchen, gave Sadie a reassuring pat, and headed out of the house.

She heard sirens as she ran down the hill. Thank God the fire department was only a few miles away. Gabe was spraying water on the flames leaping out of the boatyard, which seemed to be the center of the fire. He waved her away as she moved past him, yelling at her to stay back, but she had no intention of standing around and doing nothing while her business was burning to the ground.

Her eyes burned as she breathed in the smoke, but she pushed past the discomfort, turning the fire extinguisher on the edge of flames closest to her. Within minutes, the extinguisher was done, and the fire was still burning too fast for their meager efforts.

She dropped the extinguisher on the grass and backed up, relieved to see the fire department on the scene. Within minutes, they were on top of the fire.

One of the guys told her to get back, but she was so mesmerized by the fire that she couldn't move. Then Gabe grabbed her arm and pulled her up onto the lawn until they were far enough away that she could breathe again. He put his arm around her shoulders, holding her tight. She glanced up at him, seeing the hard set of his jaw, the anger in his eyes, and it was only then that she began to realize what was really going on.

"Oh, my God," she muttered, feeling suddenly sick. "You don't think this was an accident, do you?"

"We don't know yet," he said, but there was no conviction to his words.

"I think we do," she muttered, watching the firemen attack the flames.

For sixty years, Hayden River Adventures had been housed

in that building. They'd launched thousands of river trips off the pier. All of their equipment was in that boatyard, and it was going up in flames.

"I need to call my father," she said. "I need to tell Keith to keep Justin at his house. I don't want him to see this. I don't want him to be afraid." But as she made an attempt to move, her head began to spin.

Gabe pulled her up against his chest. "One step at a time. You're in shock."

"I don't know what to do."

"What you just said," he replied. "We'll make the calls. And then we'll make a plan."

"A plan to do what? Someone is working really hard to make sure we don't go back on the river."

"That doesn't mean they get to win."

"They've already won," she said despairingly.

He shook his head. "No, they haven't. We're not done fighting. We just need to regroup, Alicia. Why don't you go into the house and make your calls?"

"I don't know what to tell my dad. Should I act like it's some random incident, or should I tell him what's been going on?"

"You should be honest with him."

"But he's been hurt. He's had a hard year. You don't know the kind of pain he's had to live through."

"I know you love him, and you've been protecting him ever since the accident. But he needs to know. And frankly, he needs you to respect him enough to let him know. This is his business, too."

His words sank in, and she knew he was right. She *had* been protecting her father, because she'd come so close to losing him, and she'd wanted to make his recovery as easy as possible. But she couldn't hide the truth anymore.

Unfortunately, before she could make the call, a car pulled up next to the house. It wasn't her father. It was Keith, Justin, and David. They all broke into a run as they crossed the grass.

Keith reached them first. "Alicia, are you all right?"

He gave her an odd look, and she realized that she was still holding Gabe's hands. She abruptly let go and stepped back. "I'm fine. The fire started in the boatyard. I was just about to call you."

"What happened, Mom?" Justin asked.

"I don't know yet, honey. I'm waiting for the firemen to tell me. Why don't you and David go into the house? Sadie is going crazy in there by herself. And it's too smoky out here, anyway."

As the boys went into the house, Keith moved closer to her, and Gabe walked down the hill to talk to one of the firemen.

Keith put his arm around her. "You're cold. You're shaking. You should go inside, too."

"I will. I just want to make sure the fire is out, that it's not going to spread."

"It looks like it's just about out. At least your house is okay."

"I'm grateful for that."

"You have no idea how it started?"

"No," she said with a shake of her head. "But my gut tells me that someone set the fire."

"What?" he asked in shock. "Are you serious?"

"How else could it start?"

"I don't know, but arson is a big accusation."

"You know how many people don't want us to reopen the business."

"I do, but I can't believe anyone would try to burn the place down."

Was he right? Had she been letting Gabe's cynicism take over her thinking? But Keith didn't know about the cut fuel line or the fact that Kenny Barber had been wandering around the yard the night before with a flashlight. She really hoped Kenny wasn't responsible for this. But even if he wasn't, whoever had done it was probably someone she knew, and that thought stung.

"I need to call my father," she said. "There's a good chance we've lost pretty much everything."

"Maybe you will have to give up the business," Keith said.

As she stared at the smoldering remains down the hill, a wave of anger ran through her. "I don't know about that."

"It's going to cost a lot to replace everything."

"We have some insurance."

"Will it be enough?"

"I don't know, but it's one thing to quit a business and another thing to have someone try to rip it out from under you."

Keith's brows knit in a worried frown. "If someone set this fire on purpose, then maybe you should back off. Do you really need this kind of trouble in your life?"

"No, but it's here, and I have to deal with it. Great, here comes my dad," she said with a sigh as her father and Bill made their way across the lawn.

"What the hell is this?" her father bellowed, shock in his face. "Why didn't you call me, Alicia?"

"I was just about to. It's almost out."

"Where's Justin?"

"He's in the house. He's all right, and so is Sadie."

Her father took off before she was finished, hobbling on his cane as quickly as he could down the hill. Gabe intercepted him, for which she was grateful. She didn't need her father yelling at the firemen until the fire was out.

Bill shook his head. "I heard the sirens earlier but never imagined they were coming here. When we saw the smoke from down the road, your father almost had a heart attack."

"I know the feeling," she said.

"I'm glad everyone is okay and that it's not the house," Bill said.

"Me, too."

"This shouldn't have happened." He muttered the words below his breath, but Alicia heard them.

"It sounds like you're not that surprised," she said.

Bill's head swung back around. "I told your dad earlier that I was having second thoughts about encouraging him to re-launch the river tours. I thought folks would have gotten over their bad feelings by now, but I don't think they have."

"You think someone set this fire?"

"I sure hope not, Alicia." He paused. "I'm going to get back to town. You let me know what you need to rebuild or repair. I'll give you as much of a discount as I can."

"Thanks, Bill. I appreciate it."

"Why don't we go inside?" Keith suggested. "Let your father deal with something for a change."

"I can't. I need to know what happened. You can go in."

He frowned but finally nodded. "I'll wait inside with the boys until you come back."

She gave him a thankful smile. "I really appreciate that."

"No problem."

After Keith left, she walked down the hill. Her father and Gabe were already talking with Blain Colley, a fireman who had been one of Rob's closest friends.

"Hey, Alicia," he said with compassion. "I was just telling your dad that we found a gas can and some rags. Your father said you don't keep gas in the yard."

"No, we don't."

"It looks like it was probably arson."

Her heart sank. "What will happen now?"

"We'll see if we can pick up any clues to identify the arsonist, but I have to warn you that it's unlikely we'll find anything."

"So they can just burn down our building, and nothing happens?"

"Let's take it one step at a time," he said diplomatically. "I'll talk to Ronnie tomorrow, too, tell him what we found."

"You can also tell him that Kenny Barber was out here last night with a flashlight and some lame story about looking for a backpack," Gabe put in.

Blain looked from Gabe to Alicia. "That true?"

"Yes. He claimed he was looking for something he left behind." She hated to think Kenny had done this, but he was the last person who'd been in the yard.

"I'll pass that on to the chief," Blain said. "We're going to stay here a bit longer, make sure everything is out."

"Thanks, Blain."

"I can't believe they took it this far," her father said.

"Who's they?" Gabe asked. "Do you have any specific ideas?"

"Wild River Tours. They have to be behind this. They want our runs. We weren't backing down, so they tried to ruin us. But they're not going to succeed. This is just a setback. I've come back from worse than this." He turned to Gabe. "You'll help, right?"

"Whatever I can do," Gabe said quietly.

"We'll start in the morning," her father said. "I'm going inside."

Alicia waited until her father was out of earshot to say, "I wish you'd try to discourage him instead of supporting him."

"Right now, he seems like he needs some support."

She let out a sigh. "You're right. He's shaken up, and this isn't the time to fight with him. But tomorrow—"

"Will be here soon enough," Gabe said. "You should go inside, too. It's cold. I'll wait out here until they're done. I'll make sure they do everything they're supposed to do."

"You're a good man to have around in a crisis."

"You were pretty impressive yourself. You jumped right into action."

"I'm used to taking care of myself and my family."

"Someone needs to take care of *you*." He paused, his gaze a bit distant. "Isn't Keith waiting for you at the house?"

She started. "Yes, he is." She turned to leave, then looked back at him. "Thanks, Gabe. Maybe this won't look so bad in the morning."

Gabe stared at the still-smoking wreckage as the sun crept up into the sky. He'd spent the night in a chair on Alicia's porch, watching over the yard long after the firemen had left and the Haydens had gone to bed. He'd let them down. He should have realized after the incident with Alicia's car that there was going to be more trouble. Hell, he should have understood the depth of the problem when he'd gotten into a fight with Russell Farr on his second day in town. But he'd fucked up. And now Alicia's business was in ruins, and her life wasn't too far behind.

He was supposed to be helping the Haydens save their business, not standing by idly while it burned to the ground. Well, that stopped today.

Getting up with a groan and a stretch, he walked down the hill to what was left of their office building and deck. The wall closest to the yard was gone, but three-quarters of the building still stood, although there was a huge hole in the roof. Someone had stretched yellow tape across the door to caution anyone about entering what was probably an unsound structure. He kicked open the door and peered over the tape. It was dark inside. He could see the metal filing cabinets on the far wall, along with a desk that appeared to be intact, although the room had been battered with fire and water. He doubted that they'd be able to salvage much.

A snap of twigs brought his head around. Alicia was barreling down the hill, wearing boots over brown leggings and a thick, oversized cream-colored sweater. Her long blond hair flew out behind her as she moved quickly toward him. It was barely seven, but he wasn't surprised to see her up so early. He doubted that she'd gotten much sleep, either.

She climbed the stairs to the deck, stopping a few feet away from him, shaking her head as she stared at the devastation. "I was hoping it was all a nightmare." She let out a breath as her gaze moved across his face. She frowned. "Were you out here all night?"

"I was on the porch," he admitted, running a hand over his stubbled jaw. He needed a shower and a shave.

"You didn't have to do that. I'm sure whoever set the fire didn't stick around to see it burn."

"I wouldn't be so sure of that. Arsonists often like to enjoy the show. It's part of the adrenaline rush."

"But this wasn't just a run-of-the-mill arsonist."

"No, this was personal, another reason someone might stick around or come back."

"So you sat up all night watching over us?"

He shrugged his shoulders. "It wasn't a big deal. I don't sleep that much, anyway."

"And you made a promise," she said quietly. "But I don't think Rob expected to send you into this mess."

"Actually, I think he did. That's why he was so desperate for me to agree to come."

"He was desperate?" she asked, homing in on his words with a sharp gaze. "You didn't say that before."

He swallowed hard, seeing the fear in Rob's eyes, feeling the plea in the strength of Rob's hand in his. Rob had stayed alive to get that promise, but he couldn't tell Alicia that. He just hoped she couldn't see it in his face, because she was looking at him very intently. He tried to think of something he could say that would satisfy her.

"You made that promise to him just before he died, not when he wrote the letter," she said, breaking into the tense silence. "He knew what was happening."

"Yeah, he knew."

Tears filled her eyes. "But when you made the promise, he felt better, didn't he?"

He had to fight hard to hang on to his own composure. He hadn't cried in more than twenty years, not when his mother had died or his father had abandoned him, not when any of his friends had died, not when he'd taken a bullet to the hip, not even when Rob had taken his last breath, but now . . .

He cleared his throat and managed to look Alicia straight in the eyes. He needed to tell her this. "Rob smiled, and then he closed his eyes."

"Oh, God." She put a hand to her mouth, her lips trembling, tears sliding down her cheeks.

He pulled her into his arms as she cried, her tears soaking through his shirt. He stroked her back, wanting to comfort her, but nothing he could say would take her pain away. So he just held her until the storm passed.

Finally, she lifted her ravaged face to his and wiped her eyes with her sleeve. "I'm sorry for falling apart on you. I'm glad you told me. I know it doesn't seem like it, but it makes me happy to know that Rob was at peace with your promise. Thank you for giving him that."

"It was the least I could do."

"I didn't tell Rob much about what was going on here. I didn't want to worry him. But I guess he read between the lines. He was always good at that."

"Some of his other friends in town probably shared things with him that you didn't."

"That's true." She looked over at him. "I never really thought much about who else he was in contact with." She glanced toward the burned-out building. "I'd like to take a look inside and see if anything escaped the fire. Although the worst has already happened. Even if we can salvage some paperwork or some files, our rafting equipment is gone, including the two new rafts we picked up yesterday."

"Did your father have anything to say last night?"

"He ranted and raved and drank half a bottle of Scotch and then ranted and raved some more, swearing he was not giving up. He would not be forced out of a business that he'd spent his entire life building. I've never seen him so angry. And he's going to have a hell of a hangover this morning."

"Did you tell him about your car?"

"No, and I think I'll hold off on that. The fire was a much bigger warning shot. If that doesn't stop him from wanting to reopen the business, my cut fuel line won't even register." She paused. "I wonder if this is the end, though."

"That probably depends on how you react. But whoever is doing this hasn't gotten caught yet, and the acts are escalating. You have two choices: surrender or fight."

"I want another choice. One that doesn't sound like war."

"This is war, Alicia. You just don't know who your enemy is, and that's the most difficult kind of war to win."

"I have a child, Gabe. Whatever I do affects Justin. I have to be careful."

"I agree. It might be smart to walk away, close down the business."

"But then I'd be letting the person who did this win, and that's unthinkable."

He saw the conflict in her eyes. "I understand."

"What would you do?"

"I would fight, but I don't have a kid, or a father who's still disabled—or a dog," he added as Sadie came running down the hill to greet him. He leaned over to pet her as she jumped up, licking his hand, his face, whatever she could reach.

"She certainly likes you," Alicia commented.

Gabe grinned. "I've got a way with the ladies."

"The four-legged ones, anyway. Sadie, down." The dog stopped jumping, giving Alicia an expectant look. "I know you're hungry," Alicia told her. "I guess I'll start the salvage operation after breakfast."

Before they could start back to the house, Justin came running down the hill in his pajamas.

"You're up early," Alicia said in amazement. "On school days, I can barely drag you out of bed."

"I wanted to see what the fire did. Wow. It's really bad," Justin declared. "How did it start?"

"We're not sure yet," she said. "But we'll be fine. We can rebuild." She ran a hand through Justin's hair. "Are you hungry?"

"I'm starving. And you need to make me a lunch, too. Because Keith is going to take us hiking at McClaren's Park, and we're going to have a picnic."

"That sounds like fun."

"And we're still doing the sleepover tonight, right?" Justin's face scrunched up in concern as he looked at her. "Are you sure you don't want me to stay with you today? I don't want you to be alone on your birthday."

"I'm not alone. And I have a lot of things to do today. Your gift to me is to go out with Keith and David and have a fantastic time."

"But you're going to be sad, because it's Uncle Rob's birthday, too."

She squatted down so she could look him in the eyes. "I will miss Rob today, but I know he wouldn't want us to be sad. Rob was always happy. So I'm going to honor him today by not being sad, and you should do the same."

179

Justin didn't look completely convinced but said, "Okay. When do you want me to give you your present?"

"How about after breakfast?"

"All right," he said, then took off up the hill.

"I forgot it's your birthday," Gabe said as they walked toward the house.

"I wish everyone would forget," she said with a sigh. "I asked Keith to take Justin today and tonight because I didn't want to spend all day pretending to be happy."

"Keith does seem like a good guy." He hated to admit it, but so far, he hadn't found anything to actively dislike about the guy. "But he wants you to give up your business, you know that."

"I do. Keith doesn't like conflict. He likes people to like him, and that usually happens, because he's really likable. The animosity toward me and my father, and even the kids at school toward Justin, is getting to him. He thinks it would be easier for all of us if we just moved on. And maybe it would be. Sometimes I don't even know why I'm fighting, because going out on the river is actually the last thing I want to do. But I feel compelled to save my business, too, because I don't want to let some cowardly, fuel-line-cutting arsonist win."

He smiled. Alicia was good at bouncing back. "Of course you don't want that. You want to kick someone's ass, and I'm going to help you."

She nodded. "Yes, because frankly, an almost-ten-year-old and a crippled sixty-year-old are not enough firepower."

"Speaking of firepower, I saw two rifles in Rob's closet."

"Yes, Rob loved guns. My father does, too."

"Do you know how to shoot?"

"I used to go with Rob and my dad to the shooting range. But I'm not going to shoot anyone," she added, her gaze narrowing. "It's one thing to aim at a target, but a person—I couldn't do it."

"What if they had a gun pointed at you—or your son?"

"Well, that's completely different. If Justin's life was in danger, I could do anything. But I'm sure no one's life is at stake here." She frowned. "Are you trying to scare me?"

"I would have thought the fire would have done that."

"I don't think anyone was supposed to get hurt."

"Probably not. But I'm not going to let anyone get this close to you again, Alicia."

"I have no idea how you're going to do that," she said wearily.

He didn't, either, but he'd just made another promise that he was not going to break.

Twelve

The kitchen at the Blackberry Inn smelled like cinnamon and maple syrup. Kelly finished up the last of the breakfast orders with a weary sigh. They went all out on Sundays, offering pancakes and waffles with blueberry and strawberry toppings, a vegetarian frittata, a slow-cooked flaxseed oatmeal sprinkled with brown sugar, along with fresh pecan rolls and an array of colorful fruit.

As the server took out the last of the plates, Kelly tucked a loose strand of hair back into her ponytail and set her skillet in the sink.

"That was fun," Nora said, returning to the kitchen with empty plates. "Everyone loved your food. Most people practically licked their plates clean."

"That will make the washing up go faster. But you know that clearing the tables is not your job."

"I do what's needed. I enjoy talking to our guests. It's so interesting meeting people from all over the country. Your mother used to love it, too. I hope when she's feeling better, she'll be back in the dining room chatting it up."

"I took her some breakfast earlier, but she said she wasn't hungry. She's nervous about the surgery."

"That makes sense. Last time she was in the hospital, your dad died."

"Yeah, but this is completely different."

"Of course it is," Nora said with a reassuring smile. "Lynette just has to deal with some memories, that's all. But I know she's relieved to have you here, even if she hasn't been up for much conversation."

Kelly picked up a sponge and wiped down the counter. "I'd forgotten how much fun it was to run my own kitchen."

"How's the restaurant in Sacramento?"

"It's all right. Sometimes they go for quantity instead of quality."

"That must be hard for a perfectionist like yourself."

"I try not to care too much."

"That doesn't sound like you at all. You've always been very particular about your cooking. It's your passion."

"I'm not interested in passion anymore. It hurts too much. So now I protect my heart."

"Oh, honey, protecting your heart isn't the same as letting it heal. Sometimes you need open air and sunshine to close a wound. Hiding it away just makes it fester."

She sighed. "Leave it alone, Nora."

"I have been leaving it alone, and I'm thinking that was wrong."

"You? You're never wrong," she teased, trying to lighten the mood and change the subject. "Have you seen Ian this morning?"

"Nope."

She set down her sponge and leaned against the counter. "I'm worried about him, Nora. He seems so angry and withdrawn."

"He's been that way since Brian died," Nora said. "I thought he was acting out because he was grieving."

Brian and Ian had gotten close. Ian had finally gotten a brother, and they'd joked about how he wouldn't be outnumbered by women anymore. She'd been so caught up in her own pain that she hadn't really thought about what her brother had gone through. "I need to talk to him."

"Well, you'll have to catch him first. He's probably in town at the carnival. It's all anyone is doing this weekend."

And it was the last thing she wanted to do, but sitting around the inn with nothing to do but think also didn't seem very appealing. "I guess I'll go into town and look for him."

"Really?" Nora said with surprise. "I thought you were avoiding town."

"I was. But the one person I wanted to avoid showed up here yesterday, so I might as well go check out the carnival."

"Who showed up here?"

"Alicia. Her car broke down a few blocks away. She couldn't get cell-phone reception, and it was raining, so she came here."

"Oh, my. How was that?" Nora asked curiously.

"It was awkward, uncomfortable, sad, bittersweet. We had one kind of nice moment, but it was mostly bad."

"But not all bad?"

"Stop it, Nora. I'm not making up with her. The wall between us is too high and too big."

"You can tear it down."

"I don't want to tear it down. I just want to ignore it."

"The problem with walls is if you try to ignore them, you just keep bumping into them."

She took off her apron and tossed it at Nora. "I'll see you later."

"You are so stubborn."

"Just like you," Kelly retorted as she headed toward the door.

Nora's words rang through her head as she jogged up the stairs to her attic room. She wasn't being stubborn. She was just moving on with her life. Some friendships didn't last forever. And right now, she had a more pressing concern. She needed to make sure that Ian wasn't in any trouble. Then, once she got her mom through surgery and back on her feet, she could return to Sacramento without any regrets.

Twenty minutes later, Kelly parked at the edge of downtown. There were a lot of tourists in town for the festival and far more cars and people than she was used to seeing on Main Street. In one way, it was good. It was easier to blend in with so many strangers around, people who didn't know her or Brian. She wasn't in the mood for carnival rides or games, so she decided to take a walk and see what had changed in six months. It soon became clear that nothing had changed. Her life had been spun off its axis, but River Rock had simply gone on without her.

As she passed friends and neighbors on the street, she said hello, exchanged pleasantries about the weather and what she was doing with her life now, cooed over a few babies, and pretended that she was doing fine. No one probed too deeply, and for that she was grateful. She was just starting to relax when she turned the corner and saw Brian's photography studio.

He had opened the studio three years ago with his cousin, and apparently, Randy had decided to keep it open. Her steps slowed. She wasn't quite ready to see Brian's photographs in the large display windows on either side of the front door. Then again, she couldn't hold herself back.

Pausing in front of the window, she drew a deep breath as the beauty of Yosemite greeted her. Brian had taken the shot when they'd gone on a weekend getaway, and he had truly captured the majesty of the mountains and the water-falls. He'd had such an eye for the perfect shot. Even though he'd made a living taking school pictures and photographing weddings, his true gift had been his artistic photographs. And he'd made some nice money on the side selling his pictures online.

The other photographs on display were just as beautiful. Brian had left behind a legacy of art. He'd made his mark on the world. That was something most people didn't get to do.

She was so caught up in the pictures that she jumped back when the store door opened.

"Kelly?" Brian's mother gave a shriek of surprise and then rushed forward, embracing her in a big hug. "Oh, my God. I heard you were back. It's so good to see you. So good," she repeated as she pulled back and gave her a long, searching look. "How are you? You look pale and thin. Have you been eating, sleeping?"

"I'm doing all right," she replied with a smile. Dina Farr was a tall woman with white-blond hair, bright blue eyes, and a perpetual tan. Like Brian, she was outgoing and full of energy. She'd been very close to her youngest son and had been devastated by his shocking death. But it looked like Dina had managed to pull herself together in the past six months. Or maybe, like her, Dina was just pretending to be normal.

"How's your mother?" Dina asked. "I heard she's about to have hip surgery."

"Yes, and she's quite nervous about it."

"I'll bet she's glad to have you home. And I'm sure the hip replacement will be great in the long run. I know she's been hobbling around in pain for a few years now."

It was amazing how different in agility her mother and Dina were, even though they were about the same age. Dina played golf and tennis and hiked on the weekends. Her mother pretty much puttered in her garden and talked to her guests at the inn.

"I'm hoping the surgery will allow her to be more active," Kelly said. "So, what are you doing here?"

"I've been helping out the past few months. Randy is busy with the photography side, and he needed some help with the bookkeeping. I'm only working three days a week in the school library now—cutbacks, you know. So I was happy to help out. I came in today to pull out the proofs from Jordan's wedding. She just got back from her honeymoon and is dying to see the pictures. I was going to wait until Monday, but when I ran into her this morning at church, she looked so wistful I told her she could come down and pick them up." Dina checked her watch. "I hope she's not late, because I have to judge the pie contest at the carnival."

"You?" Kelly asked with a smile. "Do they know you can't cook?"

"They know I love to eat." Her eyes sparkled. "I'm so glad I ran into you. I want you to come to the house for dinner.

Lowell is in Scotland with his ailing sister, so I'm all alone. I'll ask Russell and his girlfriend to come over, too. It will be just like old . . . well, it will be good," Dina said quickly, catching herself.

"I'd love to come," she said, even though the thought of sitting down at the Farrs' and seeing Brian's empty chair made her feel nauseated. But they'd been so good to her, welcoming her into their family. She couldn't say no.

"I'm kind of hoping you might decide to move back here. I hate to think of you in Sacramento all alone."

"I have friends there now. It's a good change for me."

Dina gave her a look that said she wasn't quite buying her story, but she didn't press. "I guess we all do what we have to do."

"Yes," she agreed. "Speaking of doing what we have to do, I'm worried about Russell. He seems so angry still. And I know he got into a fight the other day at Mullaney's."

Dina's smile faded. "I heard about that. Apparently, some friend of the Haydens said something to him."

"Or Russell said something. He needs to find a way to work through some of his anger. I'm afraid it's going to eat him alive." She paused as a familiar figure called her name and then came running down the street. Before she knew it, she was being swung around in a tight hug.

"Kelly!" Jordan declared with a big smile. "I'm so glad you're here. I was going to come down to the inn later."

Jordan looked amazing, with a light tan to her normally fair skin, a sparkle in her green eyes, and a short sundress that showed off her long legs.

Kelly smiled. "I'm so happy to see you," she said with

genuine pleasure. Jordan had been one of her closest friends. They didn't go back as far as she and Alicia, because Jordan's family hadn't moved to town until the end of middle school, but they'd still shared many wonderful moments and memories. "You look radiant."

"I'm in love. I guess it shows."

"Absolutely. So, the honeymoon isn't over?" she teased.

"Not by a long shot. We've just moved it back to River Rock. Married life is so wonderful. I never imagined it could be so good. And my parents are ecstatic that I've finally settled down and that there might even be grandchildren—" Jordan stopped somewhat abruptly, as if she'd suddenly realized that she was a little too happy for this particular conversation with these particular people.

That's what Kelly hated the most, the fact that people couldn't just be normal around her anymore. They kept tripping over themselves not to say something hurtful. But it didn't matter what they said, because the hurt was always there.

"The proofs are inside," Dina said, her expression strained. Obviously, Jordan's words had reminded her of the wedding she would never attend for Brian. "Why don't you both come in?"

Jordan grabbed her hand and pulled her into the studio before she could say no.

It took her a moment to catch her breath. In this room, where Brian had invested so much of his time and his life, she could feel his presence more strongly than anywhere else. She could picture him sitting at the consultation table, talking to prospective clients as he'd done so many times. She'd always been amazed at how good he was with people, even the nervous brides who were afraid that their precious pictures would get screwed up.

"Sit down with me while I look," Jordan said, drawing her attention back.

Dina took the proofs out of an envelope and spread them across the table. "I have to run over to the carnival for a while. Do you still have your key, Kelly?"

"Oh, I guess I do," she said. Brian had given her a key when she'd started helping out in the studio a couple of days a week, and she'd never taken it off her key ring. "I should have given it back to you."

"Don't worry about it. Just lock up here when you're done. And, Jordan, let me know what you want to order, and I'll pass it along to Randy. He'll take care of everything tomorrow."

"Thanks, Dina. I appreciate the early preview," Jordan said.

"Well, I don't blame you for wanting to see your pictures. You two have fun."

As Dina left, Kelly glanced down at the first photo of Jordan and her husband, Philip. It was a shot taken at the altar of the local church, and Jordan looked spectacular in an off-the-shoulder gown. But it wasn't Jordan's beauty that captured her attention; it was the look of love in her eyes as she gazed up at Philip. It was clear that she adored him.

A rush of moisture filled Kelly's eyes. "You look beautiful. I wish I'd seen you walk down the aisle."

"I wish the same thing," Jordan said.

She lifted her guilty gaze to Jordan's. "I'm sorry. I thought about coming. I just couldn't make myself do it."

"You should have been there, Kelly," Jordan said with hurt

in her eyes. "I understood why you didn't want to be a bridesmaid anymore, and I understood that it would be hard for you to attend, because we made so many of our wedding plans together. But I thought you'd still show up for me."

"I just couldn't do it," she repeated helplessly, wondering when she'd become such a coward.

"Because Alicia was there?"

"And everyone else. I didn't want to ruin your day with my sadness."

Jordan didn't look convinced. "I don't think that would have happened."

She blinked away a tear. "I am really sorry."

"Oh, don't cry," Jordan said hastily. "You know what a sympathetic crier I am."

Kelly sniffed. "I feel so bad. I was wrong. I was scared to face everyone. I hate how people look at me with pity. They don't know what to say to me, and I don't know what to say to them. It's so awkward."

"Is that why you moved away?"

"Yes, because in Sacramento, no one knows who I am. They don't have expectations or opinions, and I can blend into the woodwork."

"But don't you miss everyone here?"

"I miss some people—like you."

Jordan's expression softened. "I miss you, too. And now it's my turn to apologize for being so hard on you. You're here now, and at least I can share the photos with you." She held up a picture. "What do you think of my flowers? I ended up using Lori Rudowsky, and I think she did a good job."

"She did a great job," Kelly said, her mind flashing back

to the day they'd visited three florists to get bids on wedding flowers. Jordan had gotten engaged just a month after she had, and they'd made a lot of their preliminary plans together.

Jordan smiled as she studied another photograph.

"What's so funny?"

"Philip's uncle." She turned the picture around to reveal a very large man with a drink in his hand and a red flush on his cheeks. "He got wasted at the reception and tried to pick up Lois Marblestone."

"I don't think anyone has tried to pick up Lois Marblestone in twenty-five years." The stone-faced sixty-plus woman was a vice president of the local bank and had a dour expression and a sharp tongue. Her first husband had disappeared one night, and no one had heard a word from him since.

"Mrs. Marblestone gave him a shove, and he landed ass-first in the water fountain," Jordan continued with a grin. "It was pretty funny. He's kind of a prick. But you can't choose the family you marry into, only the man."

"True." She'd been lucky with the Farrs. Not a bad apple in the bunch. She flipped through several more photos, her hand stilling on a picture of Jordan and her bridesmaids, Alicia and Jordan's younger sister, Robin. "Pretty dresses," she said, careful to keep a neutral tone. "I'm glad you went with these." Another memory took her back. They'd spent more time laughing and trying on bad dresses than seriously looking for the right fit. At the time, they'd also been shopping for bridesmaids' dresses for Kelly's wedding.

"You don't really want to do this, do you?" Jordan said quietly.

"Yes and no," Kelly said, lifting her head to meet Jordan's gaze. "It is nice to see your pictures and share in your day."

"But it reminds you of the day that didn't happen. I'm such an idiot." Jordan gathered the photos and returned them to the envelope. "That's enough of that."

"You don't have to stop on my account," Kelly protested.

"It's fine. I'll look at them with Philip and my parents. When am I going to see you again?"

"Uh, I don't know. I'll be around for a few months."

"That's too vague," Jordan said. "We need to plan a dinner. I miss you." She took a deep breath. "And Alicia misses you, too."

She stiffened. "I can't talk about Alicia."

"If you can't talk about her, then talk to her. I want this feud between my two best friends to be over."

"That won't happen, Jordan. And I did talk to Alicia yesterday, but we didn't get very far. She's going to reopen her business, and I can't stand the thought of that, not to mention the fact that she's still insisting she did nothing wrong."

"Well, I don't know what happened that day on the river, but I'm not sure Alicia will be able to reopen after the fire last night."

Kelly sat up straight, her nerves tingling. "What fire? What are you talking about?"

"You didn't hear? Someone set fire to the Haydens' office and boatyard. The rafts and all the equipment went up in flames."

"Oh, my God. Was anyone hurt?"

"No. Apparently, Alicia saw the flames, and the fire department got out there fast, but they couldn't really save much. I called her earlier, but she couldn't talk long. She did say it's clear that it was arson."

"Who would do that?"

Jordan's gaze fixed on hers. "Probably someone who really loved Brian and doesn't want to see the Haydens reopen their business."

"You don't think that I—"

"No, not you," Jordan said quickly. "Maybe Russell or one of Brian's other friends."

Russ was a bitter man filled with rage, but the idea that he would set fire to Alicia's business made her sick to her stomach. It couldn't be him. And she couldn't imagine who it could be. All of Brian's friends were good, honest, caring people.

"Alicia's father must be devastated," Jordan said. "His whole life just went up in smoke. Ever since I've known him, he's been in love with his life as a river guide. Alicia used to say her parents' marriage broke up because of her father's devotion to running the river."

Kelly got to her feet, too restless to sit. She knew all too well how much the Haydens loved the river. She'd grown up in their house. She'd been on rafting trips with them, too—none of the more dangerous runs like the one Brian had taken, but she'd shared the river experience with them. It wasn't her favorite thing to do. She'd rather be someplace where she had solid ground under her feet, but she could appreciate how much the river meant to them, because it meant a lot to many people in town. You didn't live by a river that flooded every decade or so unless you loved it, unless you were willing to risk losing everything just to have a place at the water's edge.

But maybe George had given up his right to be on the river, she told herself, trying to hang on to the anger that had been getting her through the past six months. Maybe he'd run the river one time too many, and he deserved to be bound to the land for the rest of his life. At least he was still alive.

"Kelly?" Jordan's questioning voice brought her head around.

"I can't believe Dina didn't say anything about the fire," Kelly said. In fact, Dina had been cheerful, happy. Was that because she knew the Haydens were probably done?

"Maybe Dina doesn't know, although that's doubtful. It's all over town, and you know how quickly news spreads around here. Dina might not have wanted to bring it up to you, because of your past connection with Alicia."

"Russell couldn't have done this. It had to be someone else. Perhaps one of those guys from Wild River Tours."

Jordan gave her a doubtful look. "Do you really think a big, successful company would have to resort to those kinds of tactics to drive away a business that was already sinking? This feels more like revenge to me. There were twelve guys on that trip, and all of them were there for Brian. It could have been any one of them."

But those twelve guys were all her friends, too—at least, most of them. A couple had been Brian's college friends, whom she'd barely met.

"I have to go," she said.

Jordan went with her to the door. "Do you want to get some coffee or something? You look upset."

"I just need some air," she said, stepping outside with relief.

"Don't forget to lock the door," Jordan reminded her.

Kelly pulled out her keys, another painful reminder of the past. When would they stop coming? She locked the door with a shaky hand and slipped the keys back into her bag, very aware that Jordan was looking at her with concern.

"I wish I could make things better," Jordan murmured.

"No one can, but I appreciate the sentiment. I just need to find a way to fix things and move on."

Jordan smiled. "You know who used to be the fixer in the group? Alicia."

She shook her head. "Stop."

"Just stating a fact."

"And you used to be, and still are, the one who doesn't know when to shut up."

"True," Jordan agreed with a smile. "But I do know when to make an exit. So I'm going. I will be in touch." She leaned over and gave her a quick hug. "I'm glad you're back."

Kelly watched Jordan walk down the sidewalk, wishing she felt glad to be back, but all she felt was turmoil and a certainty that things were going to get worse before they got better. She needed to do something, but she wasn't sure what. Talking to Russell was probably a good idea, but she wasn't sure she was ready for that. Did she want to ask a question when the answer might not be what she wanted to hear?

A horn honked, and she jumped.

It was Jared in his tow truck. He pulled up alongside the curb and lowered the window on the passenger side. "What are you up to?" His gaze moved past her to the studio window. "Checking out the old haunts?"

"Not intentionally. I just ended up here." She moved closer to the truck. "Do you know anything about Alicia's business being burned down?"

His expression turned somber. "No more than what you just said."

"You don't know who did it?"

"Should I?"

"No, I just . . . I don't know what to think. Who would do that to them?"

"Get in the truck, Kelly."

"Why?"

"Because you need someone to talk to."

"I should talk to the Farrs."

"I'm a better choice right now."

"Why is that?" she asked suspiciously.

"I'll tell you after you get in. Come on, Kelly. Don't try to pretend you have someplace else to go. We'll take a ride."

"The last time we took a ride, you ran your father's car into a fence."

He grinned. "Selective memory, sweetheart. You were driving."

"Correction—you were teaching me how to drive a stick, and you neglected to tell me where reverse was, so technically, it was your fault."

"Tell me, who was your scapegoat when I wasn't around?"

"I didn't need one, because I only got into trouble when I was with you."

"But we had some fun along the way."

She shook her head but found herself opening the door of his truck and sliding into the passenger seat. "Aren't you supposed to be working now?"

"It's a slow day. The weather is good, and most people are at the festival. But if we get a call, you might have to help me change a tire."

"Yeah, like that's going to happen."

"I forgot. You're a girlie girl. Alicia was the one who loved to get dirty."

Her smile faded. "We're not talking about her."

He put up a hand. "Sorry, it just came out."

"I'm still mad at you about what you said the other day."

"I figured. Anywhere you want to go?"

She let out a sigh. "Every time I make a plan, it goes haywire, so just drive, and let's see where we end up."

They ended up near Miller's Creek, a longtime picnic area under a canopy of towering redwood trees about five miles out of town. It was a popular place in the summer, but today there was no one around. Jared parked the truck on a dirt road, and they walked down a well-trodden path to the creek.

"I haven't been here in years," Kelly said as they wandered through the trees and bushes, the hum of the creek just up ahead. "My dad used to bring me here when I was a little girl. It was one of his favorite places. He used to take his notebook out and write poems while I played on the rocks."

"I didn't know your dad was a writer."

"Just a hobbyist, but he was pretty good. He said these woods inspired him. I don't think I realized it at the time, but I always wanted to be just like him." She cleared her throat. "Anyway, this place looks pretty much the same."

"Not a lot changes around here, Kelly, but you know that. And you used to like it."

"Well, this place may not have changed, but I have."

"You really like it in Sacramento?"

"It's a beautiful city. It has its own river but not nearly as rural. I like the action. The traffic sometimes makes me a little crazy, but it's been a good change for me."

"Still, it's not home."

"Are you trying to get me to say I miss River Rock?"

He gave her a teasing smile. "Among other things."

She shook her head. "I can't believe you're flirting with me." In fact, it was a little shocking to be flirted with. She felt like she'd been in a deep, dark cave the last six months, more like a ghost than a woman.

"Sorry, Kelly." His smile disappeared. "I forgot for a minute."

She held up a hand. "Please don't apologize. It's kind of nice to be treated normally. Most people still tiptoe around me. When I go into town, I feel like everyone is looking at me."

"It must be uncomfortable. You like to hide in the background."

"Excuse me?"

"Like you used to do in school," he said with a shrug. "You were always the girl behind the curtain instead of onstage. You were sewing costumes or painting the scenery, memorizing everyone's lines for them."

"I was the stage manager. And if I hadn't been doing all that, you wouldn't have been able to ham it up onstage."

"True, but it didn't end there. In the last couple of years, you've always been the woman in the kitchen doing the cooking, not the one out front entertaining. You cooked at your own engagement party, for God's sake. The only time I saw you and Brian together that night was when Russell made his toast."

"I'm a chef. I wanted to make the food for my party, and I spent plenty of time with Brian that night," she said defensively. "You are so annoying, Jared."

"Yeah, because I know you too well, and you don't like it."

She didn't like it. She was shy and private by nature, and most people took that at face value, but Jared always liked to get in little digs at her. "This was a mistake. I should have known that five minutes with you would make me want to hit you."

He smiled. "I'd like to see that."

"Don't push me, or you might," she warned.

He held up his hands in surrender. Turning her back on him, she walked over to the creek, hoping to find some calm in the nature that surrounded her. A moment later, Jared approached with a bouquet of wildflowers in his hand.

"Truce?" he asked.

She accepted his bouquet with a reluctant smile. "Yes, but only because I have a lot of other people to worry about besides you." She walked over to an old bench and sat down. "These will make a nice centerpiece," she said, inhaling the sweet floral scent. "They're very pretty."

He sat down beside her. "Like you," he said with a smile.

"Save it for some girl who cares." She paused, suddenly curious. "Is there a girl?"

"Not at the moment."

"Why not? As I recall, you've never had trouble getting a date."

"Dates are easy to come by, but more than that—not so much."

The yearning note in his voice surprised her. Jared had been a player since he was fifteen. He'd always had a different girl on his arm. But he had been coming alone to more events in the past two years. "Whatever happened to that woman you were seeing last year—Elizabeth, right? I thought you were talking about living together."

"For a while, but she decided River Rock was way too small for her."

"You didn't consider moving?"

"I considered it. But I don't think it was just River Rock that bothered her. She got married last month."

"Whoa, that was fast."

"I guess when you know it's right—it's right. To be honest, I think she made the right decision in leaving."

"Probably. You *are* a pain in the ass," she teased. "Did she break your heart?"

"Not at all."

She shivered as a gust of wind blew past. Where they were sitting, the tall trees blocked out most of the sunlight, reminding her of what Jared had said about her liking to be in the background. "You know, just because I don't like to be front and center doesn't mean I'm hiding," she said. "I'm not some wimpy, shy girl who can't speak up for herself."

"I didn't mean it that way. I just think that once in a while, you should take yourself out of the shadows."

"I came out of the shadows when Brian died. I couldn't hide from all the sympathetic stares, even though I wanted to. I had to sit in the front row at his funeral, and I had to shake hands and receive hugs and do what I could to support his family."

"That's true." Jared paused. "Maybe after Brian's death, you came out of his shadow, too."

Kelly gave him a glare. "Really? Are we going there?"

"You told me on Friday to stop being neutral, stop having no opinion. I always had an opinion about you and Brian. I just didn't share it."

"And what is that opinion?"

He shrugged. "I never got why you two were together."

She was surprised by his words. "You were friends with Brian. How can you say that?"

"Because Brian was my friend. I know what he was like."

"And I don't?"

Jared sighed, staring out at the creek for a moment, and then said, "Brian was on his best behavior around you."

"I know Brian liked to party, that he was wild when he was younger, but he was past that stage. He wanted to move on to the next phase of his life, marriage and children and a house. He wanted the same things I did, Jared. And he loved me, I have no doubts about that," she added forcefully, feeling the conversation had gotten way out of hand.

"He did love you, Kelly." Jared paused. "You said you didn't have any doubts about *that*. What *did* you have doubts about?"

"Nothing. That was the wrong choice of words." She didn't like the way Jared was looking at her, as if he could see into her head, and he knew what she was thinking. That was the problem with him; he'd always gotten a little too personal with her, a little too in her face. "There's no point to this conversation. Brian is gone. So whether we were right for each other or not isn't worth discussing."

"But your life isn't over. You deserve to be happy, Kelly. And I hope someday you'll be able to move past this, maybe even come home for good."

She drew in a big breath and slowly exhaled. "I will be happy, and I want to feel normal again. Unfortunately, it's a little hard to move past what happened when it's still happening."

"You're talking about the fire."

"Yes. Who would have done that?"

His gaze darkened. "I have some ideas but no proof."

"You don't think it was an accident?"

"No, especially not after what happened to Alicia's car yesterday."

Her pulse leaped at his expression. "She said she ran out of gas."

"Someone cut her fuel line."

"No." She started shaking her head. "This doesn't make sense, Jared. Things like that don't happen around here."

"It makes perfect sense. Rafting season is about to open, and some people in town don't think the Haydens paid for Brian's death. They want their business shut down permanently. And I'm guessing this latest blow might be fatal. It will be hard to replace all their equipment. And even if they do, will they get any customers?"

"I don't like this," she said, the sick feeling coming back to her stomach. "I don't want Brian to be used as an excuse for destruction. He wouldn't have wanted that."

"Maybe Brian wouldn't have wanted that, but Russell is a different story. He wants revenge. I kept thinking time would heal, but time is only making him crazier. I tried talking to him the other day after he punched Alicia's friend, but he couldn't hear me. He didn't *want* to hear me."

"You think he did it, don't you?"

He met her gaze. "I wish I didn't, but I don't know who else would go that far."

"Let's get back to town," she said, getting to her feet. "Someone has to talk some sense into him. Maybe he'll listen to me."

Thirteen

Are you sure you don't want to come with us, Alicia?" Keith asked as Justin and David hopped into his car. "Get away from all this?"

"I just want to get Justin away from all this." She frowned as she saw her father heading down the hill. She'd been trying to keep him away from the ashes all morning, but there was no stopping him now. He was moving faster than he had in a long time, as if anger had given him renewed energy and a will to be well again.

"I'll make sure Justin has a good time, but I'm worried about you."

"I'll be all right, and I have a lot to do."

Keith shut the car door so the boys couldn't hear their conversation. His gaze was extremely serious now. "Alicia, you're a fighter, and I respect that about you, but maybe it's time to give up."

"Even if I did, my father wouldn't quit."

"Would he have a choice? You're his only hope of bringing his business back to life."

"Not just me—Gabe."

"Does Gabe know anything about rafting?"

"He'll do whatever it takes to learn. He made a promise to Rob, and he's determined to keep it."

"I'm betting Rob asked him to promise to keep you safe. Encouraging you to reopen your business won't accomplish that."

"I hear what you're saying, but you don't know what my father and I have been through, Keith. You don't know how much he loves this river. Being on it is when he's the happiest."

"He can still be on it without leading tours. You can get him a kayak, and he can paddle around all he wants."

"My father would never be happy with just paddling around."

"But you could be fine with it. You have your garden, your friends, Justin, and me. You can have a wonderful life without being a river guide."

Everything he said was true, and a part of her wanted to have that wonderful existence just as he'd described. But the other part of her didn't know how to give up something she'd clung to her entire life. "I want it to be my choice to quit. I don't want it to be someone else's."

"Now it's about pride?"

"Honestly, I don't know what it's about. I'm worried and overwhelmed. I need some time to think."

He leaned over and kissed her gently on the lips. "I'll see you later."

"Okay. Have fun with the boys."

"I always do. Although I have to admit I'm getting a little tired of hearing about Five Arrows Point and the challenges to becoming a great warrior."

She smiled. "Justin is obsessed with that story. I'm going to have to find some time to take him out there. I just don't know when."

"That's what you should be thinking about—all the things you could do with Justin if you didn't have to rebuild your business."

"Hey, I still need to eat. That's our livelihood you're talking about, Keith."

"You would find a way to make money," he said confidently. "One thing I know about you, Alicia, you always find a way to make things work."

She was still thinking about Keith's words long after he'd left. She'd been able to make things work in the past, but she wasn't the only one involved now. She walked down the hill to join her father.

Gabe had pulled some items out of the building earlier: a melted laptop computer, piles of paperwork, the desk chair, and one of the side tables that was charred on the top. To think this was all that was left of their business added another weight to her shoulders.

Her dad leaned heavily on his cane, staring at the water as if his beloved Smoky River could give him strength. She hoped it could, because they were both going to need all the strength they could get.

"Don't say it," her dad said abruptly.

"Don't say what?"

"That you're quitting." He turned to face her. "That's what you came down here to say, isn't it?"

She saw the pain in his eyes and wanted to erase it. "No. I think we should rebuild."

He jerked as if he couldn't believe he'd heard her right. "What did you say?"

"Don't make me say it twice, or I might change my mind."

He eyed her with approval. "I'm proud of you, Alicia, proud you're not buckling under. I knew I didn't raise a quitter."

"It would probably be easier if we both knew how to quit, because there's no guarantee that this is the end of the sabotage, Dad. If we start buying new equipment, someone might come back."

"We'll have better security. Gabe already told me he would help with that. And Bill said he might be able to store some equipment at the hardware store. No one is going to go after his store."

That was probably true. Bill was beloved in the town. Although the Haydens used to be well liked, too.

"Gabe said he'd go through the rubble today, see if we can salvage anything else." Her father paused. "We're going to be getting some money from Rob's life insurance, but if you'd rather put that away for Justin's college, I wouldn't blame you. We need to make sure he's taken care of. We own the houses outright, so we won't be homeless, but things will be tight for a while if we can't get the business going again."

"Maybe we can split the difference," she said slowly, wanting to be a good mother, a good daughter, and a good sister. "Rob would want us to rebuild. He loved rafting, and he loved this river, and, more important, he loved you, Dad. And he knew how much it meant to you. I love you, too," she added, her eyes tearing up. "Gosh, it's still smoky out here, isn't it?" she lied as she wiped her eyes.

"Yeah," he said gruffly. "I—" Whatever else he was going to say was cut off by the sound of a car turning into the drive.

"That's Bill," he said with an edge of relief in his voice. Her dad didn't handle emotion very well. "We're going to go to his store and look online, see what kind of deals we can get on new equipment."

She was happy to hear that her dad was going to get away from the house for a few hours. It would give her time to start in on some cleanup.

They walked up the hill together. Bill got out of his car and gave her an empathetic smile. "How are you doing, Alicia? Sad business, this is."

"I'm hanging in there."

Her father opened the passenger door, then paused. "Damn," he said regretfully. "I didn't say happy birthday to you, Alicia. I thought about it when I got up, and then we moved on to other things. We should have a nice dinner or something."

"I have plans for later," she lied. "I hope you don't mind."

"No, okay, good," he muttered awkwardly. "Then I'll probably catch a bite with Bill."

"That's fine."

She watched Bill's car pull out of the drive. When she turned around, she saw Gabe. He'd showered and shaved, his hair still damp, his cheeks glowing, and he'd changed into clean jeans and a long-sleeved T-shirt that clung to his nicely formed chest. She drew in a quick breath. Now was not the time to have a physical reaction to him. She just wished he wasn't so damn good-looking, that he didn't make her heart beat a little faster every time he came around.

He gave her an odd look as he drew closer, and she quickly schooled her expression. "I thought you might be taking a nap after your long night on the porch," she said.

"I did for about a half hour. Did your dad take off?"

"He and Bill are going to order some new equipment."

"I guess that means you're rebuilding."

"How could we not? My dad loves the river and loves his job, and he doesn't know how to do anything else. I don't know how to do much else, either."

"Did you ever want to do anything else?"

She shook her head. "I never really had time to think about it. I dropped out of school when Justin was born, and I love being a mom. Working for my dad gave me a schedule that I could handle and still have plenty of time for my kid. Anyway, we're getting off track. Just because we replace equipment doesn't mean we're going to have any customers."

"Oh, you'll have customers. I've already got some lined up."

"I thought you were a marine, not a miracle worker."

He smiled. "Sometimes I have to be both. And speaking of the Marines, I called a few buddies. I've got six guys so far who would love to shoot the rapids with you and your dad. I gave them a couple of dates three to four weeks out, and they're going to get back to me with a confirmation."

"Wow, you *are* a miracle worker," she said, both touched and impressed. "But I don't want you bringing anyone out here under false pretenses. They should know what we've been through."

"I told them what they needed to know."

She tilted her head, giving him a considering look. "And what was that, exactly?"

"Semper fi."

"Always faithful," she murmured.

"Exactly. I told them a marine's family needed help, and most of them knew Rob, so I didn't have to say any more."

"'No man left behind,' Rob used to say. What builds that bond?"

"It starts from the first day of boot camp, and it's unbreakable."

"I can't imagine what that's like," she said, her thoughts drifting to Kelly, the woman with whom she'd thought she shared an unbreakable bond.

Gabe dug his hands into his pockets and gazed out at the river. "I never believed that someone would put down his life for me until I joined the Marines." He turned back to her. "Rob saved my life five years ago."

"I didn't know that," she said in surprise.

"He wouldn't admit to it, but I knew it was him who knocked me out of the way."

"Rob was fearless. You should have seen him run the river. He and my dad were exactly alike. They lived to take on Gambler's Chute and Wilderness Falls."

He raised an eyebrow. "The rapids have names?"

"Yes. The river has multiple personalities. Sometimes she's calm and peaceful, and other times she's a woman scorned."

Gabe smiled. "Now you sound like your father."

"Well, I've listened to enough of his stories. They couldn't help but rub off."

"I want to go out on the river with you."

She drew in a quick breath. "Well, we'd need a raft for that, and we're fresh out."

"What about the rafts in the garage?"

"I don't even know if those are still intact. They're just rafts we used for family trips, and I don't have time to check them today." She tried not to look at him, but it was impossible. His quietness was more compelling than any words would have been. "I don't," she repeated.

"Alicia, you're going to have to face the river."

He was right, but she could only take one monumental hurdle at a time. "I will, but today I just want to clean up a little."

"I want to make sure the structure is sound before you start digging around in there."

"That's fine. I need to clean up the house, anyway."

As Gabe disappeared around the corner of the house, Jared's tow truck pulled into the drive. Maybe he had news on her fuel line. She walked toward the driveway, stopping abruptly when she realized that Kelly was with Jared. Her heart thumped against her chest. What was she doing there?

Kelly and Jared got out of the truck. Kelly walked across the drive, while Jared hung back by the truck, apparently wanting to give them some space.

Kelly gave her an uncertain look and then turned toward the devastation. "Oh, my God," she said, looking back at Alicia. "I didn't think it would be so bad."

Alicia didn't know what to say to that—or what to say about anything, for that matter. Their last conversation hadn't gone too well, and Kelly had made it clear that she wasn't interested in a truce.

"What are you doing here?" Alicia asked.

"I heard what happened, and I had to come by."

"So you could gloat?"

"No! God, no!" Kelly said, her brown eyes shocked. "I'm sorry about what happened, Alicia."

"Really? Why would you be sorry? You don't want us to go back on the river."

"But I didn't want this."

"Do you know who did it?"

"Of course I don't know who did it. I just heard about it a little while ago."

"Well, whoever did it probably did it for you." The angry words burst out of her. She'd wanted to make peace with Kelly. For six long months, she'd thought of nothing else, but numerous apologies hadn't been enough. And after their conversation the day before, it was clear that nothing she could do or say would ever be enough. Kelly was done. And maybe Alicia was done, too.

"You can't think I would condone something like this," Kelly said, disbelief in her eyes. "You know me, Alicia."

"And you know me," she retorted. "But that didn't stop you from accusing me of all kinds of terrible things. You weren't even on the rafting trip, but you believed what everyone else told you—everyone except me." Pain and fury filled her. "You wouldn't even listen to me, Kelly. We were best friends, and you wouldn't even talk to me, take my calls, answer my letters." Now that she was rolling, she couldn't seem to stop. "And then the worst thing in the world happens to my brother—someone you supposedly loved. But where were you? You should have come to Rob's funeral. He would have been there for you. No one could have kept him away, because he loved you. And I thought you loved him."

"I did love him," Kelly protested.

"But you couldn't honor him by coming to his memorial service. And I don't believe the bullshit you gave me yesterday that it would make things harder for me. You were only thinking of yourself. That's all you've been doing the last six months."

She shook her head, feeling overwhelmingly frustrated. "I felt horrible for you, Kelly. I know how much you loved Brian and how much he loved you, but I can't do this anymore. I can't keep saying I'm sorry. I can't keep asking you to listen, to think, to forgive, and to understand that it was just a tragic accident. If you want to hate me, that's fine. There's a whole group of haters in this town. You're not alone."

Kelly's face was white, her eyes wide, her lips parted, but she couldn't seem to come up with a reply. It was just as well. There was nothing left to be said.

"Go home, Kelly—wherever that is." She turned and walked back into the house.

Once inside, she shut the door and collapsed against it, bursting into tears.

She slid down along the door to the floor, crying for everything she'd lost, including the best friend she'd ever had. There was no way in hell they were ever getting back together now.

"You okay, Kelly?" Jared asked quietly as he pulled away from Alicia's house.

She stared out the window, not seeing anything because her eyes were blurred with tears. She'd never anticipated Alicia attacking her like that. She'd been so angry, so hurtful.

Was she also right?

"Kelly?" Jared repeated.

"I should have come back for Rob's funeral." She glanced over at him. "I knew it at the time. I told myself it would be too awkward, too uncomfortable, but Alicia was right; I was only thinking about myself. I didn't want to face everyone. But Rob was as much my brother as Alicia was my sister. He looked out

214

for me in school, he listened to my problems, he was there for me. Even after he joined the Marines, he always kept in touch. He was so good about that. After the accident, he wrote me e-mails every day, and he sent me this beautiful poem about life and death and grief. It meant so much to me. I must have read it a hundred times. I should have been there for him."

"Memorials are more for the living than the person who is gone," Jared said quietly. "Rob knew how you felt about him."

"I hope he did, but I pulled back from Rob after Brian died. He wrote me, but I didn't always write back, because he was connected to Alicia."

"For what it's worth, I don't think Alicia meant what she said."

"Yes, she did. She meant every word. She's always been direct and honest, but I've never seen her so angry, so bitter." She paused. "How can she be mad at me when she's the one who's wrong?"

He gave her a half smile. "Obviously, she doesn't believe she did anything wrong. Maybe you should cut her a little slack, at least for today. Someone is trying to hurt her and her family. You caught her at a bad moment."

"We can't seem to find a good moment." She thought about their conversation the day before. "Alicia was different yesterday, trying to make peace, but I shut her down. And today she shut me down. She thinks I'm part of whatever is going on." She stared straight ahead for a moment, then looked at Jared. "And the thing is, maybe I *am* a part of it. I've heard Russell and others put her and her father down, and I've done nothing to try to change their minds."

"Because you agree with them, right?"

"I did." She frowned, wishing she didn't feel so confused now. "But you've put doubts in my mind about Brian's behavior during the trip, and now so has Alicia. She was right when she said I didn't listen to her after the accident. I refused to hear her explanations. I didn't defend her to anyone. I just did nothing but cry. I was so caught up in my own grief I couldn't see anyone else."

"Of course you couldn't think of anyone else. You'd just lost your fiancé, Kelly."

"You're letting me off the hook."

"And you're beating yourself up for something that isn't your fault. You didn't set fire to Alicia's property."

"No. But was I wrong to blame Alicia?"

He shrugged. "I don't know, Kelly. A lot of time has passed since that day. I'm not even sure what I remember or what people told me. There was a lot of chaos, a lot of people in the water."

"But you still think it's a possibility that Brian drank during the lunch break?"

"Like I said, it's just a gut feeling."

"If he was drinking with someone else, why didn't that person come forward and say that?" Jared didn't reply, but she could see the answer on his face. "Because they were protecting Brian?"

"And maybe themselves. You should talk to Marco and John. They were with Brian."

"I'll have to see if I can track them down." Marco and John were two of Brian's friends from college, and they didn't live in the area. "But why didn't you ask them, Jared?"

"I did ask Marco. He said Brian was just taking photographs from higher up."

"Why didn't you believe him?"

"I didn't care much for Marco and John. They were friends from a different time in Brian's life."

"I don't know them, either. I only met them for a few moments before they left that morning."

"I probably shouldn't have said anything. My doubts are just hurting you more."

"I'm starting to have my own doubts. Alicia isn't perfect, but she's never been a liar."

"Just because she thinks it was an accident doesn't mean it was. She was in the water, too."

She sighed. "You're very good at arguing both sides."

"I've had a lot of practice."

There was an odd note in his voice that made her curious. "What do you mean?"

He didn't answer right away, then said, "You want to know why I try to stay neutral? Because picking sides never got me anywhere. I learned that when my parents divorced, and they fought over everything. I wanted to bring them back together, but my involvement backfired. When they wanted to prove a point, they brought me in to be the mediator, the judge. I had to decide who was right and who was wrong. But picking one of them only hurt the other one. It was a no-win situation. And I couldn't stand it. I was relieved when they each finally remarried. Now I make it a point not to get involved in their relationships or anyone else's. And frankly, what's going on with you and the Farrs and the Haydens feels very much like a no-win situation to me."

Kelly felt like someone had just turned on a light over her head. She'd known his parents to be possessive and loud, their fights well documented by the gossips in town, but she hadn't known the position he'd been placed in. No wonder Jared had turned into Switzerland. "I'm sorry you grew up feeling like a wishbone, and I apologize for taking my frustration out on you. I seem to be misreading a lot of situations these days. I used to think I had good instincts—not so much anymore."

"You just need to find a way to move on. Because the past is gone."

"I wish that were true. But it's not going to be gone until the attacks on Alicia and George stop." She drew in a deep breath, feeling that she was about to take an irrevocable step. "I need to make them stop. I was Brian's fiancée. I loved him, and I lost him, and I don't want there to be any more pain associated with his death. We should go by Russell's house."

"We?" he asked with a raised eyebrow.

"Yes. You're friends with Russell, too. I need someone to help me figure this out."

"I thought I irritated the hell out of you."

"You do—sometimes. But you'll help, right?"

"Yes, but before we get to Russell's house, you should think long and hard about what you're doing. You have a relationship with the Farrs, and they're loyal to Brian. They want you to be loyal to him, too."

"Wanting the truth isn't being disloyal."

"It could be."

He was right. The Farrs wouldn't like her defending the Haydens in any way, but Alicia's words rang through her head: *You believed what everyone else told you—everyone except me.*

"I need to do this, Jared. Not just for Alicia but for myself."

Fourteen

Gabe had expected Alicia to be on his heels all day, wanting to get into the office, to dig through the rubble, but the front door to her house had remained closed for the past two hours. It was just as well. He had a hard time concentrating when she was around, he thought as he ripped off some drywall so he could determine whether the walls of the office were structurally sound.

Alicia was even more beautiful now than she'd been three years ago, which seemed strange considering all she'd been through in the past year. Maybe that was part of it. She'd grown into a woman, strong, courageous, and independent.

When he'd first met her, he'd been torn between reupping and getting out of the service, and he'd chosen to go back to the Marines, which had hurt her deeply. He just hadn't had the courage to make a different decision back then. He'd gone with his comfort zone instead of the woman who'd taken him way out of that zone.

The attraction certainly hadn't gone away—not on either

side. Even when she said she hated him, he could see the desire in her big blue eyes. But she was fighting it as much as he was. Because neither one of them wanted to go down that road again.

Maybe this time would be different.

But would it? Once Alicia's business was going again and he was confident that she was going to be all right, he was leaving. He wasn't a small-town guy. And he was horrible at relationships. The only commitment he'd ever made was to the Marine Corps. And he'd made that commitment because there was no doubt in his mind that if he was there for his fellow soldiers, they would be there for him. He'd needed that certainty after eighteen years of unpredictability.

What Alicia needed was a family man. That wasn't him. He didn't have the first clue how to fill that role. So he would move on. He had a job waiting—a job he knew how to do.

Still, the last couple of days had been a nice change. Despite the animosity Alicia was encountering from some of the people in town, he liked the small-town feel of River Rock. It was a simpler life by the river. He could see why Alicia liked it. He could also see why Rob had been a little bored. No doubt, he'd be bored, too, if he stayed for too long. Or would he?

The doubt surprised him. He'd been focused for the last twelve years, knowing exactly what he had to do and how to do it. But now there were a lot of options, and it had been a long time since he hadn't been following orders.

He pulled off another large chunk of drywall, then stepped back to look at what he'd done so far. He needed to get some lumber and put up some supports before he let Alicia or anyone else inside. The roof was going to need work, too. It was doable. They could recover. They could reopen.

But when they did, would Alicia be ready? Her fear of the river was not going to be fixed as easily as the building.

His gaze drifted to the house again, wondering what the hell she was doing. He had a bad feeling. Something was wrong. She'd been gung-ho earlier to get going on the cleanup. So, where was she?

Stripping off his work gloves, he headed toward the house.

He was almost to the porch when Alicia opened the front door, a rifle in her hands.

"Good," she said briskly. "I was just coming to find you."

"With a gun?" he asked.

"I need a refresher course. If whoever torched our building comes back, I'm going to be ready."

"Why don't you let me handle security? And would you mind putting the gun down?" he said, seeing the angry fire burning in her gaze. Her eyes and nose were a little red, as if she'd been crying. Had something else happened, or had the events of the past twenty-four hours finally caught up to her?

"You can't guard our house twenty-four hours a day, and I'm not going to let anyone get this close to my home again."

She was right, but he didn't like the idea of her watching over the property with a loaded gun, especially since he doubted she really had the mettle to shoot someone, someone she might even know.

"We can set up a target or go to the shooting range," she said. "There's one about twenty miles from here."

"The range sounds like a better idea," he said slowly, still trying to think of how he could talk her out of it. "But don't you want to focus on cleaning up today?"

She shook her head. "Right now, I really want to shoot

something. You'll have to drive. My car is still in the shop." She headed across the grass, and he had no choice but to follow.

Alicia put the gun behind the seat in his cab, then buckled her seatbelt while he slid in behind the wheel. Instead of starting the car, he said, "You're going to have to tell me what happened, and don't say *nothing* again," he warned. "Because your mood has gone from bad to worse since I saw you earlier. And I'm not taking you anywhere to shoot a gun while you're this pissed off. You'd probably shoot me."

"Fine. Kelly came by. We had a big fight."

"When was that?"

"While you were in the garage."

"I was gone ten minutes."

"Yeah, it was a great ten minutes," she replied sarcastically. "When I saw Kelly, I just snapped. I've tried to make peace with her, to understand her attitude, to be patient with her grief. But she can't give one inch. Yesterday I tried to talk to her again, but she wouldn't listen to me. It's as if she's completely forgotten everything we shared. We were best friends since kindergarten. But when Brian died, she turned her back on me, and that was that. She blamed me for his death, and she still does. It hurts." She blinked rapidly as her eyes filled with tears. "So, when she showed up today, I just let her have it."

"What did you say?"

"I don't really remember, but I think I asked her if she was happy now, if she'd come to gloat."

"Do you think Kelly had something to do with the fire?"

"I don't think she lit the match, but she's with the haters who want to destroy my family. If my best friend can turn on me, then I can't trust anyone in this town."

He understood where that feeling came from. When his father had walked out on him, he'd felt exactly the same way.

"Start the truck, Gabe," Alicia ordered.

"I still don't think this is a good idea. If you want to get away, we'll go somewhere else."

"I want to shoot," she said firmly. "And don't try to handle me or calm me down. I don't like it."

He smiled, recognizing a no-win situation when he saw one. "I wouldn't dare."

"Now you're making fun of me like Rob used to do."

"Believe me, I do not think of you like a sister." The air between them suddenly crackled with a new kind of tension. He mentally kicked himself for taking things in that direction. And suddenly, shooting a gun seemed like a damn good idea. They both needed to release some stress, and the other ideas he had for doing that were far more dangerous. He started the truck and backed out of the driveway.

Alicia's anger slowly ebbed away as Gabe drove down the highway. Once they left the outskirts of River Rock, she shifted into a more comfortable position, her gaze fixed out the window. She'd spent too much time crying that day; she needed to take action, to take back control of her life, and this seemed like a good way to start. She was tired of being a victim. That was going to change now. She had let others' doubts become her own.

Last year's accident had been just that—an accident. She'd gone over and over in her head what she could have done differently, but riding the white water was always fraught with an element of danger. Brian's death had been a tragedy, but she had to move on.

She glanced over at Gabe. He'd been wonderful the last few days. Was it just because of his promise to Rob? Or because he cared about her, too?

That was a dangerous thought but one she couldn't get rid of. Or maybe she didn't want to get rid of it, because she liked him. He'd dumped her before, but she was finding it hard to drum up that old anger anymore. A lot had changed in three years. She'd changed; perhaps Gabe had, too.

But so what? She was seeing Keith now. And he was a good man, an excellent father, and a caring boyfriend. Maybe he didn't send her over the moon, but she'd already taken that ride, and look what it had gotten her: a heart full of pain. She needed to be smart this time, make good choices—not just for herself but for Justin, too. Justin adored Keith and David. He would love to have Keith as his stepfather and David as a brother.

What about her? Was it enough to give her son the family he wanted and deserved?

It should be enough. She should only be thinking of Justin. He was the most important person in her life, and she owed him more than a biological father who was never around. And she cared about Keith. Maybe he was a little impatient when it came to her father and the business, but that was understandable. He didn't really know what the river meant to them. He hadn't been around before the accident. He hadn't rafted with them, hadn't experienced the thrill of the white water.

A voice from deep down inside suggested that maybe he didn't know her as well as he should.

But if that was the case, it was her fault. She was the one who put up walls. Keith just hadn't figured out how to maneuver past those walls.

Would Gabe be as patient as Keith if the two of them were involved?

Memories of their one night together flashed through her head. Gabe hadn't been at all patient. He'd ripped the buttons off her shirt with the same desperate, hungry need to be together that she'd felt.

She drew in a quick breath, her cheeks warming as the memories came alive in her head, the feel of his hands on her breasts, his mouth trailing down her stomach . . .

She reached for the air-conditioning and turned on the fan. "It's hot," she said as Gabe looked at her. Then she quickly glanced away, afraid of what he could see in her eyes.

"Not much development out here," he commented.

"I'm sure it will happen in time, but I hope not for a while. There are enough condos and highways in the world, don't you think?" She felt better now that they were talking about nothing important.

"In some parts of the world. In other parts, our basics are someone else's luxury items."

"Rob used to say the same thing, that he never realized how much we had until he saw how little others possessed."

"It's an eye-opener."

"The Marines have taken you all over the world, haven't they?"

"I never would have seen it otherwise."

"What were you like before you became a marine?" she asked curiously.

"An angry teenager on the road to nowhere. The day before I enlisted, I was driving around in a car with a couple of guys. We stopped at a gas station, and one of the guys went in. I didn't realize until he came out that he'd robbed the place. I'd never been so scared in my life. Not just because I was afraid I was going to pay for his crime but because I realized where I was headed. The next day, I enlisted. I figured a roof over my head, food to eat, and a salary were a step up from nothing. I didn't have any other options."

"You were so young," she said. "Did you even realize that you might die?" Her voice broke a little on the last word.

"No," he said quietly.

"Rob never thought about that possibility, either. Or if he did, he didn't share it with me. He saw the Marines as the biggest adventure of his life."

"He loved being a soldier, and he might not have thought of that possibility when he enlisted, but it became clear soon after."

"He had opportunities to quit, but he couldn't. He was addicted to risk, and I think you were, too."

"Maybe, but it wasn't that simple."

"Rob was only quitting because of what happened to my dad and me. He finally realized that we needed him more than the Marines did." She paused. "Why did you decide to give it up now, when you couldn't give it up three years ago?"

He didn't answer right away, and for some odd reason, she found herself holding her breath.

"I don't know," he said finally.

She was disappointed. "Don't know or won't say?"

"It's complicated."

She let out a sigh but decided not to push her luck. Gabe had shared a little of his history with her, and for the moment, that was enough. "You need to take the next exit."

"Got it," he said, changing lanes. "You're still in the mood to shoot?"

"Absolutely," she said, her mind returning to the devastation she'd left behind. "If someone comes after me, I'm going to be ready."

A frown crossed his face. "I don't want you to end up with a false sense of power. Knowing how to shoot a gun and actually doing it are two different things. It's one thing to shoot at a target and another to actually pull the trigger against a person—maybe a person you know."

"You think I know my enemy?"

"Don't you?"

Kelly couldn't find Russell. He wasn't at home, and he wasn't returning her calls. Frustrated, she gave in to Jared's suggestion that they take a look around the carnival. Maybe Russell would be there.

At first, she'd been worried that she'd be the focus of attention again, but there were so many tourists that it was easy to blend into the woodwork. After a lunch in the beer garden that included two beers, she felt a lot more mellow.

"Okay, I think you've finally relaxed," Jared said with a grin. He glanced down at his watch. "Three hours and forty-two minutes. We probably could have shortened the time if we'd come here first."

She sipped the last of her beer. "I do feel better, but I haven't forgotten about Russell. I really hope we can find him."

"Maybe it's good that you've had a chance to calm down. It won't take much to send Russell off."

"He didn't used to be so short-tempered, did he?"

"He's definitely gotten worse since Brian's death."

"I wonder who he gets that temper from. His mom and dad are lovely people, and Brian rarely got angry. He didn't let things get to him the way Russell does." She paused, her pulse jumping as the object of their conversation came into view. Russell was walking with his girlfriend, Amanda, his arm draped around her shoulder. He certainly didn't look like a man who had just committed arson. Then again, he also looked happier than she'd seen him since she'd returned to River Rock. Was that because he knew the Haydens had suffered a huge setback?

She hated the direction of her thoughts, but she couldn't deny reality. Someone had gone after Alicia's business, and it was more than likely that that someone had done it for Brian.

"Looks like you're going to get your chance to talk to Russell," Jared said, his gaze somber.

"I don't want to talk to him with his girlfriend around."

"I could distract her for you."

"That would be nice." She paused. "In fact, you're being amazingly nice to me, and I don't think I've said thank you."

"No thanks required." He got up, calling Russell over.

As Russell and his girlfriend approached their table, she realized that while Russell was all smiles, Amanda's expression was a little strained. An attractive brunette, Amanda worked as a pharmacist at the local drugstore. She'd moved to town a year earlier, and Kelly had gotten to know her pretty well during her engagement. She'd thought Amanda was a good match for Russell, because she wasn't into drama, and he needed someone like that in his life. But now she wondered if Russell's anger was taking a toll on his relationship.

"Kelly, it's great to see you," Amanda said. "Russell told me you were in town. I hope we can have dinner one night soon."

"That would be great," she said as Jared and Russell greeted each other.

"Amanda, I'm so glad you're here," Jared said. "Because I need a partner for the Cake Walk, and Kelly refuses to do it with me."

Amanda didn't even hesitate. "Sounds like fun. Let's do it."

As Amanda and Jared left, Russell sat down at the table across from her. "How did you and Jared end up here together? I thought you didn't like him much."

"I just ran into him," she said, catching something in his tone that bothered her. He was looking at her as if she were cheating on Brian, which was ridiculous. "I called you earlier. Did you get my message?"

"Yes, but I didn't have a chance to call you back. What's up?"

"The fire at Alicia's house," she said shortly.

He nodded. "Yeah, I heard about that," he said, a gleam in his eyes. "Looks like they won't be able to get back on the river."

"Unless they buy new equipment."

"I'd be careful if I were them. New equipment could end up the same as the old."

Her stomach began to churn at his words. "Russell—did you set that fire?"

He didn't seem surprised by her question. "No, but I can't say I'm sorry it happened. In fact, it was a damn good idea. I wish I'd thought of it."

She frowned. "It wasn't a good idea. Alicia or her father or, God forbid, Justin could have been hurt."

"From what I heard, the fire was only in the boatyard."

"It could have gotten out of control. There are tons of trees around there. If a spark had flown, it could have landed on the roof of the house."

"Well, it didn't."

The steel glint in his eyes told her she wasn't going to get a different reaction from him no matter what she said. "Do you know who did it?"

He shrugged. "It could have been anyone. Brian had a lot of friends."

"Brian wouldn't have wanted something like this to happen."

"I think I know what my brother would have wanted a little better than you, Kelly. No offense, but I grew up with him. You were only with him for a few years."

"I was engaged to him, and I do take offense," she snapped back. "Brian was a good man, and he liked Alicia and her father."

"Maybe before they killed him."

She sucked in a quick breath at his harsh words. "It wasn't like that."

"Now you're on their side?" he asked sharply. "I never thought I'd see the day that you'd betray Brian. I thought you loved him."

"You know I did, Russell, and I'm not on their side. But I also won't support illegal and dangerous actions against them. I don't want to see anyone else get hurt. Nothing anyone does to the Haydens will bring Brian back."

He shook his head, his lips tightening. "You've changed."

"You're the one who has changed, Russell. You're letting your anger get the best of you."

"I didn't do it, Kelly," he said, getting to his feet. "But like

I said before, I'm not unhappy about it, and I'm not going to pretend I am, not for you, not for anyone."

She let out a breath as he left. Her heart was racing from their exchange, her hand shaking a little. Was Russell lying? Or was he just trying to cover himself in case she went to the police?

That seemed unthinkable. She didn't want to go against the Farrs. She cared about them a great deal. She never should have come back to town. If she hadn't, she'd be none the wiser about what was happening. But she was there, and she had to deal with what was going on. She didn't want to see anyone else get hurt.

She looked up as Jared sat down at the table.

"Well?" he asked.

"He denied setting the fire, but he was almost giddy with delight that it happened." She paused. "I have to figure out who did it."

"Why you?"

"Because I have the best chance of getting the truth. I'm one of the—what did Alicia call them?—the haters."

"But you don't hate Alicia."

She shook her head. "No, though I gave it a good try."

"What changed?"

"I finally came out of the fog of grief I've been hiding in." She paused. "Russell accused me of changing sides, betraying Brian's memory. He even acted like I had something going on with you. That's crazy."

His smile didn't quite reach his eyes. "Yeah, crazy."

The indoor shooting range was a one-story building about the size of a football field. Inside the range were twelve soundproof shooting booths and automated targets that could be switched in and out with the push of a button. After renting ammunition, protective glasses, and hearing protectors, Alicia and Gabe proceeded to their cubicle.

"Let's go over some basics first," Gabe said.

She sighed. "I've done this before. You heard Harry. I was one of the best female shooters he's ever seen."

"Harry is an old man with bad eyes and likely a bad memory." The owner of the shooting range had been happy to see Alicia and had spent almost twenty minutes telling Gabe about how Alicia and Rob used to come to the range with their dad when they were barely in their teens.

"He is old, but I was good. Stop stalling, and give me the gun."

Ignoring her request, Gabe went over the safety procedures. Then he put on the required goggles and ear protectors before handing her the gun.

Alicia lifted the gun with sure hands, aiming it at the target with confidence. Then she pulled the trigger. The blast sent her backward, but he was ready, catching her against his chest.

"I forgot about that," she said rather loudly, giving him a big smile. She stepped away and took another shot, absorbing the blast this time.

She might not need him to catch her again, but he still stayed close, watching her take out her frustration and anger on the target. She was better than he'd expected, but while she might be able to shoot a target with precision, it was nothing like pulling the trigger on a person—maybe a friend.

He wished he had a better idea of who could be involved. He felt like he was flying blind.

Well, not completely blind. There was Kenny Barber and Russell Farr. But who else? Maybe after Alicia got some of the anger out of her system, she'd be in the mood to talk it out or at least give him a list of names to investigate.

They needed to start acting instead of reacting; he just had to figure out how to do that.

It would be easier to concentrate if he wasn't always with Alicia. She was a beautiful distraction. Last night, they'd danced and kissed, and he'd been tempted to forget all of the reasons they shouldn't be together and just be with her one more time.

But would once be enough? And what about Keith? He didn't poach other men's women. That wasn't his style. He had to keep his distance.

The thought had no sooner crossed his mind than Alicia set down the rifle and gave him a hug. She pulled the ear protectors off his head and said, "Thanks, Gabe. This was exactly what I needed."

She looked so pretty. All he could think about was how her sweet and soft lips beckoned to him. And suddenly, it wasn't about what she needed but what *he* needed. He pulled off her protective gear, framed her face with his hands, and kissed her, his tongue sliding between her parted lips, using her surprise to his advantage. One kiss wasn't enough. He wanted to devour her, run his hands and his tongue all over her body, but his need for air finally made him lift his head to catch his breath.

Alicia looked at him through dazed, glittering eyes, shimmering with the same sensual haze that surrounded him. It had always been like this—from the first second he'd seen her, he'd wanted her.

"Gabe."

Her voice was soft and breathy. He moved to kiss her again, but she stepped away, backing up against the wall of the booth.

"We shouldn't," she said. "Look where we are."

It took a moment for her words to register, for his brain to start working again. "Right," he said finally. "Let's get out of here."

"You don't want to shoot?"

"Hell, no."

She gave him a wary look. "You're pissed off at me?"

"No, I'm mad at myself." He was too wound up to argue. He needed to move, to walk, to get some air. So he headed out the door and didn't stop until he reached the parking lot. Alicia stopped to talk to Harry, so he had a minute to himself, for which he was intensely grateful. He needed to retreat, regroup. He didn't want to go through all the pain that had followed the last time they'd been together. He couldn't let himself believe in a future with Alicia, because she came with a kid, with needs that he couldn't fulfill. And thinking otherwise would only get him into trouble. He'd learned early in life to keep expectations low, so the fall wouldn't be that bad.

He got into the truck and slammed his fist against the wheel, relishing the bruising pain. That hurt he could handle. Falling for Alicia . . . he couldn't go there.

Fifteen

Alicia took her time talking to Harry. She needed to regain her composure after Gabe's fiery kiss, but she could barely keep her mind on what Harry was saying. Her senses were still tingling with Gabe's taste, his scent, the rough edge of his voice. It had taken every last ounce of strength she had to pull away from him.

"Alicia?" Harry asked, a quizzical gleam in his eyes.

"Sorry, I didn't hear what you said."

"I was talking to Ian Palmer about you the other day."

"Ian was in here?" she asked, surprised that Kelly's little brother would be spending time at the shooting range.

"He's been a regular the last couple of weeks. I'm a little worried about him. He's got something gnawing at him, and I can tell he's about ready to burst."

"Maybe shooting a gun isn't the best thing for him to be doing right now."

Harry smiled. "In here, it's safe and controlled, just the right place for him to be. Ian told me that you're planning to be in business again this season."

"That's the plan. We'll see how it goes." She paused. "Can I ask you, was Ian upset about our business reopening? Brian, the man who died, was going to marry Ian's sister."

Harry nodded. "Yeah, that was a sad business. Like I said, Ian just seemed mad at the world."

Mad enough to set fire to my boatyard?

It was a crazy thought, but she couldn't shake it out of her head. Maybe he'd done it for Kelly.

But she'd been like a sister to Ian. They'd spent tons of time together. The thought of him being involved was worse than the Farrs being responsible. As Gabe had said earlier, it was likely that she knew her enemy. She just didn't want it to be Ian.

"So, who's your fellow?" Harry asked, tipping his head in the direction of the parking lot.

"Gabe? He's Rob's friend, another ex-marine."

"I figured. He had that look about him. He's sweet on you."

She shook her head. "You don't know anything about him."

"I got eyes. That's all I need."

"Good-bye, Harry," she said with a smile.

"You take care of yourself, Alicia. And tell your dad I send my best wishes. Hope to see him in here again soon. He used to be one of my best customers."

"I'll tell him," she said, then headed out to the truck.

The radio was blaring when she slid into her seat and fastened her seatbelt. Apparently, Gabe wasn't in the mood to talk.

As they drove toward home, she started to feel restless when they got closer to town. The sun had gone down, and the moon was still low in the sky, reminding her that she still had something important to do that day.

"I need to make a stop," she said.

"Where?"

"Just take the next exit." Five minutes later, she directed him into a parking spot in front of J&M Liquors. "I need to get a very special bottle of tequila."

Recognition sparked in his eyes. She didn't wait for a reply, just got out of the car and hurried into the store. She felt a wave of relief when she saw a bottle of Don Julio Blanco, one of the best tequilas on the market and Rob's favorite. On her way to the register, she impulsively grabbed some plastic cups.

Back in the truck, she set the bag on the floor. "I have somewhere else I want to take you."

"Care to be more specific?"

"Not at the moment. But we can park at the house and walk from there."

As Gabe pulled away from the curb, her cell phone rang. It was Keith. She didn't really want to talk to him in front of Gabe, but he had Justin, so she had to answer.

"Just wanted to see how things were going," Keith said.

"Fine. How are you guys? How is Justin?"

"He's having a blast. I'll let him say hello in a second. I tried your house. Are you out somewhere?"

"Yeah, I had some errands to run. I'm almost home."

"Are you sure you haven't changed your mind about spending your birthday alone? We can come and get you."

"Not unless you've changed your mind about keeping Justin."

"No, the boys are fine. I just hate to think of you sad and on your own."

"It's not like that, and I really appreciate your taking Justin tonight. It's the best present."

"If you say so. I'll put Justin on."

A moment later, Justin's excited voice came over the phone. "Hi, Mommy."

"Hey, how's it going?"

"Good. We're going to barbecue and roast marshmallows."

"That sounds like fun. Have a good time, and I'll talk to you in the morning before school, okay? I love you."

"Love you, too."

She hung up her phone. "He's having a good time."

"Nice of Keith to give you the day off. Sounded like he was trying to change your mind, though."

"A little, but I'm not in the mood to be sociable, and I don't have to pretend with you."

"No. You don't ever have to pretend with me," he said, meeting her gaze.

She licked her lips and glanced away, hoping she wasn't making a mistake.

A few minutes later, Gabe pulled into the driveway of Rob's house. All was quiet on the two properties. There were no lights on at her house, so she assumed her father was still out.

"Where to now?" Gabe asked as they got out of the car. "It's getting dark."

"There's a lantern in Rob's house. I'll grab it."

"You're being very mysterious," he said.

She smiled. "You just don't like to be the one not in charge."

She entered Rob's house and took the lantern out of the closet. She turned it on, relieved to see that the batteries still worked, then turned it off again. As she walked through the living room, she swiped the afghan off the back of Rob's couch. Looking around, she was surprised at how the house was beginning to feel more like Gabe's place than Rob's. How odd was that? He'd only been there a few days, and Rob had lived there for years. Shaking her head, she met up with Gabe on the porch.

"You can carry this," she said, handing him the lantern. "Follow me."

She led him through the woods about a half mile. There were no houses beyond Rob's for at least two miles, just a lot of trees and the constant hum of the water running downstream. Gabe stayed on her heels, not asking any more questions. He was a lot different in that regard from Keith. Keith was more of a talker, which she usually liked, because it meant she didn't have to work too hard to keep the conversation going.

Sometimes she wondered just how much Keith listened. But how many men were good at that? She certainly hadn't met too many. Connor had loved the sound of his own voice, whether he was singing his songs or telling Irish tales over a shot of whiskey. Justin took after his father, too; he loved to talk. Whenever she went to a parent-teacher conference, they always said Justin was a great kid, but he needed to learn how to listen.

Maybe he could learn that from Gabe. But would Gabe be around long enough to form a relationship with her son? That was still to be determined, but she didn't want to think about the future right now. Tomorrow would come soon enough.

Gabe turned on the lantern, throwing some light over their path. She didn't really need it; she'd roamed these woods since she was a little girl.

"We're almost there," she told him.

Five minutes later, she took a left turn and headed toward

an old abandoned dock by the river. "This was the original launching pad for Hayden River Adventures," she said.

"No kidding. Why the move upstream?"

"This part of the river is more prone to flooding. Everything got wiped out in the early sixties in a monster storm, so they moved to higher ground."

"Not that high. I'm sure you could still flood."

"Twice, but that's part of living by a river." She spread the blanket out on the dock and sat down, motioning for Gabe to do the same. Then she pulled the bottle of tequila out of her bag.

Gabe leaned over to read the label. "Don Juan Blanco. I thought so."

"It was Rob's favorite tequila, and my dad's, and my grand-father's, another male tradition passed down. Rob had his first taste of it on his eighteenth birthday."

"When did you have your first taste?"

"My eighteenth birthday," she said, meeting his gaze. "Rob brought the bottle to me later that night, and we came down here and we had a shot together. We did the same thing every year after that, until Rob went away. We made a promise that if we weren't together, we'd still take a drink and toast each other." Her eyes watered a little, but she sniffed back the tears. She wanted to celebrate Rob, not mourn him. "I don't really know if he found this particular brand when he was overseas, but—"

"But he always took a shot of tequila on his birthday," Gabe said. "Or as close to his birthday as he could get."

"You were with him some of those times?"

"A lot of those times. So, what are you waiting for?"

He ripped open the bag of plastic cups and pulled two out while she unscrewed the bottle cap. She poured two cups half full and handed him one.

"To Rob, the best brother in the world."

Gabe held up his cup. "To Rob, the best friend in the world."

She smiled at him as they clicked their plastic cups together, and then she drank it all down in one long shot. It burned down her throat, warming her from the inside out.

"Very good," Gabe said. He held up his empty cup. "I need some more. I have another toast to make."

"In that case . . ." She refilled their cups. "What's your toast?"

"To you, Alicia. Happy birthday."

She clicked her cup to his and drank again. "Thank you." She drew in a deep breath of fresh, cool air. "I don't want to be sad anymore. Does that sound bad?" She couldn't believe she'd said the words out loud. They seemed so wrong. "It's only been a few weeks, but I feel the sadness dragging me down, and while part of me wants to sink into the misery and just hide under the covers, I have a son, and I don't want to drag him down with me."

"That's why you didn't want him to spend your birthday with you."

"Exactly. I wanted Justin to have a good day with no sad moments. But let's talk about something else, something besides me and my problems. In fact, let's talk about you."

He handed her his empty cup. "I'm going to need another shot."

She poured some tequila into his cup and then refilled her own. She took only a sip this time as she studied Gabe's face. The lantern was hard-pressed to compete with the night shadows, but maybe shadows were better for tonight. "Tell me something about yourself that I don't know. What did you like about being a marine?"

"I was proud to serve my country. It gave my life some honor."

"You don't think you would have found that without the Marines?"

"I'll never know."

"I think you would have. You have a core of strength that's there no matter what you do." His jaw tightened as if he weren't comfortable with the compliment. "You just need to loosen up a little," she teased. "So, what's your favorite food?"

"Spaghetti and meatballs."

"Not particularly imaginative but not bad."

"I'm so glad you approve," he said with a grin. "What about you?"

"I have a lot of favorites. Chicken marsala, the way Kelly makes it. She does this special kind of sauce . . ." Kelly was another topic she needed to avoid. "And for dessert, fresh strawberries on angel food cake."

"Hot apple pie with vanilla ice cream for me."

"You are an all-American guy."

"I'll drink to that." He raised his cup and drank.

She followed suit, feeling a lot more relaxed.

"What was it like getting pregnant so young?" he asked.

"Terrifying."

"Did you ever consider not having the baby?"

"Not for a minute. Thankfully, Connor didn't push for that. My dad was so upset when I told him the news. But he surprised me with his support. And Rob, too, was great about it. He was there in the delivery room with me. Well, actually, he hung out by the door with Connor, who was having a major panic attack at the idea of being a father. Kelly was the one who held my hand through the contractions." She drew in another breath. "Anyway, it was hard at first, but I kind of grew into the role. I didn't know much, but I knew I loved Justin, and I wanted to be there for him every second of every day. I made a promise that I would never leave him the way my mother left me."

"I have no doubt that you will keep that promise."

"I thought it would get easier as Justin got older, but there are always new challenges. Just when I think I've got one thing conquered, something else comes up. Someone once told me 'bigger kids, bigger problems,' and they were right. But I'll deal. I just wish Rob was going to be here to see it all unfold."

Gabe reached for the bottle and poured two more shots. Handing her back her cup, he said, "Okay, your turn. Favorite book?"

"*Little Women*. I loved those girls, and I always wanted sisters. What about you?"

"*The Red Badge of Courage*."

"Of course, a war story," she said with a grin. "And you didn't even hesitate to come up with that title."

"I could give you a dozen more. *The Adventures of Tom Sawyer, The Island of the Blue Dolphins, The Chronicles of Narnia*."

"You've surprised me. I wouldn't have taken you for a reader."

"When you don't have a home you want to go to, you have to find somewhere to hang out, so I went to the library. It was free and warm, and sometimes they even had food in there. I would read until I got kicked out."

It saddened her to think of the kind of childhood Gabe

had lived, but the hardships had made him the man he was today, someone she respected. The more she got to know him, the better she understood why Rob had been so willing to follow Gabe into any battle.

"I had to find my heroes in books," Gabe continued, tossing back his shot of tequila. "They certainly weren't present anywhere else in my life."

"You were Rob's hero."

"No," he said sharply. "That's the last thing I was."

She stared back at him, surprised at the sudden anger in his expression. "I don't blame you anymore, Gabe."

"Well, you should."

She shook her head. "I don't think you let Rob die. I think you did everything you could to save him, because that's who you are."

"You don't know what it was like out there."

"No, but I knew my brother, and he had good instincts about people."

Gabe let out a sigh. "Why are you being nice to me now? You hated me before. You should stick with that."

A moment of tense silence passed between them. "If I hated you, Gabe, it was only because I loved you, too."

"We only knew each other a week," he ground out. "It wasn't love; it was great sex."

"I can have my own opinion of what it was. Obviously, you didn't feel the same way."

"I didn't want to feel that way. You had a kid."

"You didn't want to see me again because of Justin?"

"Not because of him—because I couldn't be a husband or a father."

"I wasn't asking you to marry me back then. I just wanted to keep things open, but you were determined to shut it all down. You tried to make me hate you."

"I thought I'd succeeded," he said.

"For a while," she agreed, meeting his gaze. "And then you came back."

"But I'm leaving again," he quickly pointed out.

"You could leave right now."

"Not until things are settled around here."

"Is that a warning—don't get involved, because you've still got one foot out the door?"

"Do you need a warning? I thought you were with Keith."

His words startled her. He was right. She was with Keith. What the hell was she doing? "I think I'm a little drunk."

"Yeah, me, too, or we wouldn't be having this conversation," he said dryly.

She lay back on the deck and stared up at the sky. The stars had come out in full force, and there in the dark woods, there was nothing to dim their shine. "Do you know the constellations?"

"Yes."

"From books or from being a marine?"

"Both. The stars can be a good compass."

"What's the most amazing place you've ever been?"

He stretched out next to her, staring up at the sky. "Cairo was fascinating, all that history. Dubai is also an amazing city."

"I can't even imagine."

"They're both a lot more crowded than here."

"Just about any place is."

"But not nearly as peaceful. The river is like a song that lulls you to sleep. I can hear it at night."

"A reassuring beat," she agreed. "Like someone else's heart next to yours."

Gabe turned onto his side. "What was it like being a twin?"

She thought for a moment. "It was amazing and weird and sometimes a little irritating. I adored Rob, but we were always together, always being compared. My parents would buy two of everything. It was easier than picking out something for me and something for him. I got a lot of boy presents, especially after Mom took off to find herself. When she was around, she used to try to give me some girl stuff, but the truth is that I was always kind of a tomboy. And she was a girlie girl. We didn't have a lot in common."

"Do you keep in touch?"

"She sends me cards now and then, e-mails, the occasional phone call that's usually polite and awkward and we're both relieved when it's over. I was angry with her for a long time, but once I had Justin, it changed me. I understood more what it meant to have a kid and how hard it could be. I still don't think she was right to move away. It would have been great if she could have at least stayed in town, but she just didn't like River Rock. She wasn't from here, and she missed her family, and we weren't enough for her."

"You sound very well-adjusted."

She uttered a short laugh. "I'm glad I come off that way. Like I said, I was mad for a long time, but I can't hate her forever, right?"

"Well, hate doesn't change the facts."

She sat up, hearing the gloom in his voice. "You need another drink."

"I don't know about that."

"It's traditional to finish the bottle," she said, slurring her words a bit.

Gabe smiled. "Who usually finished it, you or Rob?"

"Who can remember? We were drunk," she said with a laugh. She poured two more cups. "Let's drink to you this time." She lifted her cup. "To the man who . . ." She thought for a moment, trying to find the right words.

"It's taking you a little too long to think of something," Gabe said.

"Sh-sh, I've almost got it." She raised her cup higher. "To the man who makes me believe everything is going to be okay."

"It will be okay," he said as their cups met.

She drained her cup. "It could be better than just okay," she said, the liquor setting off the sparks that had been simmering all night.

He tossed back the rest of his tequila. "You're looking for trouble, Alicia. I can see it in your eyes."

"Have I found it?" she asked, feeling reckless.

A split second of indecision, and then he tossed his cup aside. She did the same, her gaze never leaving his.

Then he reached for her, but his kiss was far too brief. He immediately pulled away. "What am I doing? You're drunk."

"I know what I'm doing."

"Do you?"

"Yes."

"You're going to hate me," he said with cynical certainty.

"Well, didn't you say that would be easier?" This time, she reached for him, wrapping her arms around his neck as her mouth sought his. She needed his heat, his touch, his taste. She needed it all. She wanted to lose herself in him.

After his initial resistance, Gabe met her kiss for kiss, each one lasting longer, going deeper, making her head spin and her body ache for more than just a kiss. She shrugged out of her sweater and pulled her top over her head. Then she lay back on the dock.

He stared at her for a long minute. "You're beautiful," he murmured.

"You're too far away."

He pulled off his shirt, revealing a strong, powerful chest, not an ounce of fat anywhere. She wanted to slide her hands over those hard abs and then down his jeans to the bulge that was growing larger by the second.

Before she could move, Gabe was on top of her, his tongue sliding into her mouth, kissing away what little sense she had left, which was fine with her. She didn't want to think or worry; she just wanted to feel something besides sadness, to be with the man who had haunted her dreams for three long years.

Gabe's mouth left hers. She immediately felt an empty ache, but then his mouth trailed down her jawline, her neck, his tongue tracing the line of her collarbone, and she found herself holding her breath as his mouth slid lower. His lips moved along the edge of her bra, and she willed him to push it aside, but he didn't seem to be in as big a hurry as she was.

She ran her hands through his hair, guiding him a little with her hands, so there would be no mistake about what she wanted.

He finally flicked open the front clasp of her bra and pushed the edges aside. The air was cold against her breasts, but the heat that came with his mouth as his tongue swirled around her nipple drove an electrical charge down the rest of her body.

She squirmed under him, feeling the weight of his body and still wanting more.

His hand slid down her belly, playing with the snap on her jeans. She helped him open it, and his fingers slipped inside her panties. Her breath came fast, her heart pounding against her chest. It was too much and yet not enough.

"I need you, Gabe," she said.

He lifted his head, his dark eyes glittering with desire, his rough features so handsome in the moonlight.

"No clothes," she whispered. "Just you and me."

He kissed her hard on the mouth as she slid out of her jeans and then helped him off with his. Then she pulled him back on top of her, reveling in the power of his body as he parted her legs and slid inside. They moved together as if they'd never been apart, as if their bodies had found their way back home.

Sixteen

Alicia woke up to the bright sun shining in her eyes. It took her a minute to realize that she was still on the dock, wrapped up in Gabe's arms and the blanket he'd pulled around them after they'd made love for the second time. "Oh, my God," she said, sitting up abruptly. She glanced down at her watch, and her heart sank even more. "It's almost eight. I told Justin I'd call him before school started."

Gabe stretched, giving her a smile, then handed her the phone that had slipped out of her jeans sometime in the night. "You look beautiful."

She tucked her hair behind her ears, feeling both pleased and a little self-conscious to be naked in the morning light. She pulled the blanket up over her breasts and stared down at the phone. As Keith's number popped up, she felt an overwhelming wave of guilt at what she'd done.

"What's the problem?" Gabe asked.

"You know the problem." She set down the phone. "I need to get dressed."

"Clothes are required for phone calls?" he asked dryly as she scrambled to get her bra and top from where she'd thrown them the night before.

"For this phone call, yes."

Gabe didn't make any move toward his own clothes, his eyes on her as she tried to get her bra on under the blanket.

"You know I've already seen everything," he drawled.

"Last night was different."

"That's obvious."

She struggled with the clasp, thinking that her clothes had come off a lot easier than they were going on. But then, she'd been drunk on tequila and passion, and the shadows had made everything easier. She hadn't really had to look at him or at herself.

Gabe got up without any hint of modesty, and the sight of his beautiful body only made her fumble her clothes more. He gave her another smile and then grabbed his boxers and jeans and pulled them up over his long legs. He tossed her panties and jeans to her and turned his back to her. "Will this help?"

Without his gaze on her, she quickly finished dressing. She pulled on her shoes and walked several feet away from the dock, searching for a signal. Turning her back to Gabe and the memories of the night before, she waited for Keith to answer.

"Hello, Alicia. We're just heading to school," he said a moment later. "I tried your phone earlier, but it went to voicemail."

"I had the ringer off," she said.

"Didn't want to get any birthday calls?"

"Exactly. Can I talk to Justin?"

"Is everything okay, Alicia? You sound kind of funny."

"I'm still a little sleepy. I slept in."

"Well, you probably needed a good night's sleep after everything that's been going on. I trust it was a quiet night at your house."

Another wave of guilt ran through her. She should have been at home keeping watch over the property, looking out for her father. She really hoped it had been a quiet night.

"Do you want to get together tonight, Alicia?" Keith continued. "I'll make you dinner. It won't be a birthday celebration, exactly, but maybe we can toast to a new year."

He was being super nice, and she felt like the most horrible person in the world. "I'm not sure. I should probably spend some time with Justin at home tonight. You've done a lot for us lately. I have not been keeping up on my end of things."

"You've had quite a bit going on. We'll discuss it at the baseball game. I'll see you there this afternoon, right?"

"Yes, I'll be there."

"Great. Here's Justin."

"Hi, Mom," Justin said a moment later.

"Hi, honey. Did you have fun last night?"

"Yes! Keith helped us go on the Internet, and you know what we found? The story of the five arrowheads online. There was even a map. We printed it out so we can use it when we go to look. Isn't that cool?"

"Very cool," she said, her mind barely registering his words as she turned around and saw Gabe folding up the blanket and gathering up the tequila bottle and cups. "Have a good day. I'll pick you up after school and take you to the baseball game."

"Don't forget my cleats," he said.

She heard the unspoken words: *like you did the last time.* The thing about having a kid at nineteen was that sometimes you grew up together, and sometimes the roles weren't as clearly defined. She did have a tendency to forget things, usually because she was trying to do ten things at once, but Justin was insistent about having everything he needed when he needed it.

"I won't forget," she promised.

"'Bye, Mom. I love you."

"I love you, too." She slipped the phone into her pocket and walked back to Gabe.

"Everything all right?" he asked.

"Justin had a good time."

"And Keith?"

She looked away from his questioning gaze. She didn't know what to do about Keith, and at the moment, her head was pounding too hard to make any decisions. She rubbed her temple. "Let's go back to the house."

"In a minute. Did you really just tell Keith you love him?"

His question took her by surprise. "I was talking to Justin."

"Good. You need to break up with Keith."

The pounding in her head grew worse. She rubbed her temple. "I'm not going to talk about Keith with you."

"You can't seriously pretend last night didn't happen!"

"But are we going to have more than last night, Gabe? Or is this going to be like the last time?"

His lips drew into a tight line, conflict shading his eyes. It took him way too long to come up with an answer, and her pride wouldn't let her wait any longer.

"Your silence says it all."

She tried to move past him, but he grabbed her arm. "Alicia, wait."

"Why?"

He drew in a long breath. "If I was going to be with someone, it would be you. Last night was amazing. I'll never forget it. But I'm not good at relationships."

"Maybe that's because you've never had one." She paused, wondering if she was wrong about that. "Or maybe you have. Have you been in love?"

Another long pause. "I fell in love once, but I didn't act on it."

His gaze bored into hers. Was he talking about her? Or was she misreading him?

"I know myself, Alicia," he continued. "I know my limitations. And I want the best for you."

"Then why did you tell me to break up with Keith?"

"Because I don't think he's the best."

"Isn't he? Isn't Keith all the things you aren't? He knows how to be a husband and a father, a family man."

"If you were in love with him, you wouldn't have slept with me."

"I was drunk."

"Is that the excuse you're going with?"

She ran a hand through her tangled hair, realizing that she probably looked as messy as she felt. "Does it matter?"

"You shouldn't settle, Alicia. It's not fair to him or to you. Rob was worried about you doing that. He said he didn't want you to marry just to give Justin a dad."

"Is that why you had sex with me last night, Gabe? To show me what it could be like if I didn't settle?"

His jaw tightened. "I wanted you," he said roughly. "That was my only reason."

Her body tingled with his words, with the memories. "You're the one who's settling, Gabe. Not for a woman but for a life that's safe and won't break your heart."

"I don't have a heart left to break."

"Yes, you do, or you wouldn't be trying so damn hard to protect it." Shrugging her arm out of his grip, she started walking down the path. After a few feet, she stopped and looked back. He hadn't moved. "And I don't want you thinking you took advantage of me, that you betrayed Rob in some way, because I know that's what you're thinking right now. I bought the tequila, I poured the drinks, and I took off my top. I take responsibility for what I did. And you know what? It was great. It was really great. But it's over now. We have to live in reality, whatever that turns out to be."

There were things he wanted to say, probably should say, but he couldn't find the right words, and as Gabe followed Alicia back to her house, he thought it was just as well.

They parted company in front of Rob's house. He headed straight into the bedroom and flopped onto the bed, staring up at the ceiling. He was exhausted, but it was the ache in his heart that was most disturbing. How could he miss her already? He had a stiff neck from holding Alicia all night and an ache in his lower back where the bolt from the dock had been pressing into him, but it was totally worth it. The night before had been amazing. She'd been great. He hadn't felt that kind of passion since . . . well, since the last time he'd been with her.

And it wasn't just the physical attraction. He liked her. He liked talking to her. And he admired her even more for taking responsibility for what happened. She hadn't blamed the tequila or him. She'd owned up to what she wanted. She had a hell of a lot more courage than he did.

She was also damn good at reading him. He was used to guarding his thoughts, hiding his feelings, and he'd believed he was good at it. But somehow Alicia saw into his head in a way that no one else could. Another reason to stay away from her. He didn't need anyone getting that close.

But a voice inside his head asked why. Wasn't that really what he'd always wanted—that kind of closeness that came from a deep emotional connection?

Shit! She was making him crazy, and he was tired. He closed his eyes. Maybe when he woke up, he'd be ready to take her on again. Because one thing he knew for sure: he wasn't leaving until he'd done what he'd come to do.

Gabe woke up just before two o'clock. After a shower, a shave, and some eggs and toast, he felt ready to take on the day.

He walked through the woods toward Alicia's house, not sure what he'd say when he saw her again, but he wasn't going to hide at Rob's place. There was work to be done.

When he got to the house, he found George on the porch. He was talking on his cell phone but motioned for Gabe to wait.

George hung up a second later and gave him a weary smile. "I was wondering where you were."

"I'm getting a later start today. I apologize."

George waved his words away. "Don't be ridiculous. Alicia told me you sat on this porch all night after the fire to make sure no one came back."

Yeah, but what about the night before? He hadn't given one

thought to the property being unprotected. So much for doing his duty.

"I saw that you got a start on the rebuilding, too," George added. "What do you think?"

"It's going to take work, but everything can be redone."

He nodded approvingly. "I like that attitude. Bill and I ordered some equipment. It should be here in a couple of days. Alicia has been working on our Web site this morning, getting the reservation system up and going. Now we just need some customers."

"I have some buddies who want to come down. I spoke to Alicia about them."

"Good, very good. And I spoke to Simon, our top guide. He's been delayed, but he should be here by Friday. He's a hell of a river guide. With him and Alicia on the runs, we should be fine for a while, until I can get back out there."

He wanted to tell George that Alicia wasn't ready to handle any runs, but he couldn't break her confidence, so he said, "Sounds good. I need to get some wood. I want to put in some supports so you can go into the office without anything falling on your head."

"I really appreciate that, Gabe. Didn't know you were a builder."

"Just basic stuff, but I can at least make it safe to go inside. Can you tell me where the nearest lumber yard is?"

"Elm Street. Just take the main road into town, but turn right on Poplar, left on Tallway, and then right on Elm. There's a big sign by the highway. You can't miss it." George paused. "We'll reimburse you, Gabe."

"Don't worry about that. We'll settle up later. Is Alicia around?"

"No, she went into town. Justin has a baseball game after school. It's at McClaren's Park. You'll actually pass it on the way to the lumber yard."

"I'll see you around, then." He headed back to his house, got into his truck, and drove into town, telling himself that he was not going to stop at the baseball field. But the field was very near the lumber yard, and despite his better instincts, he pulled into the parking lot and got out.

There were two fields in action and kids everywhere dressed in blue and gold, red and white, purple and black uniforms. There was a snack bar selling candy and drinks and sign-up sheets to help with the upcoming baseball tournament.

He saw Alicia and Keith standing by the fence talking to Justin and David, and his steps slowed. They looked like a family, mom and dad and two kids. He paused by the snack-bar table, watching their conversation. Keith was leaning over, talking to the boys with great enthusiasm. Then he gave them each a high five, and the boys ran out to the field. Keith put his arm around Alicia's shoulders, and they stood together, watching their children.

A knot in his throat began to grow. He'd watched this kind of scene before when some foster parent had dropped him off at the field the few times he actually made it to a game. All of the parents were in the stands cheering on their kids, some even arguing with the umpires, but he'd always been alone, always on the outside. Just like he was today.

This wasn't his scene. What he'd told Alicia earlier was absolutely true. He didn't know how to be the kind of guy who did this—but Keith did.

He really hated Keith.

But he hated himself more for getting in the way of their relationship.

What the fuck had he been thinking?

He was so caught up in his thoughts that he didn't realize that Keith was leaving to talk to someone, and Alicia was walking in his direction.

He should have left when he had the chance.

"What are you doing here? Is everything all right at home?" she asked.

"Yes. I was on my way to the lumber yard, and your dad said you'd be here. Justin plays third base, huh?"

"He does sometimes. I don't really like it because the ball comes so fast. I'd rather he was in the outfield, but Keith says he's a really good infielder."

He noticed that Keith was now in the coach's box at third base. "He coaches, too?"

"He helps out."

"He's quite a helpful guy, isn't he?"

She gave him a steady look. "Do you want to watch the game?"

"No, I'm going to leave you to it."

"You can stay, Gabe. If you want to . . ." she added a little awkwardly.

"I should pick up the lumber. I hope Justin has a good game. I'll see you later." He turned and left before he could give in to the temptation to spend a little more time in a life he was never going to have.

She'd fallen back into her old life, Kelly thought as she sorted through the laundry in the house her mother shared with her brother, Ian. After cooking breakfast for the guests at the inn, she'd driven her mom to the local hospital for her pre-op consultation, stopped by the market to pick up supplies, and now was hoping to do a few loads of laundry before dinner service. She didn't really mind the busywork. It kept her from thinking, and ever since she'd spoken to Russell the day before, her thoughts had been going down a path she didn't want them to take.

Russell's attitude about the fire at Alicia's house had been disturbing. He'd been almost gleeful. She wanted to believe his denial, but she couldn't help wondering who else might be feeling as much anger as Russell.

Her mother stepped into the laundry room. Lynette was a tiny brunette who never gained a pound, no matter how many desserts she ate. It was unbelievable that as thin as she was, she would have such bad hip problems. It would be good to see her moving more freely and without any pain.

"You don't have to do the laundry," her mother said. "I didn't bring you here to work nonstop, Kelly. I appreciate your help in the restaurant, but you don't need to do all this."

"I don't mind. Although I wouldn't mind making Ian sort through his own smelly socks." She made a face as she tossed her brother's socks into the washer.

"I don't know where Ian is. He didn't come home last night. I've been calling him all day, and he hasn't answered. I'm getting worried."

"You know how he is with his phone. Half the time, he doesn't have it or it's not charged." She could see that her rationalizations were not easing her mother's mind. "I can try to find him."

"Would you do that? I don't know what's going on in his head these days, but he's changed since he dropped out of school. He used to be so focused on his studies. He wanted to be a veterinarian. Now I have no idea what he wants to be."

"He's confused, a little lost. That happens to kids around his age."

"I wish your father were here. He'd know what to do."

"He probably would," Kelly said. "I'll try to find Ian as soon as I get this laundry started."

"Is everything all right with you, Kelly? I know it's been hard for you to come home. I probably shouldn't have asked, but I really wanted you here."

"And I want to be here. I'm glad I came back. Not just for you, either. I'm starting to feel like I don't know what happened with Brian's accident."

Her mother looked surprised by her words. "What don't you know, honey?"

"Whether it was just an accident or if the Haydens were responsible."

"Maybe you'll never know that."

"Alicia said I listened to what everyone had to say but her."

"You did shut her out."

"I was angry and devastated, and everyone thought Alicia and her father had screwed up. But maybe she didn't do anything wrong. I'm still trying to sort it all out. I'm really worried about what's going on. The fire at her place was pretty bad."

"You went out there?" her mother asked in surprise.

"It was a spur-of-the-moment decision. She was not happy to see me."

"I wish the two of you would find a way to make up."

"Well, right now, I'm more concerned with crimes being committed on Brian's behalf. He wouldn't want that, and I need to stand up for him—and for myself."

Her mother smiled. "Good for you. Just be careful," she added, her smile dimming. "If people think you're switching sides, you could end up in the middle of a nasty fight."

"It will still be better than standing on the sidelines." She thought about what Jared had said about her staying in the background. "I do that too much, don't I, Mom? I let others take the lead."

"You're sometimes more quiet than your friends, but I don't think you've ever been led somewhere you didn't want to go."

Kelly smiled. "Thanks for that. You should lie down and rest. And don't worry about Ian. I'm sure he's just being a normal, irresponsible, self-centered twenty-year-old."

As her mother left, she scooped up another pile of laundry and tossed it into the washer, then dug through the hamper for more colors to add in. As she pulled out a pair of Ian's jeans, she was assaulted by a very strong smell. For a moment, she couldn't place it, and then she realized it was gasoline.

Her heart jumped. *Gasoline?*

Ian could have gotten gas on his hands while filling up his car and maybe wiped his hands on his jeans, but the smell was really strong.

Or he could have gotten the gasoline on his jeans when he cut Alicia's fuel line.

Or when he set the boatyard on fire.

Oh, God! She needed to find Ian fast.

Alicia had trouble concentrating on the baseball game. She kept thinking about the odd yearning look on Gabe's face. And it wasn't just her he'd been looking at but the field, the crowd, the kids, as if he'd just landed in a foreign country and couldn't speak the language.

He'd never had this kind of childhood. Her heart ached for the lost, lonely, neglected boy he'd once been. He would never get his childhood back. But she hoped he could one day move forward, have kids of his own. As a parent, you got to do childhood all over again, from a slightly different perspective. It was one thing she loved about being a mom. She could celebrate the holidays, get dressed up at Halloween, talk to Santa, share with Justin all the fun, silly things she'd done as a kid.

She doubted that Gabe had ever celebrated the holidays. They'd probably just reminded him of what he didn't have. No wonder he'd found such comfort in the Marines. He'd gotten an instant family, a band of brothers. He didn't have those brothers anymore, at least not in the same way, and losing Rob had to have left a huge hole in his life. Only she knew how big that hole was.

Being with Gabe had made her feel like she was coming back to life. Maybe it had been reckless and stupid to make love to him, but she didn't have regrets. They might not have a future, but they would always have a past.

She started as people around her began to clap and realized that one of the kids on Justin's team had just hit a home run. She needed to start paying attention. But as the teams changed pitchers, her gaze drifted across the field, and she wondered if Gabe might have come back to sneak a peek at the game.

But it wasn't Gabe she saw by the trees near the outfield fence; it was Ian Palmer. He was dressed in jeans and an oversized sweatshirt. On impulse, she got up from the stands and walked toward him. Aside from their brief encounter the other day at the carnival, she hadn't talked to him since Brian's death.

When he saw her, he straightened, glancing around quickly as if he wanted to leave, but she wasn't about to let him run away. She needed someone to give her an insight into the enemy camp. Kelly was out, and the Farrs definitely wouldn't talk to her, so Ian was her best bet.

"Hey there," she said. "What are you doing out here?"

"Just watching the game," he said with a shrug.

"I remember when Kelly and I used to watch you play. You were an All-Star pitcher."

"A long time ago," he said grimly.

Her gaze narrowed as she noted the pallor of his face, the growth of beard on his jaw, the messy hair and wrinkled clothes. "You don't look so good. Are you feeling all right?"

"I'm fine. I gotta go."

"Ian, wait."

He kept walking. She followed him toward the parking lot.

"You owe me," she said.

He paused, turning. "For what?"

"Our friendship."

"We're not friends anymore. You killed Brian."

His words stabbed hard and deep. She should have been used to the accusation by now, but every time it came, it hurt. "It was an accident."

"Everyone else says otherwise."

"Who is everyone else, Ian? I need to know who's after me. Someone set fire to my office and boatyard. The fire could have spread to our house. We could have been hurt. Justin could have been hurt," she added. "I can't imagine you'd want that."

His face was white now. "I didn't do it, Alicia."

"I wasn't accusing you," she said, surprised that he'd jump to that conclusion.

"You need to shut it down. Then it will all stop. Just close the business and move on, or someone is going to get hurt."

"Is that a threat?" she asked in shock.

"It's a warning. You should take it."

He walked away, leaving her to wonder why his warning felt so personal. He'd denied setting the fire, yet he'd assumed that she was accusing him. Why was he acting as if he were guilty? Was he lying? Had he done it for Kelly? For Brian?

Her stomach churned. Never in her wildest imaginings would she have considered that Ian could turn on her in such a way.

"Alicia?"

She turned her head to see Keith walking toward her. The two teams were shaking hands. Apparently, the game was over.

"Who were you talking to?" he asked.

"Ian Palmer."

Keith raised an eyebrow. "What was he doing here?"

"He said he was watching the game, but he gave me a warning. Shut down the business before someone gets hurt."

Keith sighed. "I don't think this will end until you do."

"You really believe we should just give in to these threats?" She was disappointed in his reaction but not surprised. He'd been saying much the same thing even before the fire.

"You're going to work really hard and waste a lot of time and money and end up at the same place that you're in right now."

"Possibly, if you want to go with the worst-case scenario."

"I know that's not what you want to hear, and I'm trying to support you, Alicia, but it's getting to be too much. This business is consuming our lives."

"It doesn't have to consume yours," she said shortly.

His lips tightened. "What does that mean?"

"I've been dumping Justin on you, and you've been great. If it's too much—"

"It's not," he said quickly. "I don't want to break up with you, Alicia. We were just getting to a good place when Rob died, and I know you need time to sort things out."

They had been getting to a good place, but her brother's death had made her realize that life was short, very short. And Gabe's arrival and her ridiculous, insane attraction to him had reminded her that passion was very important to her. She cared about Keith. She loved many things about him. But she wasn't in love with him. And suddenly, it was very, very clear.

"I don't think I can be the woman you need," she said slowly.

"I think you can. It's too soon to cut things off."

"Too soon is better than too late. It will hurt less."

He shook his head. "No, not now, not while you're upset about the fire and Rob. We'll discuss this later, when we've had a chance to really be together."

Justin and David ran over with their bat bags and snacks, so this was clearly not the time to have a serious conversation.

"Did you see my catch, Mommy?" Justin asked eagerly.

Luckily, it was one of the few plays she had seen. "I did. It was awesome."

"The team is going for pizza, because it's Carson's birthday. Can we go?"

She'd been disappointing Justin a lot lately; today was going to be different. "Pizza sounds great."

Keith gave her a reassuring smile. "It's all going to work out, Alicia. You'll see."

Kelly stopped in at Jared's auto shop, finding him on his back underneath Alicia's car. He rolled out when she called his name, surprise in his eyes.

"What's up?" he asked, sitting up. He grabbed a nearby rag and wiped off his hands.

She looked around at the other men who were working in the area. "Can I talk to you somewhere more private?"

"That sounds interesting."

"It's not like that," she said, catching the teasing glint in his eyes.

"Let's go out back." He led her through the shop to a back patio that was used as a break area. "What's happened now?"

"I was doing laundry, and Ian's jeans smelled like gasoline. I don't know what it means, but my gut tells me it means something."

Jared gave her a long, thoughtful look. "You think Ian set the fire at Alicia's place?"

"Or cut the fuel line. He's pretty good with cars."

"Did you confront him?"

"He isn't answering his phone. I've left a couple of messages, and my mom said he didn't come home last night. What do you think I should do?"

"We have to find him. I'm about done here. If you can give me about fifteen minutes, I'm all yours."

"I'm sorry I keep running to you with my problems."

"I'm happy to help, Kelly. And don't jump to any conclusions. If Ian had been involved, I doubt he would have just tossed his clothes into the laundry bin for anyone to find."

"Really? Because I feel like that's exactly what Ian would do, never expecting that my mom would notice a thing. Or if she did, she wouldn't say anything. She always gave him too much freedom. After my dad died, she just couldn't say no to him. I was the one who had to do that."

He put a hand on her shoulder. "We'll figure it out."

"I hope so." She tilted her head to give him a smile. "It's so strange. I don't find you nearly as annoying as I used to."

He grinned. "Well, that's something. You can wait for me here. I'll get done as soon as I can."

She sat down in a chair. Jared had a way of making her problems seem a lot less important. She always took things too seriously. She needed someone to balance that out. Brian had done that for her, too, she realized. But Brian had never been quite so involved in her problems.

Sighing, she rolled her neck around on her shoulders and wondered how her life had gone from being so simple to being so complicated.

Seventeen

Dinner at the pizza parlor was noisy and crowded, giving Alicia no time to speak to Keith alone, which was probably a good thing. She needed to have a heart-to-heart talk with him, but she was relieved to put it off for a while. She was tired, and she needed to get her thoughts together before they talked.

Just after seven, Alicia drove a tired Justin home. As they walked toward the front door, she could see the progress Gabe had made on the office building. He'd stripped off some of the outer walls and inserted some new posts. It felt good to see something other than ashes. It made her feel more hopeful.

Justin ran ahead of her into the house, where an excited Sadie greeted them with wet kisses. Alicia set down her bag on a side table and walked into the living room. She wasn't surprised to see Gabe sitting with her dad. She also wasn't surprised at the way her pulse leaped and her nerves tingled. Being around Gabe always put her a little on edge. Even when she knew she was going to run into him, she still wasn't quite ready.

As she said hello, Justin flopped down onto the couch next to Gabe. She took a seat in an armchair.

"How was the game?" her dad asked Justin.

"I got a hit and a walk, and I only struck out twice," her son said.

"It was a good hit," Gabe put in. "I thought you might get a triple out of it, but that kid in left field had a good arm."

Justin sat up a little straighter at Gabe's praise. "You saw my hit?" he asked, his face a picture of pleased surprise.

"You saw his hit?" she echoed. "I thought you'd left."

"I watched a little from the car," Gabe said. Turning back to Justin, he added, "Rob told me you were a good hitter. Said you had a good eye for balls and strikes."

"I'm not bad," Justin said, his eyes sparkling with pride. "Uncle Rob taught me how to hit."

"He gave me a few pointers, too," Gabe said. "We used to play behind our barracks sometimes."

"I didn't know you could play baseball in the Marines."

"On occasion. Your uncle had a very good swing."

"That's cool." Justin turned to his grandfather. "You know what else we did today, Grandpa?"

"I have no idea," George said with a smile.

"The library lady at school helped David and me go on the Internet, and we found more stuff on Five Arrows Point and a way better map than the one we found before. It will be easier to find when we go out there."

Alicia sighed. Her son had a one-track mind. "Justin, I told you that's going to have to wait."

The boy gave her a mutinous glare.

"Why don't you tell me more about the arrowheads," Gabe

said, drawing Justin's attention back to him. "Each one stands for something, right?"

"Yes. There's Courage," Justin began, counting off on his fingers. "Wisdom, Perseverance," he added, stumbling a bit over the long word. "Patience and Sacrifice. The braves were left in the middle of the woods, and they had to find five arrowheads along the way to the big rock. Then they had to climb to the top with all the arrowheads. When they got there, they became warriors."

"That sounds a lot like boot camp," Gabe said. "When you join the service, they teach you how to be a marine. You have to be courageous, smart about your actions, willing to persevere through hard times, sacrifice yourself for your fellow soldier, and patiently wait for the right moment to strike or to retreat." He paused. "Seems like you already have a lot of those traits, Justin. You were smart enough to look on the Internet and get more information, and you're certainly determined, but I'm not so sure about the patience. When you're a marine, or a warrior, you have to follow the leader of your unit or your tribe, right?"

"Yes," Justin said warily.

"Well, around here, your mom is the leader, and you have to respect her decisions."

"But she's not a warrior."

"No? She's got a big battle on her hands trying to rebuild after the fire the other night and get the business ready to re-open in a few weeks. Maybe you can practice patience and give her a break."

Justin frowned, obviously not liking the answer, but she could see that he also wanted Gabe's respect. "I guess," he said finally.

"Why don't you go take a shower, honey, and then you can do your homework," Alicia said.

Justin got off the couch with a heavy sigh. "Okay, but we're still going to go, right?"

"As soon as we can," she promised.

As Justin left the room, her dad gave Gabe an approving smile. "Nicely done."

Gabe shrugged. "I should get going. Thanks for the beer. I'll see you both tomorrow."

Alicia followed him out to the porch. "You were good with Justin," she said. "You didn't talk down to him. You respected him, and he responded to that."

"Most people do. Adults don't always give kids enough credit for being as smart as they are."

"Probably not. You could have sat in the stands, you know—at the game."

"I didn't stay long."

She hugged her arms around her waist. "I feel like I should say something, but I don't know what."

"Then don't say anything, Alicia."

"Last night—"

"Let's not go there. Let's just let it be."

Their gazes met, held. "I don't know what to do about you, Gabe."

He gave her a small smile. "Maybe you'll come up with an answer tomorrow."

"I doubt that. You are going home to sleep, right? You're not planning to spend the night on this porch?"

"I haven't decided yet. Don't worry about me." He surprised her by reaching out and brushing a strand of hair away from her face. The brief, tender touch made her want to throw herself into his arms, but then he was moving down the stairs, pausing on the grass. "Good night, Alicia."

"Good night," she whispered, watching him walk through the trees.

A few minutes later, she saw the lights come on in Rob's house and thought how natural it felt now for Gabe to be there. And how empty it would feel when he left.

"He has to come home sometime," Jared told Kelly as they sat on the front porch of the inn, waiting for her brother to show up.

They'd been waiting for hours. After they'd checked all of Ian's favorite places, she'd invited Jared back to the inn, where she'd cooked dinner and fed the guests and Jared, and then they'd settled out on the porch. "I hope that's true, but he didn't come home last night."

Jared shifted, rocking the swing back and forth with his foot. "Maybe he was with a girl."

"He hasn't mentioned any girls."

"There are some things a guy can't tell his sister."

"I suppose." As they rocked back and forth in the porch swing, she started to relax. Maybe she was worrying about nothing. But she couldn't get past the thought that something was wrong, something she should be seeing but wasn't. "The other day, you said that you thought Brian was acting funny after lunchtime. I can't completely dismiss the possibility that something happened when Brian went off with John and Marco." She thought for a moment, something niggling at the back of her mind. Finally, it broke free. "The camera," she said abruptly. "You said they went to take pictures."

He gave her a confused look.

"I have the camera."

"You do?"

"It was in a waterproof bag. Someone gave it to me after the trip, and I just stuck it in my closet. I didn't want to be reminded of what had happened. We need to look at the camera."

"Maybe you want to do that in private?"

"I don't think I can do it alone. Come on." She led him into the house and up the stairs to her attic room.

He looked around with interest. "This is where you used to sleep?"

She was a little embarrassed by her girlish décor, some of it left over from her teen days. Brian had made fun of her when he'd first seen the room, telling her it was time to move out of her childhood bedroom, which was why she'd moved in with him, probably a little sooner than she should have. Her mother had not been happy about it. She'd liked Brian, but she was old-fashioned when it came to living together before marriage.

"It's kind of a mess," Kelly said as Jared checked out her photographs.

"I like it. It's you," he said with a grin. "The you no one ever gets to see."

"Brian wasn't too impressed. He did not want to spend the night here."

"Seriously? I'd spend the night anywhere with you, Kelly."

His words sent an unexpected tingle down her spine. "You're flirting again. You just can't help yourself, can you?"

"Is it getting me anywhere?"

"No."

"Too soon?"

For some reason, this question seemed more serious than the previous one. "Yes," she said.

He nodded. "With you, Kelly, it's either too soon or too late."

"What are you talking about?"

"Timing," he said. "Every time I was free, you had a boyfriend or a date to a dance. And every time I was with someone, you were suddenly single."

"I didn't know you were paying attention."

"Didn't you?"

"I thought I rubbed you the wrong way."

"Because I wanted you to rub me the right way," he said with a smile.

She smiled back, glad to see the tension lightening. "I think you just look at me when you're bored and lonely. And the rest of the time, you have your eyes on someone else, usually someone blond, as I recall."

"And you liked the guys who talked a lot, probably so you wouldn't have to bother."

"Okay, enough with the psychoanalysis. Let's just say we've both made some good choices and some bad ones."

"And we can also agree that we're both single."

"But it's still too soon," she said, not sure if she was repeating the warning for Jared or for herself. It was far too early to contemplate getting involved with someone else. She went to her closet and dug around through the boxes she'd dumped there when she moved out of the apartment she'd shared with Brian. She found the bag at the back, still zippered as tightly as it had been when she'd received it.

She pulled it out of the closet and set it on the bed, staring at it for a long moment.

Jared sat down on the bed, watching her, waiting.

"I don't know if I can do this," she said. "It's the last thing he touched. I can see his smile, his laugh, the joy he experienced every time he took a picture. He loved it so much."

"You don't have to do this. It probably won't prove a damn thing."

"But I can't keep putting my head in the sand. Maybe that's how this all got out of control. If I had stayed here, if I had kept in touch with Russell and Ian, perhaps they wouldn't be so filled with anger and recklessness."

"You're not responsible for how they act. And you don't even know if either of them has done anything wrong."

"I feel it in my gut."

"You want me to open the bag?"

"It's stupid that I can't."

He reached for the bag, but she stopped him. "No, I'll do it." Taking a breath, she unzipped the bag and pulled out the waterproof plastic container that held the camera. "It's strange to think that his camera made it to safety but not him."

Jared put his hand over hers. She gazed into his eyes, finding warmth and reassurance there.

"Brian would be happy that you have his camera," he said.

She nodded, then opened the container and pulled out the camera. Amazingly, it still had enough charge to turn on. She flipped to the photos, seeing the last moments of Brian's life flash in front of her eyes. Sinking onto the bed, she felt too weak to stand, too scared to see what might come next.

Jared sat down next to her, and as her hand shook, he took the camera from her and moved to the next shot. There were a lot of pictures before they got on the rafts. The men were all smiling, laughing, making faces into the camera. There were some shots taken from the raft during the early part of the trip, where the river was calm and peaceful.

"He had no idea what was coming," she murmured.

"Yes, he did," Jared countered. "We all knew what was coming, and we were looking forward to the challenge. Don't ever think that Brian wasn't exactly where he wanted to be. That trip was as much his idea as Russell's. They loved rafting."

"Almost as much as Alicia loved it. Brian really liked Alicia. He used to tell me how much he admired her for being a strong single mother." She glanced down at the camera. "Keep going."

Five more shots, and then they both stiffened. There was a shot of Brian and Marco taken during the lunch break. They were clicking plastic water bottles together and laughing. The next shot was of them chugging the liquid in the bottles. It could have been water, but there was something about the way they were drinking.

And then there was nothing. The story stopped there.

She stared at Jared. "Was it vodka or water?"

He shrugged. "How the hell would we know?"

"Marco would know. I have to call him again. I have to get him to tell me the truth—the truth he should have told me before."

She started to get up, but Jared grabbed her arm. "Kelly, even if that was vodka or something else, it doesn't mean that it affected the outcome."

"But it could have." She rose from the bed, looking for her cell phone. As she crossed the room, headlights in the parking lot made her glance out the window. "Ian's home. I should try to catch up with him."

"Go," Jared said. "You can call Marco later—if you still want to."

Her brother was already heading upstairs when she walked into her mom's cottage. Her mother's door on the first floor was closed. She'd said she was going to have an early night before her surgery, and Kelly hoped she was asleep.

She caught up to Ian on the second-floor landing. "Ian."

He jerked at the sound of his name. "What the fuck, Kelly? What are you doing here?"

"Looking for you. I've been calling you since yesterday. Where's your phone?"

"I don't know. I lost it," he said, heading into his room.

She followed him inside and shut the door. "Where have you been? Mom and I have been worried about you."

"I was out. I'm an adult. I don't need to check in with you."

She stared at his sullen face and didn't just see anger; she saw fear. And suddenly, he wasn't the twenty-year-old who now towered above her but her little brother, the brother she'd always protected. "What did you do, Ian?"

"Nothing."

"That didn't work when you were six, and it doesn't work now. I know when you're in trouble."

"Then where the fuck have you been the last six months?" he shouted.

"Hiding," she said honestly. "I'm sorry, Ian. I know I haven't been here for you. I've just been—frozen."

The anger fled from his eyes and he sat on the bed. "Why are you apologizing to me? You're the one who lost Brian."

"You were close to him, too." She paused. "I'm here now. So talk to me."

He drew in a heavy breath. "It's not your problem."

"We're family. You can count on me."

He stared down at the floor. "I got into some trouble gambling. I owed some guys some money."

She wanted to ask him why he hadn't learned his lesson the last time, but now that he was talking, she didn't want him to stop.

"Someone came to me with a deal. I just had to do one thing, and my debt would be canceled."

Her heart sank. "What did you do?" she asked again.

He slowly lifted his head to meet her gaze. "I cut the gas line under Alicia's car."

Her heart thumped against her chest. "Oh, Ian. Why?"

"I just told you why. I needed the cash."

"Who paid you?"

"They didn't pay me. They paid my bookie. I didn't ask any questions, Kelly."

"And the fire? Did you set that, too?"

"No." He immediately shook his head. "I swear I didn't do that."

"I smelled gasoline on your jeans in the laundry room."

"That was from the car. I had to make it a slow leak, so she'd get out of the parking lot but not too much farther."

"You put her in danger."

"She just ran out of gas. It didn't seem like a big deal."

"Oh, it's a really big deal, Ian." She couldn't believe he was downplaying what he'd done.

"Well, I didn't set the fire. I don't know who did that, but it wasn't me."

"Where were you last night?"

"I was just walking around. I needed to think. I didn't want to come back here. I had a feeling you were going to interrogate me." He looked up at her. "I knew it was wrong. I was in a bind. I didn't think it would matter, but then, when I heard about the fire, I started to worry that someone was going to pin it on me."

"What's the name of your bookie?"

He shook his head. "I can't tell you."

She sat down next to him. "Ian, you know you're going to have to make this right. At the very least, you're going to have to pay for Alicia's car to be fixed. And you're going to have to tell the cops what you told me."

"I can't do that."

"I know you're scared, but we can fix this."

"I don't see how."

She stared at him. "Is Russell behind what's happening?"

"I told you, I don't know. The guy I make my bets with came to me with an offer: cut the fuel line, and we'd be good. I didn't have any other way to pay him off. I didn't want to tell Mom with her surgery coming up. And I couldn't ask you for the money."

"You could have asked me for the money. Ian, you have to realize that you have a problem with gambling. I thought you'd learned your lesson the last time. What happened?"

"I was in a bad place. I didn't know what to do when I got kicked out of school."

"I thought you dropped out."

"Same difference."

"Ian, what's going on with you? Was it a girl? Some other problem?"

"School just didn't make sense anymore. I don't know what I want to do, so why am I sitting in a classroom learning about things I don't care about?"

"Maybe so you can figure out what you want to do."

"It's different for you, Kelly. You always wanted to be a chef. And you were always good at it."

"Well, I want to help, but the first thing we have to do is take care of the car situation."

"If I turn over the other guy's name, I'll not only owe him the money again, but I'll probably get the shit beat out of me for talking. I'm thinking about just leaving town. Maybe you could give me some money or let me stay in your place in Sacramento for a while? No one has to know."

As much as she wanted to protect him, she couldn't let him run away. "You have to be honest about what you did."

"Why do you care about Alicia's car? She killed Brian. Everyone knows that. She's just getting what she deserves." He gave her a pleading look. "Don't turn me in, Kelly. Nothing happened to Alicia. She just ran out of gas. Big deal."

"That wasn't the end of it."

"It was the end of it for me."

"You must have some idea—"

"I didn't ask questions. I didn't want to know." He took a breath. "What are you going to do?"

That was a hell of a question and one to which she didn't have an answer. "I need to think."

"I'm your brother, Kelly. You can't turn your back on me."

"You crossed a line, Ian." She got to her feet. "We'll talk in the morning. I can't do this right now. Just don't go anywhere. Promise me."

"As long as you promise not to turn me in without talking to me first."

"I promise."

Kelly felt completely shaken. Was he lying about the fire? But even if he didn't set it, he'd still sabotaged Alicia's car, and a lot of bad things could have happened. He needed to take responsibility.

She left her mother's cottage, crossed the quiet courtyard, and entered the inn, going up the stairs to her attic room. When she pushed open the door, she was surprised to see Jared stretched out on her bed, sound asleep. She stared at him for a long minute and then sat down next to him. After a minute, she stretched onto her side.

Another minute, and he lifted his arm, inviting her to move closer. She slid into the crook of his body, resting her head on his shoulder.

He was the wrong man at the wrong time . . . or maybe he was the right man at the right time.

She needed a shoulder, and his suited her just right. She'd kick him out in a minute . . . or two.

Eighteen

Alicia woke up to the sound of hammering. After getting dressed, she made coffee and took a cup down the lawn to Gabe, who had apparently decided to get an early start on the day. She was shocked at how much progress he'd already made.

"Coffee?" she said, holding out the mug as he paused.

He set down his hammer and came over to her. "Thanks."

"You've really done a lot. Where did you learn construction?"

"In the Marines, of course," he said, taking a sip of coffee. "Sometimes we help communities rebuild. It's goodwill, and I've picked up some tips along the way. It won't be perfect, but it should work until you get a real construction crew in here."

"Maybe I won't need one. We don't use the office for that much. It's more the boatyard."

He nodded. "I talked to your dad about that last night. You can buy some preconstructed metal storage sheds that might do the trick for you as a stopgap measure."

"So, we're putting this business together with tape and glue."

"Whatever it takes. Come with me to the garage for a minute."

She reluctantly followed. The garage door was open. It soon became clear what he'd wanted her to see. He'd blown up one of the inflatable rafts they'd used on family trips.

"I thought I'd see if this was river-worthy," he said.

"That's just for family stuff; we don't use it in the business."

"I wasn't thinking about the business but about you. We need to get you in a raft, Alicia, and out on the water."

"There are a lot of other things to do first."

"Are there? If you can't guide, then you're going to need someone to replace you, and it seems like you're a little short on guides as it is."

"I just came out to give you some coffee," she said, feeling too much anxiety for this early in the morning. "We're not going to fix everything in a day."

"Why leave for tomorrow what you can do today?"

"Because I'm not ready."

He gave her a steady look. "I know. You went through a terrifying ordeal. A lot of people on that trip would think twice about putting themselves in the same situation."

"But I ran that run before without any problems."

"That's what you need to focus on. I'd love to go out on the river with you. Just around here. Nothing too challenging, just you and me in the boat."

When he put it like that, it sounded a lot more appealing.

"I'll think about it, but right now, I need to make breakfast."

An hour later, she dropped Justin off in front of the school and waved hello to a couple of mothers who seemed a little more friendly than usual. Since the fire, it seemed like people were starting to feel more sorry for her than angry.

Her next stop was Jared's garage. She found him in the office handling a customer. He gave her a smile and said he'd be right with her.

As she waited, she thought that Jared was one of the few people who hadn't been totally against her since the accident. Despite his friendship with the Farrs and with Kelly, he'd managed to stay amazingly neutral.

"Hi," he said when they were alone.

"I'm hoping you have good news for me."

"I did a service on your car since it was here, no extra charge. I wanted to make sure everything was in good shape. I did notice a sensor that wasn't operating correctly. I ordered a new one, and I should have it tomorrow if you can leave the car one more day."

"Of course, and I'm happy to pay for it. The car needed to be looked at. The Check Engine light kept coming on."

"And you were ignoring it, right?"

"Sort of hoping it would go away on its own," she admitted. "It's been a busy couple of weeks."

"Yeah. I'm sorry about all the trouble you've been having."

"And I'm sorry that you saw the ugly scene with Kelly yesterday. I don't think I even said hello to you."

"You were upset. I understand that. How are things coming along after the fire?"

"Pretty good, actually. Gabe has been a huge help, and he's already working on the building, and my dad and Bill have been ordering new equipment, so we're regrouping." She paused, realizing what she'd just said. "You probably don't want to hear that."

"I never wanted to see you run out of business, Alicia. I

don't really know what happened last year, and I was there. But the more I think about it, the more I believe it was probably just an accident."

She was surprised. "Wow, I don't even know what to say. I guess, thank you."

"Just be careful, Alicia. I don't want to see anyone else get hurt."

"I don't, either."

Kelly spent all day Tuesday in the hospital waiting room about thirty miles away from River Rock. She hadn't told anyone about Ian's confession, not even Jared. He'd been gone when she woke up, which was a relief. She didn't know what she'd been thinking, sleeping with him the night before. Not that anything had happened. In fact, she'd slept better than she had in a very long time.

There was something so comfortable about Jared. He knew her well, and she didn't have to pretend to be someone she wasn't. He didn't annoy her nearly as much as he used to. She was starting to like him . . . although that thought scared the hell out of her. It was far too soon for her to be feeling anything for another man. She owed Brian that much—didn't she?

Shaking her head, she set down the magazine that she wasn't really reading and leaned her head back against the wall. Her mother's surgery had been delayed because the doctor had had an emergency to tend to first, so she still had probably another half hour to wait until her mom was in recovery. She wasn't anticipating any problems, but it was hard not to worry. Lately, it seemed that anything that could go wrong did go wrong.

She pulled out her cell phone and tried Ian's number again.

He hadn't been at the house when she'd picked up her mom, which wasn't a good sign. She really hoped he hadn't taken off somewhere, but she knew he was scared. She was scared for him. She didn't know what kind of consequences he would face for cutting Alicia's fuel line, and it hurt to think that her little brother might go to jail. How could she let that happen? But how could she stay quiet over something so serious, so important?

The door to the waiting room opened, and she looked up in surprise as Jared strode through the door with two cups of coffee in a tray and a paper bag under his arm.

She got up to greet him. "What are you doing here?"

"Thought you might want some coffee and some company."

"That's so nice of you," she said, taking the coffees and setting them down on the table. She resumed her seat. "Are they both the same?"

"Latte on the left, nonfat, plenty of caffeine, and mocha on the right, also nonfat."

"Both favorites," she said. "Very good choices. Are you having one?"

"Whichever one you don't want." He sat down next to her. "How's it going here?"

"It's probably going to be another half hour, I hope not more than that," she replied, taking a sip of coffee. "This is much better than what's in the cafeteria."

"I figured."

"Aren't you supposed to be at work?" she asked, noting that he'd traded in his work overalls for clean jeans and a long-sleeved button-down plaid shirt.

"It was a slow day. I took off early."

"Is your dad okay with that?"

He gave her a smile. "I'm not sixteen anymore. My dad and I are partners."

"He's still your dad, and as I recall, he was always tough on you."

"He's mellowed a little. In fact, he spends more days fishing with his buddies than at the shop."

"Is the shop going to be enough for you?"

"I didn't think it was, but in the last year or two, I find myself enjoying it more and more. It's nice to be my own boss, and I'm good at what I do. I like cars. I enjoy working on them." He paused. "I know you think I settled."

"I don't think that," she said quickly. "I was rude when I said that before. Who am I to judge your choices?"

"Well, I used to think I was settling, too, taking the easy way out by working for my dad, but the business has grown on me."

"Sometimes what we think we want isn't really what we need."

He tipped his cup to hers. "I'll drink to that." He took a sip. "By the way, I spoke to Alicia earlier. She came by to check on her car."

"Is it fixed?"

"The gas line has been repaired, but I have to replace another part, so I told her she'd have it tomorrow."

"I'm sure she'll be glad to get it back." She took another drink, debating whether she wanted to tell Jared about Ian.

"So . . ." he began. "Sorry about crashing on your bed last night."

"It was fine. I was tired, too," she said, feeling a bit awkward under his thoughtful gaze. "I was going to kick you out, but then I fell asleep. When I woke up, you were gone. I didn't hear you leave."

"I didn't want to wake you."

"It wasn't a big deal," she said, feeling as if she needed to make that point.

"I didn't think it was." He glanced down at his coffee cup and then lifted his head. "What did Ian have to say?"

"He admitted that he's gotten into some trouble gambling and that he owes some guy a lot of money."

"That's not good."

She took a deep breath. "What would you do if someone you were close to had made a big mistake? Would you turn him in?"

His gaze narrowed. "How big a mistake—like setting fire to someone's house?"

"No, but maybe cutting someone's gas line."

He blew out a breath. "Shit, Kelly. That's bad. Ian did it?"

"I didn't say that. We're just talking theoretically. I wouldn't want to put you in the position of feeling you needed to do anything."

"You won't be able to live with yourself if you don't find a way to make this right."

"Make it right for whom?" she asked in frustration. "Ian, myself—Alicia?"

"All of the above."

She paused. "I know I have to do something."

"Or get Ian to come clean if he theoretically did something," he added dryly.

"He was gone when I picked up my mom this morning.

I told him not to go anywhere, to let me help him, but he obviously didn't listen. I don't know where he went or if he's coming back."

"How much money does he have?"

"I'm not sure about that, either."

Jared stared at her for a long moment. "Did Ian come up with this idea on his own?"

"He said the guy he owes money to said his debt would be forgiven if he cut the line."

"Who's that guy?"

"He didn't give me a name. But he referred to him as a bookie." Something flashed in Jared's eyes. "Do you know who I'm talking about?"

"I have an idea."

"Want to give me a name?"

"Since we're speaking theoretically, I don't think so."

"Jared," she said, frowning, "if you know something, you have to tell me."

"Let me do a little research first."

"You can't tell anyone about Ian until I figure out what to do."

"I won't. You can trust me, Kelly."

For a few minutes, they sat quietly, sipping their coffee.

"I really hate hospitals, especially this one," she said. "Being here reminds me of when my dad died of cancer. He was in this hospital off and on for months. We kept thinking he'd beat it, but he didn't. I still remember the day he died. It was horrible."

He put his hand on her leg. "Your mom isn't going to die today. Everything will be fine."

She met his gaze. "You really are the nicest man, Jared."

"It's about time you figured that out," he said with a smile. "It's taken you long enough."

"Maybe you weren't always this nice."

"And maybe you just never noticed. By the way, next time we sleep together, we're going to do a lot more than sleep."

She choked on her coffee, coughing so hard tears came to her eyes.

Jared laughed and patted her back. "Just think about it," he said.

As if she'd be able to think of anything else.

Alicia arrived at Justin's school a few minutes before dismissal. She'd borrowed her dad's car again, a fifteen-year-old Jeep that her dad loved but hadn't been able to drive since the accident. She hoped her dad would be able to reclaim his driving privileges soon.

She got out of the car and leaned against it, taking a minute to enjoy the unusually warm spring day. It was so lovely under the trees that she could almost forget all of the problems waiting for her back home. Then a sedan pulled up behind her car, and she was surprised to see Keith.

"I thought I was picking David up," she said as he joined her.

"My last conference canceled," he said, leaning over to kiss her.

It was a light, friendly kiss, but his lips felt wrong, and in that moment, she knew that she was just kidding herself thinking that she could go back to Keith now that she'd been with Gabe. Whether she ended up with Gabe or not, she wasn't going to be with Keith. He was a perfectly nice man, but he didn't rock her world, and while she'd once thought that life would be easier without that kind of rocking, now she knew it wouldn't be enough.

She wanted passion with love. One without the other wasn't enough. With Gabe, she had passion, but did she have love? With Keith, she had love but not enough sparks.

Was she being too picky? Did she want too much? How many men would be willing to commit to a single mother with an almost-ten-year-old son? Especially since she lived in a town where single eligible men were a hot commodity.

"Alicia?" Keith asked.

She started. "Sorry, what did you say?"

He gazed back at her, his normally easygoing smile absent from his face. "Where were you?"

"Just daydreaming."

"About us?"

"Partly." As she spoke, the bell rang. Kids would be pouring through the door in less than a minute, and she really didn't want to have a serious conversation with Keith right then.

He actually looked a little relieved by her answer, which made her feel guilty. It was one thing to string herself along; it was another to take someone with her. Keith deserved to be with someone as great as he was, someone who wasn't panting after some other guy. But Gabe wasn't staying forever. Did she really want to break up with Keith when Gabe would probably be nothing but a memory in a few weeks?

Justin and David came running out of the school together.

"Can we get ice cream?" Justin asked.

She'd been saying no to Justin about so many things lately.

Stopping for ice cream was the least of her worries. "All right. Do you two want to come along?"

"Sounds good," Keith said, and David nodded enthusiastically.

They piled into her car and headed into town to Sally's Ice Cream Parlor, known as the best ice cream parlor in the county. It was also the only ice cream parlor in the county, but that was beside the point.

Alicia had a single scoop of mint chocolate chip, while the boys and Keith ordered doubles of various flavors in waffle cones. Justin and David would be bouncing off the walls from the influx of sugar, not that Justin needed much encouragement. He was a lot like Rob, a whirlwind of energy, his mind racing from one topic to the next. But he was a lot of fun and as friendly as could be.

They took their ice cream to one of the outside tables, the boys immediately distracted by the arrival of one of their friends with his new puppy.

"I'm glad we have a minute to talk alone," Keith said as the boys joined their friend. "What's going on with your business?"

"We're rebuilding and reordering equipment."

Keith didn't look too happy with her answer. "Sounds like it's full steam ahead."

"Does that bother you?"

"I can't say I'm happy about it. I feel like you're just asking for more trouble."

"I'm not asking for it. If it comes, it comes. I have every right to run a rafting business. Despite the gossip and rumors, there has never been any evidence to prove that Brian's accident wasn't an accident."

"But with so many people in town against you, where will you get customers?"

"We've actually had a few inquiries from potential customers. Simon, our lead guide, will be back later in the week, and he may have some ideas on how to generate more business. My dad believes that with time, people will forget, or they'll finally understand that what happened last year was a tragic fluke. A lot of our customers are out-of-towners, so it depends on how much research they do or whether or not they'll be bothered by what happened. Eighty percent of our trips are not in any way dangerous."

"You're making a good argument."

"I feel like I have to prove something to you."

"I see Justin take a lot of heat from other kids, and certainly you and your dad have suffered. I can't help wondering if it's worth it."

"I don't know, but if I choose to walk away from the business, it will be on my terms."

"You've changed in the last week."

"What do you mean?" she asked in surprise.

"There's a new determination in your eyes, your voice. The last few months, you've been halfhearted about getting the business going again. Now you're practically waving a flag and marching down Main Street announcing your intention."

"I don't like being attacked. I will defend myself."

"Yeah, I get that," he said heavily. "I just wish . . ."

"What?" she prodded.

"We don't spend as much time together as we used to, and I can't see that changing once you're back out on the river." He paused. "I love Justin. He's been great for David. And I don't want you to think I don't love spending time with both of them. But I don't want to be your babysitter."

"I'm sorry if I've made you feel that way."

"It's nothing you've done, just a pattern that's developed the last few weeks."

She nodded, her heart beating a little faster. They were coming to a crossroads. Whatever choice she made could change her life.

Keith gazed into her eyes. "I didn't mean to start this now. It's not the right time or place."

"But you're feeling like things aren't right anymore."

"That sounds like what you're feeling," he said.

"My life has gotten very complicated."

"You can simplify it by making some changes." He paused. "I care about you, Alicia. I think we could be great together. We could make a family with our boys. But I need to know you're committed to making that work as much as you are to getting your rafts back out on the water. If you're not, I need to know that, too. You tried to talk to me the other day, and I blew you off. I think I sensed that I wasn't going to like what you had to say. But that was stupid, because we have two kids who are thinking that they're going to be brothers. And the longer this goes on, the more they'll think that. Neither one of us wants to hurt them."

She swallowed hard. "But we can't have a relationship just for the kids."

"No, we can't. I know what real love feels like. I had it with my wife. I'd like to have it again someday." He met her gaze. "When you know a person is right for you—you just know."

"Is that how it was with you and David's mother?"

"From the first day. Are you worried about being second to her?"

"No," she said immediately. "I would never want to take her place."

He gave her a long, thoughtful look. "Is Gabe part of your past?"

She cleared her throat. "Why would you ask that?"

"Just something about the way the two of you are together, the way you look at each other. He's very protective of you, and I don't think it's just because of his relationship with your brother."

This was her moment of truth. She needed to come clean and tell Keith about her relationship with Gabe. She couldn't possibly go forward without being completely honest with him. It wasn't in her nature to lie or deceive, but she also didn't want to hurt him.

"I do have feelings for Gabe," she said slowly. "I don't know if they're going anywhere. There are a lot of reasons why nothing could ever work between us."

Keith nodded, disappointment in his eyes. "But you need to find out."

"I do," she admitted. "I'm sorry. You are an incredible guy, so I really haven't wanted to end things with you. But I'm not being fair to you."

"Or to yourself."

She felt a wave of sadness, knowing that they weren't going to recover from this conversation, and she did care a great deal about Keith. "So, we're over?"

"It sure seems that way."

"Should we say something to the boys?" Justin was so happy playing with his friends and the puppy. She hated to bring any more sadness into her son's life.

"Why don't we wait until the weekend? Make sure that's what we both still want to do."

Nineteen

After ice cream, Alicia drove Justin home. Gabe was still working on the building, but she headed straight into the house, too emotionally spent to get into a conversation with him. She hoped she was doing the right thing breaking up with Keith, but part of her wondered if she wasn't being a romantic fool.

Keith was a good man, and she was walking away from him—but who was she walking to? Gabe didn't want to give her a commitment. She was more than likely going to end up with no one.

Her turmoil grew as the hours passed. She tried to focus on dinner and then homework with Justin, but her restlessness grew, and by the time she was cleaning up the kitchen just before Justin's bedtime, she was completely out of sorts.

Jamming a pan into the crowded dishwasher, she tried telling herself that she was better with no man than with one she didn't love or one who didn't love her.

"What's got you so fired up?" her dad asked, taking a beer out of the refrigerator.

"Nothing."

"Then stop trying to squeeze that pot into the dishwasher. Some things just don't fit."

"Exactly," she muttered, not thinking about the dishes at all. She took the pan out and set it on the counter, then shut the door and started the cycle.

Her dad walked around the counter with an agility that surprised her.

"Dad, where's your cane?"

"I'm trying not to use it so much," he said, taking a seat on one of the bar stools. "Especially around the house. I need to get back into shape as fast as possible, and I've been babying myself for too long." He looked her straight in the eye. "I've let you carry the burden around here, and that needs to stop."

"I've been happy to help. You've had a rough recovery."

He shook his head. "You're being too nice. When I look at Gabe and all the work he's doing around here and how he's watching over us, I'm reminded of how I used to be. And I'm not talking about just since the accident but even a few years before that. When Rob was gone, I leaned on you, let you take over this house and the business. I was always better on the river, and I didn't care about the rest. I let you pick up the slack, even though you had your hands full with Justin. I don't think I've ever said thank you, Alicia."

She was incredibly touched. "I—I don't know what to say."

"You're a good girl, the best daughter a man could have."

"Okay, now you're getting a little sappy, and neither of us wants me to cry," she said with a sniff.

He smiled. "I never could handle your tears. After your mom left, I didn't know what to do with you. I didn't know how to raise a girl, so I just treated you and Rob the same, but that was wrong. I should have tried harder."

"It was fine. I'm tougher than I would have been otherwise, and I'm proud of that." She wondered where her father's sudden attack of conscience was coming from.

"You should be proud." He paused, then said, "Gabe was asking me about the accident last night. I told him what I remembered, which wasn't a whole lot." He tilted his head as he looked at her. "I knew you went into the water because everyone did on your raft, but I didn't think much about it. Gabe told me you had a struggle getting back to the boat. And I started thinking that maybe it was worse than I know."

She really wished Gabe hadn't told her father that. "It all worked out."

She grabbed a sponge off the counter and wiped off some crumbs, needing something to do, some reason to avoid her father's questioning gaze. Her dad never asked questions, because he usually didn't want the answers. When she was growing up, he'd never asked her what she'd done the night before, why she'd come in late, none of the parental-type questions that most kids got. She'd never really known if it was disinterest or if he was afraid to know because then he might have to take some action, when in reality, all he really wanted was to have them grow themselves up and get on with their lives.

"Well, good," he said gruffly. "I need you on board when we reopen."

"Have I ever let you down?" she asked lightly.

"No, you never have," he said, getting up from the stool. "But I'm guessing I've let you down more times than you can count."

He didn't wait for an answer, and she was relieved not to have to give him one.

She finished cleaning up the kitchen, her irritation with Gabe growing with each swipe of the sponge. He had no business getting into the middle of her business. Just because he thought she was scared to go back on the river didn't make it true. She would get past the fear when she had to and not because he wanted her to prove something.

Her anger continued to rise as she got Justin ready for bed. When he was finally tucked in with the lights out, she told her dad that she was going to speak to Gabe and slipped out of the house.

Gabe opened the door at her knock. He'd changed into a dark green T-shirt and jeans, and one of Rob's records was playing on the old stereo.

"Can I come in?" she asked.

He waved her inside.

She noted the empty frozen-dinner package on the counter and frowned, but she wasn't going to be deterred. "You shouldn't have told my dad I was scared of the river," she said abruptly.

"Do you want to sit down?"

"I want an explanation."

"I didn't tell him you were scared. I asked him if he knew what you'd gone through, and he said he didn't."

"So you filled him in. You weren't there. You don't know."

"I know what you told me."

"It's not your business."

"I'm making it my business. Having spent the last ten hours rebuilding your office, I think I have a right."

"I didn't ask you to do the work. You volunteered. You can stop at any point. You can leave at any point, and maybe that's what you should do."

"Why?" he demanded, moving closer.

She instinctively stepped back until she ran into the back of the couch. "Because you're getting too involved."

"Really? Are you sure it isn't you who's getting too involved?"

Desire glittered in his eyes, and she swallowed hard, trying to remember why she was mad and what she'd hoped to accomplish with this visit.

Gabe took another step forward, his breath warm against her cheek as he leaned in and said, "We both know why you really came over here, Alicia."

"I came over to tell you to mind your own business."

He shook his head. "No, you came over for this." His mouth touched hers, hungry, possessive, needy, and she felt exactly the same way. She put her arms around his waist, pulling him closer. He threaded her hair with his fingers, holding her head in place in case she had any thought of escaping, but escape was the last thing on her mind. He was right. This kiss was exactly why she'd barged into his house. She might not have him forever, but she could have him now.

Her tongue danced with his, her hands working their way up under his shirt, his following a similar hot path.

As he broke the kiss, he slid his mouth along her cheekbone, his tongue swirling around the shell of her ear, shooting an electrical charge down her body. She tilted her head as he moved down the curve of her neck, kissing the sensitive spot above her collarbone.

He pressed her backward to gain better access, and she went right along with him, wanting his mouth on her neck, on her breasts, on her stomach, and lower still, remembering all the things they had done to each other the last time and all the things she still wanted to do.

Her legs weakened, her body melting into his, and suddenly, one more step pushed her over the back of the couch. She landed on the cushions in bemusement, one foot hitting the coffee table.

"God, Alicia, are you all right?" Gabe asked, coming around the couch.

She laughed. "You literally knocked me off my feet."

"I'm so sorry."

"Prove it." She grabbed his hand and pulled him close. "Make love to me, Gabe," she whispered.

"Do you want to go into the bedroom?"

"No, here, now."

He started to ask something else, and she put her finger against his lips. "No questions. No talking."

"Are you sure, Alicia? This never ends well for us."

"But it's really, really good while it's happening." And right then, that's all she cared about.

"Is that enough?"

She didn't want to think about the question. Instead, she sat up, placed her hands on both sides of his head, and kissed him hard. Then she grabbed his shirt and helped him off with it. "I love your body," she murmured, talking to herself as much as to him. "Hard, powerful, very, very male."

"And I love yours. Soft, sexy, very, very female," he said with a smile as he helped her take off her top. His gaze raked her full breasts. "Beautiful."

"Touch me."

"Try to stop me," he said, cupping her breasts with his hands. "Every time we're together, I want to go slow, but you make me a little crazy."

"And you make me a lot crazy. I don't want to go slow. I want to go fast, hard, reckless. And I want you to go with me. No control. No second-guessing. Just be with me—in this moment."

He pulled open the snap on her jeans and lowered the zipper, then slid her jeans and panties off with one quick move. Her bra followed, and then his clothes, until they were completely bare. There was no hiding in the shadows this time, not for either of them.

A while later, they lay on their sides facing each other, the blanket from the back of the couch covering them as the evening air cooled their heated bodies. Alicia had her head pillowed on Gabe's arm. She didn't want to move, but as the minutes ticked by, she knew that the moment was coming.

Gabe smiled at her. "Working up an escape plan?"

She smiled back. "You think you know me so well. Maybe you're the one wondering how you're going to kick me out without hurting my feelings."

"I'd be happy for you to stay, but we might have to take this party into the bedroom. We haven't tried out a real bed yet. The first time we made love was on the floor of your house."

"I remember—in front of the fireplace and the Christmas

tree while Justin, Rob, and my dad were at my aunt's house. We were supposed to meet them there, but we didn't make it."

"It was your fault. You had to wear that sexy low-cut red dress."

"I can't believe you remember what I was wearing," she said in surprise.

"I remember everything about that week," he said. "I especially remember trying to keep my hands off you, because you were Rob's sister, and you were untouchable. But one look at you, and all I wanted to do was touch you."

"It took me two looks. The first time I saw you, I was a little intimidated. You were abrupt and kind of cold."

"Armor. I was steeling myself against your charm. But as hard as I tried, I just couldn't stay away from you."

"We had some fun. Remember the sledding?"

"I remember you being a daredevil on a trash-can lid. It was unexpected."

"You weren't too cautious yourself."

"I like a good adrenaline rush." He trailed his fingers along her bare arms. "But flying down that hill was nothing compared with the sight of you in that dress, and then you put the mistletoe over my head, and I was gone."

"That was my plan," she said softly. "I wasn't going to let you leave without being with you."

He gazed into her eyes. "It shouldn't have happened. I knew I was going to hurt you. I couldn't tell you what you wanted to hear."

She drew in a breath. "I naively thought that making love to me would be enough to change your mind about signing up again. But it wasn't just that you were going back; it was that you were ending it without giving us a chance. You wouldn't even consider staying in touch. It had to be all or nothing, and it couldn't be all, so it had to be nothing."

"You made the decision very difficult."

"It didn't look that way."

He sighed as he looked at her with regret. "It wasn't because you weren't enough. I wasn't enough."

"What do you mean?"

"It's what I told you before. You needed a family man."

"Maybe I just needed you."

"You didn't know me."

"You didn't want me to know you," she corrected. "But I saw a little of what you were trying to hide."

"That scared me, too."

"You, the big, tough marine, scared?" she asked in disbelief.

"Of what you made me feel, hell, yes. I'd never met anyone like you, Alicia."

She looked at him for a long moment. "Do you still feel the same way about me?"

He didn't answer right away. "You still need a family man, and that's not me."

"Why couldn't it be you?"

"Because it can't."

"That's not an answer."

"It's all I've got."

"You're still scared, Gabe. You were talking to me earlier about facing my fears, but you don't want to face yours."

"It's not that simple."

"You're making it too hard."

"It's better this way."

"No, it's safer this way," she corrected, disappointed with

his answer. She got up and started putting on her clothes. "I should go."

Gabe sat up, running a hand through his hair. "It always ends with regrets, doesn't it?" he asked wearily.

She pulled her top over her head. "I don't regret what happened." She sat down next to him. "I need to tell you something." She looked him straight in the eye. "I'm in love with you, Gabe. I've been in love with you for three years."

"What about Keith?"

"Keith was my safe choice. He's a fantastic guy, but he doesn't challenge me. He doesn't shake me up the way you do. I don't spend sleepless nights thinking about him."

"But Keith is a good man," Gabe said, surprising her with the defense. "He is everything that I'm not. He's a father. He's been a husband. He coaches Little League and teaches at the school. Hell, from what I can see, he's damn near perfect. You should pick him."

"I wanted to pick him, but then you showed up and reminded me what passion felt like."

"Passion doesn't last."

"How do you know? You don't stay in a relationship long enough to find out."

"And you've had such shining examples? Justin's father walked out on you, and your parents broke up."

"But I still believe in love. Maybe that makes me crazy or stupid or both. But I can't live a lie, and I can't be happy with safe. It's not who I am. I don't really think it's who you are, either, Gabe. But only you can decide that."

She got to her feet and walked out, wishing he'd call her back, but he didn't. She shut the door behind her and let out a breath, knowing that she wasn't going to be with him again. She'd put it all on the line, and he'd let her go. Her heart ached, because the one man she really loved couldn't let himself love her back. He felt something for her, but he couldn't say it, and she needed the words. She wasn't going to settle for less. This time, she was leaving first.

Gabe couldn't sleep; Alicia's words went around and around in his head. He hadn't expected her to be so direct, so honest, so acutely aware of what was going on in his head. Not many people looked at him and called him a coward. He had a Medal of Honor and a Purple Heart, for God's sake. But she was right; when it came to love or personal relationships, he had no guts.

His life was completely up in the air for the first time in twelve years. He had no one telling him where to go or what to do. He had no unit to lead, no men waiting for him to make a call, just one very pretty woman who came with high expectations and a lot of baggage.

After tossing and turning, he got up just after dawn, threw on some warmer clothes, and took a long walk. The fog was coming off the river in a smoky mist, casting a surreal glow to the morning sun. The world was peaceful, the only sounds the reassuring rush of the water, the call of a bird now and then. No traffic, no crowds, no guns or explosions.

He should feel calm, but he couldn't shake the restlessness driving him, so he kept walking until he finally ran out of steam. He picked up a couple of rocks and spun them out over the water, wondering how he'd ended up there. The idyllic setting was about as far from his childhood home as he could get. And he'd had to go through a dozen different war zones to end up there.

Now what? Did he leave, or did he stay?

And if he stayed, for how long?

There was too much tension, too much attraction, between him and Alicia for them ever to be just friends. If either one of them was going to move on with someone else, it would have to be without the other one around.

But he couldn't go yet. He wasn't ready to say good-bye to Alicia.

After tossing one last rock into the water, he headed back to the house. It was late morning by the time he got back; he hadn't realized how long he'd been gone. The Jeep that Alicia had been using was not in the driveway. He was just about to go around to the garage to get his tools when the front door opened and George stepped onto the porch.

"Gabe, I was hoping to run into you. Any chance I could beg a lift into town? Alicia took off early, and I can't reach her on her cell phone. Bill and I are going to pick up some equipment down in Sacramento, but he can't leave his store until his assistant gets in, so I need a ride."

"Sure, no problem," he said. "I can bring the truck around."

"No need. I'll walk over with you."

"You don't have your cane," Gabe commented.

George gave him a smile. "I don't need it anymore. I was relying too much on it. When I put it away, I suddenly felt stronger."

"That's great."

"I was waiting," George continued as they walked across the grass. "Waiting for Rob to come home and fix things. All my life, I was in charge, but after the accident, I felt as weak as a baby. I had to depend on everyone, and I guess it got to be a habit—a bad habit. Then Rob died, and I wasn't sure if Alicia or I could come back from that, but after the fire, something inside me changed. I woke up. I'm not going to let someone else destroy me. If I go down, I go down on my own terms."

Gabe was impressed by the fire in George's voice, the steel glint of determination in his eyes. He could see where Alicia got her core of strength.

"Some people may think I'm a fool to throw myself into a venture that's on its last legs, but the rough water is always the most fun to ride. And whatever happens, I'll know I gave it my all. I can live with that. Giving up I can't stomach. Thankfully, Alicia seems to be on board. And I appreciate all your help, too. I can't wait to take you down the river. You're going to love it. It's a rush like none other."

"I'm looking forward to it," Gabe said as they got into his truck.

"Once we get the new equipment, we'll take a test run, get our sea legs back. It's all going to work out," George said confidently. "God, I feel good today."

"I can see that."

"And I can see you're as out of sorts as Alicia was last night when she was stomping around the house."

"She's got a lot on her mind."

"You're on her mind. I've seen the way the two of you look at each other. It's none of my business, so I'm not going to ask, but I am going to tell you this."

"What's that?"

"If you hurt her, I will kick your ass."

Gabe smiled at him. "I can hear Rob in my head saying the exact same thing."

Twenty

After dropping Justin at school, Alicia ran errands and killed some time at the local nursery picking out new plants for her garden. It was all part of a plan to avoid going home. She wasn't quite ready to face Gabe after their intense conversation the night before. Not to mention the fact that despite her declaration of independence, she wasn't all that sure that she wouldn't throw herself into his arms again the first chance she got. By one o'clock, she had run out of things to do. Fortunately, when she returned home, Gabe was nowhere to be seen.

She tidied up the house, checking her watch every now and then, knowing that there were a million things she should be doing, but she couldn't seem to concentrate. It was a shame, too, because while Justin had a half day at school, he and David were working on a school project in the library until five, so she should be taking advantage of the free time.

Her doorbell rang, and her pulse leaped in response. She was shocked to find Kelly on the porch.

Kelly gave her an uncertain look. "Can I talk to you?"

She drew in a deep breath, noting the lines of weariness on Kelly's face. While she was in town, she'd heard that Kelly's mother had undergone her surgery. She really hoped it had gone well. Kelly had had enough tragedy in her life. "Come in."

Kelly followed her into the living room. "Is your dad home?"

"No. It's just us. Why are you here?"

"To talk about what happened." Kelly sat down on the couch. "You said the other day that I never gave you a chance to explain, that I never listened to you. Well, I'm ready to listen if you still want to talk."

Alicia sat in the armchair. "I don't even know what to say anymore. I'm not going to change your mind."

"I do have a question," Kelly said, twisting her fingers together. "Jared said that Brian and two of his friends took a hike during lunch. Did you notice anything odd about their behavior?"

Alicia's heart skipped a beat. "I remember thinking that they were in a great mood and they had a lot of energy considering how long we'd already been on the river."

"More so than some of the other guys?"

"What are you asking me, Kelly?"

Kelly's lips tightened. "I'm not sure."

"Did something happen at lunch that I don't know about?"

"I don't know. I need to talk to Marco and John. They were with Brian during lunch. Is there anything else you can tell me that I might not know?"

"We checked our equipment very carefully before the trip. We knew we were taking a tough run, so we were extra careful. If there was any damage to the raft, it occurred when it hit the rocks." She paused. "As for whether I made a mistake as the guide on that raft, I don't know. I did the best job I could. The water was higher and faster than I expected. I did see my dad's boat flip. Did that distract me? Possibly." She took a breath. "I went into the water with everyone else so I didn't see what happened to Brian. I know he was a good swimmer, and he had a life jacket, but it appears that he hit his head on a rock and was knocked unconscious. That's not something anyone can prevent."

Kelly blew out a breath and sat back against the couch. "It's hard to accept that there's no reason for someone you love to die. Harder still to accept that there's no one to blame."

"Do you accept that?" Alicia asked, feeling more hopeful than she had in a long time.

"I'm trying to. I don't want to betray Brian. And I love the Farrs; they're my second family. And all of Brian's other friends were there for me after his death. They all thought the same way, and I didn't feel that I could break away from them. But the fire the other day . . ." She shook her head. "That was wrong. And I can't stand by and do nothing anymore. I talked to Russell. He said he didn't do it."

"Do you believe him?"

"He's very angry." Kelly paused. "I'm worried, Alicia, because I don't think I can stop whatever is happening. And I'm not sure it's over yet. You're rebuilding. Whoever set the fire is going to be angry that it didn't stop you. I don't know what they're going to do next."

A tingle of fear ran down Alicia's spine. It was one thing to say that she wasn't going to let anyone stop her and another to have to deal with whatever came next. She had a child to protect, along with a stubborn and proud father. She needed to be the smart one.

"Are you sure you can't just quit, Alicia?" Kelly asked.

"If it was just me, maybe. But it's my dad's life, his passion. And he deserves to live his life the way he wants to. It's strange, but his depression lifted after the fire. It's like he woke up and his anger energized him. He might actually be able to guide again. He's fighting for something now. And I guess I am, too."

"We always used to be on the same side."

"Yeah, it's strange to think of you as the enemy."

"I'm not your enemy, Alicia."

"Really, Kelly?"

"I've always loved you like a sister. I shouldn't have abandoned you. I shouldn't have listened to everyone else but you."

Relief ran through her. "I can't believe you're saying this. I wasn't sure we'd ever be able to get past what happened."

"I want to." Kelly took another deep breath. "There's something else I need to tell you. I just don't know if I should. My mom is in the hospital, recovering from surgery, and I don't want to jeopardize her health."

"Okay, I'm confused. What does any of this have to do with your mom?"

"You care about my mom, don't you?" Kelly asked.

"Of course I do. She was like my second mother. And she wrote me a really nice letter after Rob died. She had Nora drop off some food, too. She was so sweet about it." She paused, knowing that Kelly wasn't asking her if she cared about her mom just for the fun of it. "What do you have to say? Is it about Ian? Because I saw him the other day at Justin's baseball game, and I got a bad vibe. He's in some kind of trouble, isn't he?"

"Yes. I'm going to tell you something, and I'm really hoping that you won't go to the police with it yet."

Her stomach turned over. "Just say it."

"Ian cut the fuel line on your car."

"No." She sat back in her chair, feeling suddenly sick. "Why? Why would he do that?"

"He owed someone money, and they said if he did it, it would clear his debt. He told me he didn't set the fire, though, and I believe him. He was really scared."

"Where is he now?"

"I don't know. I haven't seen him since he told me the other night." Kelly paused. "Part of me didn't want to tell you. Ian is my little brother. I need to protect him, but I also can't let him get away with this."

"I'm shocked. I can't believe Ian would do that to me. No wonder he was in such a hurry to get away from me the other day."

"I want Ian to turn himself in. Do you think you could hold off telling the police what he did?"

It was a big request, considering the state of their friendship.

While she was thinking, her cell phone rang. "Hold on a second." She took the call. "Keith? I'm in the middle of something. Can I call you back?"

"No, you can't," he said tersely. "I'm at the elementary school, Alicia. I got off earlier than expected, and I thought I'd help the boys out with their project, but they're not here."

Her heart stopped. "What do you mean? They have to be there. Did you check the library?"

"The library closed when classes got out. I spoke to their teacher. She said she knows of no project and that the last time she saw them was when they left class together at noon."

"It's two o'clock now," she said, fear rushing through her. "I'm coming down there." She jumped to her feet. "We need to call the police."

"They're already here. I've got everyone in the school searching for them."

"Oh, my God, this can't be happening." Nausea flipped her stomach. She wanted to throw up, to scream. The fear of her child being missing was so overwhelming she couldn't think.

"Try not to jump to the worst conclusion," Keith said.

"How can I not? Someone cut my gas line, burned down our property, and now my son is missing!"

"Well, he's not alone. He's got David with him."

She could hear the anger in his voice. He was blaming her, but she couldn't deal with that right now. "I'll be down there as fast as I can."

"What's happened?" Kelly asked, already on her feet. "Is Justin missing?"

"And his friend David. They said they were doing a project in the library, but they're not there, and the teacher said she didn't assign them any project." She searched wildly for her keys, panic making it difficult to focus.

"I'll take you. You're too upset to drive."

"I have to find him, Kelly. I have to."

"You will, Alicia. I know you will."

Their eyes met, and for the first time in a long time, they were in perfect accord.

They ran to the car. Kelly started the engine and pulled out of the driveway with a squeal of her tires. "If both boys are missing," Kelly said, "then maybe they just went somewhere and didn't want you to know."

"I can't imagine where that would be. Justin is only nine. He's not allowed to go anywhere by himself. It doesn't make sense."

"It also doesn't make sense that someone could snatch up two boys without anyone seeing anything."

"Unless the boys knew the person." Her gaze met Kelly's. "Ian."

Kelly immediately shook her head, but there was worry in her eyes. "Ian would never hurt Justin. He considers him like a little brother. He taught him how to fish and throw a football. He wouldn't hurt him," she repeated.

"He cut my gas line. Did you think he would ever do that?"

"No, but he just wanted you to run out of gas, to be inconvenienced. That's a far cry from kidnapping."

"Unless someone had something really bad over him."

"Alicia, if Ian took the boys anywhere, it was just to worry you, not to hurt them. I'd bet my life on that."

"It's not your life you're betting. It's Justin's and David's."

Kelly blew out a breath. "I know."

They didn't speak the rest of the way.

When they arrived at the school, the police were there, and dozens of people were huddled around. Alicia zeroed in on Keith, racing across the playground to talk to him. The fear in his eyes scared her even more.

"Is there any news?"

"One of the other kids saw Justin and David go to the library after school. He said they told him that they had found a way to get to Five Arrows Point," he said. "No one saw them after that. Classes were out. Teachers were in conferences. I'm thinking maybe they're trying to find the place on their own."

"How? They don't have their bikes or even their skateboards. And it's too far to walk—they both know that."

"To kids their age, the distance probably doesn't seem real." He shook his head. "I never should have encouraged them to look on the Internet. I printed out a damn map for them."

"Somebody had to take them there," she said. She looked over at Kelly, knowing she was breaking the confidence, but she couldn't keep the secret now. "I think it might be Ian, Kelly's brother."

"Why? I didn't think Ian was even talking to you or to Justin." He paused, his gaze swinging to Kelly. "This is about your feud with the town," he added, anger filling his eyes. "My kid is in danger because you won't shut down your business, Alicia. Someone took the boys to get to you."

"Maybe they just went to find the arrowheads," Kelly suggested, moving closer. "You said they printed up a map, and they told you both a lie about where they would be this afternoon. They probably planned to be back by the time you picked them up."

"Why would I believe you?" Keith asked. "You're part of everything that's been going on. I'm going to talk to the cops and tell them to look for your brother."

As Keith strode away, Alicia looked at Kelly. "I'm sorry. I had to tell him."

"Of course you did. And he's right. I've been part of the problem. But no more. We're going to find Justin, Alicia."

Despite her optimistic words, it soon became clear that the

boys were not at the school. They'd searched every nook and cranny and interviewed whoever was still at the school.

Alicia and Kelly met back up with Keith and the chief of police, Ronnie D'Amico, in the school office. The principal hovered in the background, looking very concerned. They'd never had a child go missing in River Rock. The small-town community had always been a very safe place to live, until now.

"I'm sending some officers around the neighborhood," the chief said. "I'm going to drive down to where most people start the search for Five Arrows Point and see if anyone has seen the kids."

"That's at least six miles away," Alicia said.

Ronnie nodded. "Maybe they got a ride. Everyone at school told me the same story, that the boys were determined to go looking for the arrowheads. It's our best lead."

"I'll go with you," Keith said.

"I'll come, too," Alicia said immediately.

Keith shook his head. "You need to go home, in case the boys come back."

"I'm not going to sit at home and do nothing."

"You'll be doing something. You'll be waiting for them. I'll call you as soon as we get there. We'll check in every five minutes, okay?"

She didn't want to be sidelined, but maybe spreading out would be a smarter idea. She had no intention, however, of just going home.

"We need to talk to Russell," she said to Kelly as they walked back to the car.

Kelly nodded. "You read my mind."

"Good, because I might need you to get him to talk to me."

Russell was out. His assistant told them that he'd gone to Sacramento that morning for a meeting and wouldn't be back until later that night. Kelly tried to reach him on his cell phone, but it went to voice-mail. Ian didn't answer her calls, either.

"This isn't getting us anywhere," Alicia said in frustration as they returned to the car to debate their next move.

"Maybe the boys really did just go look for the arrowheads."

"But they had to have help. Someone gave them a ride. And I can't believe they would get into a car with someone they didn't know."

"Which brings us back to Ian," Kelly said with a sigh. "Would he know that they wanted to look for the arrowheads?"

"He was at Justin's ball game the other day. And if you were within ten feet of Justin this past month, you would have heard about his desire to follow the warrior's path. He's had everyone looking stuff up for him, even the school librarian." She stopped abruptly, clapping a hand to her mouth. "Oh, my God." She turned to Kelly and saw the same conclusion in her eyes. "Mrs. Farr works at the school library."

"Dina?" Kelly said doubtfully. "She wouldn't hurt Justin. She's a mother, and she loves children."

"She's a mother who lost her child, a mother who blames me. Let's go to her house."

"Alicia," Kelly began.

"No, don't bail on me now. I need you, Kelly. I need you to be my best friend, because no matter what you think I did, Justin did nothing, and neither did his friend. Those boys are the only important people right now. Not me or you or even Brian."

"I know that. And I'm not bailing. Whatever the truth is, we both need to find it."

It was a short five-minute ride to the Farrs' house. No one answered the bell, so they went around to the back door. It wasn't open, but it was unlocked. They entered the house, calling Dina's name.

"I don't think she's here, and I know Lowell is out of town," Kelly said as they paused in the living room. "Look at all this," she said in confusion and concern.

Alicia followed her gaze. There were photographs of Brian everywhere, stacks loose on the coffee table, others on the floor, scrapbooks on the couch, press clippings from Brian's days as a basketball star, and a box of trophies and medals. Brian's entire life covered every inch of the room. Her stomach turned over. This was no ordinary scene. This was obsession.

"I had no idea," Kelly whispered. "She seemed to be holding everything together the last time I saw her, like she'd been able to grieve and move on."

"It doesn't look like she's moved on to me."

"Lowell has been gone for a few weeks visiting his sister. The loneliness must have gotten to her."

Alicia moved over to the desk, and her heart sank even further as she saw the stack of printed pages from the Internet, all stories about Five Arrows Point. "She has to have Justin and David." Alicia held up the paper. "She must have told them she'd take them there. They told me they were going to the library. It all makes sense."

Her cell phone rang, and she jumped on it. "Keith—did you find them?"

"No, but we ran into a hiker who said he saw two boys with

a woman standing next to a car. But the car is gone, and there's no sign of the kids. We're going to search the woods."

"Tell the chief they're probably with Dina Farr," she said in a rush. "I'm at her house, and it's clear she's been obsessing over Brian's death, and there's a bunch of stuff here about the legend. She must have used the story to get them to go with her. She works in the library, and that's where they said they were going. She wants to pay me back, Keith. She wants me to know what it feels like to lose a son." Her legs felt so weak she had to put out a hand to steady herself.

"You won't lose Justin, and I'm not going to lose David. I'll tell the chief. I'll call you back when I know anything. The kids can't have gotten too far."

"If you're in the right place," she said. "No one knows exactly where the rocks are. That's why there are so many different maps."

"The chief said this is where most people come."

"By car," she said, another idea taking root in her head. "Call me as soon as you know anything."

"I will."

As she ended the call, she said to Kelly, "We need to go back to my house."

"You have a plan, don't you? I recognize that look in your eyes."

"It's a plan that has to work," she said. "It just has to."

Gabe was waiting on the porch when they returned, his face white, his eyes dark and worried. "What's going on, Alicia? I was just in town and heard that Justin is missing. I tried calling you a half-dozen times."

"I'm sorry. I was talking to Keith," she said. "We think Mrs.

Farr took the boys with the promise of showing them Five Arrows Point."

"Mrs. Farr?" he echoed. "Brian's mother?"

"She's a part-time librarian at the school. The police and Keith are searching where they think she might have taken them, but there's a lot of ground to cover, and we only have a few hours before it gets dark."

"Then let's go. We'll look wherever they're not looking."

She swallowed hard. "The road only takes us so far, and Keith and the police have that covered. The best way to get into that area would be to take a raft down the river."

He stared back at her, a question in his eyes. "Can you do it?"

She was terrified at the thought of being out on the water. Her mind flashed back to the moment when she'd lost control of her raft, when they'd flipped into the water with astounding force. And then it was over her head, the current sucking her down, down, down . . .

"Alicia, snap out of it," Gabe said, grabbing her shoulders.

"I was just remembering that day."

His fingers bit into her arms. "What you have to remember is every other day that you made a successful run. What you have to focus on is getting your son back. Failure is not an option."

His eyes bored into hers, his iron will making her lift her chin. "I can do it."

He smiled at her. "I know you can."

She caught Kelly's worried, concerned look.

"Alicia," Kelly said hesitantly, "are you afraid of the water now?"

"We'll talk about it later, when Justin and David are safe. I just need to get on the raft."

"I'm coming with you," Gabe said.

She had no intention of arguing. She needed all the help she could get.

"We need supplies," he added as they headed toward the garage. "Flashlights for when it gets dark, blankets in case the boys are cold, water, maybe a snack," he rattled off.

"I'll get them," Kelly said, running toward the house.

Alicia entered the garage, thankful now that Gabe had already inflated the raft and that it hadn't lost any air in the past two days. It was ready to go, and once she got on board, she hoped that she would be ready to go, too.

She opened the storage locker and grabbed life jackets for four of them plus the emergency radio in case they couldn't get a cell signal out on the river. Then she and Gabe carried the raft down to the dock.

Kelly joined them there a few minutes later, tossing a backpack into the raft along with two blankets. "There's flashlights, food, and water," she said.

"Thanks," Alicia said as she and Gabe put the raft into the water. Kelly grabbed the rope, holding the raft steady as Alicia took a seat in the back and Gabe got into the front.

"I'll wait here until you get back," Kelly promised.

"Try to get hold of my dad," Alicia said. "He needs to know what's going on."

"I will." Kelly met Alicia's eyes. "Be safe. And bring our boy home."

Alicia's eyes blurred with tears. "I will."

Kelly tossed the rope into the raft and pushed them away from the dock.

As they drifted away from dry land, Alicia felt a moment of

pure terror. Her heart was beating so fast the blood was pounding in her ears. Panic made her want to flee, but it was too late; she was surrounded by water as the current took them away. What if she couldn't do this? What if the river tossed them out the way it had done before? If she drowned, Justin would end up without a mother.

"Alicia," Gabe said loudly, turning sideways so he could see her face. "Look at me. Tell me what to do."

"I—I don't know," she stuttered.

"Yes, you do know. You've done this a thousand times. We need to find Justin, and you're going to take us there."

"This was a mistake." Her eyes darted back to the dock, where Kelly was getting smaller and smaller in the distance. "I could kill us both."

"That's not going to happen."

"You don't know that!" she cried. "You don't know that I didn't mess up and that's why Brian drowned."

"I know you," he said forcefully. "If you messed up, you would have admitted it. But this isn't about Brian or even about you. This is for Justin and David, and you would do anything for your child."

His words began to penetrate the fog of panic.

"You're in charge," he continued. "You're going to get us where we need to go. You're smart, and you're tough, and that's why I love you. Now, paddle the damn boat."

His determined gaze gave her the strength she needed, so she put her oar into the water, drew in a deep breath, and turned the raft downstream. Her fears began to diminish as she paddled, her overabundance of adrenaline finding release in the constant swoosh of the water. She'd done this a million times. She'd grown up on this river, and she knew it very well.

As they traveled, she gave Gabe a few instructions, the habits of a lifetime guiding her moves. But anxiety still pinched her nerves. It was calm along this part of the river. Farther downstream, the current would pick up, they would have to dodge some rocks and boulders, and the water was high, which was why rafting season hadn't started yet.

"It won't be like the last time," Gabe said loudly, his voice carrying on the wind. He flung another glance over his shoulder at her. "Hang in there, Alicia."

Was he reading her mind now? Had they gotten so close that he could tell what she was thinking before she said it?

"I'm okay," she said, trying to make herself believe it.

"I know you are."

A half hour later, the wind and the river began to pick up, the rough current matching the breeze blowing through her hair. Her muscles were beginning to ache after her six-month layoff, but she didn't slow down. She needed to stay strong, because the white water was coming up fast. There was no one else on the river, and as it wound through several tall, steep canyons, she felt as if they were the only two people in the world, as if they were going back in time to the days when the legend of the five arrows had first begun.

The first set of rapids wasn't too bad. She called out instructions to Gabe, who was quick to adapt. He was a natural on the raft, strong, quick, confident, focused—just the kind of partner she needed. And he seemed to anticipate what she was going to say before she said it, allowing her to concentrate on steering them through the boulder-strewn forks.

A few times, she questioned her choice of direction. She was going by memory and instinct. As they came to another fork, she paused for a second. She could swear she heard Rob's voice on the wind, or maybe it was just in her memory, telling her to go to the right, always to the right.

The next set of rapids was worse than she remembered, probably because the river was so high. She called out directions, and they flew down a small falls, water splashing into their faces. For a moment, the raft threatened to tip, but they both adjusted their weight, working as one until they were through the worst of it.

The river grew calm again, and Gabe glanced back at her, a light of excitement in his eyes. "That was crazy," he said. "Is there more?"

"I'm not sure," she said, scanning the shoreline. "Keep your eyes peeled for three tall trees very close together."

"Are you serious? There are trees everywhere."

"That's all I've got. It's been a long time since I made this trip. Let's get closer to the shore," she said, turning them in that direction.

For another twenty minutes, they sailed downriver, eyes glued to the winding edge of the shore. It was getting colder, and there in the canyons, where the rock walls were high and the trees were thick, it was getting darker, too. They needed to find the boys before night fell, and they had to get off the river. She took her cell phone out and tried to find a signal, but there wasn't one. When they found the boys, she'd use the radio and try to get word to Keith. It was possible that Keith and the police would find the kids before she and Gabe did. Justin and David might already be on their way home. But she wasn't going to quit until she'd covered as much ground as she could.

They hit another rapid but maneuvered their way through without any problems. She was no longer worried about handling the raft, only about finding the kids before the sun went all the way down.

Her confidence was beginning to shake as dusk fell and the shadows grew longer. It was dangerous to be on the river after dark and even more dangerous for the boys to be alone in the woods when night fell. Suddenly, she saw a flash of color up ahead. "Do you see that?" she shouted.

"What?"

"Red—through the trees." She turned the boat toward the shore, the color getting brighter as they drew closer. And then two figures broke through the shadows, one wearing a bright red T-shirt. "Oh, my God, it's them! Justin!" she yelled.

"Don't flip us now," Gabe warned as she bounced up and down on the back of the raft.

"Justin!" she screamed.

One of the figures looked up, and then the two started running toward the river. She paddled as fast as she could, Gabe keeping up stroke for stroke until they reached the shore. She jumped out of the boat before they were completely on dry land, racing to her son.

She flung her arms around both boys as tears streamed down her face.

"You're squishing us," Justin said finally.

It hurt to let them go for even a second, but she finally pulled away, raking her eyes over their tired, scared faces, making sure that there was no blood, no broken bones. They appeared to be fine. There was evidence of tears on David's cheeks, but the light of adventure was in Justin's eyes.

"I'm hungry," Justin said.

"Me, too," David added.

She laughed through her tears. Gabe handed her the backpack, and she pulled out the granola bars that Kelly had packed. She handed them each a bar and a bottle of water. They sat down on the ground together.

"You scared me to death," she told Justin. "What happened? How did you get here?"

"The library lady brought us."

Her stomach dropped. He'd confirmed her fears that Mrs. Farr was involved.

"She said she'd help us find the arrowheads," Justin added.

"She had a map," David put in.

"She showed us where the braves were dropped off to begin their journey, and she said she'd be there when we got back. But we kind of got lost."

Anger rocketed through her, but she told herself to get a grip. She would deal with Mrs. Farr later.

"Why didn't you stay where you were?" Gabe asked Justin.

"Because Grandpa said to follow the river. That the river will always bring you home."

She sighed at Justin's somewhat lopsided logic. "That's if you're in a boat, kid."

"Oh." Justin gave her a wary look. "Am I in trouble?"

"More trouble than you've *ever* been in."

"Where's my dad?" David asked.

"He's searching the woods for you two. He's been looking for you for hours, along with the police department and half the town. I need to tell him you're okay." She grabbed the backpack, tried her phone, and couldn't get a signal, then pulled out the emergency radio, which would send a signal to Kelly on the other end. Then Kelly would let everyone know that they were okay and that they had Justin and David.

"We need to stay here tonight," Gabe said, squatting down next to them. "It's too dark to go through the woods or get back into the boat."

"We're going to camp out?" Justin asked with excitement. Now that they were all together, he was looking forward to more adventure.

"Yes, until it gets light enough to make it out of the woods," Gabe said. "We need to do a few things before night falls."

"Like what?" Justin asked.

"Build a fire to get your mom's feet dry, for one," he said, sending her a pointed look.

His words reminded her that her feet and shoes were soaking wet, and her toes were already getting cold in the night air.

"Then we'll set up a shelter. I'm going to need you two to help," he added.

Both boys jumped to their feet, ready to follow Gabe's orders.

She watched in amazement as he used sticks and the tarp to build them a shelter. He didn't rub two sticks together to get fire, but his lighter came in handy, and soon there was a fire going in the middle of what was quickly becoming a campsite. She pulled off her shoes and socks and warmed her feet by the fire while Gabe taught the boys some basic survival skills. He was definitely in charge now, and she liked seeing him take command. The boys were happy to follow, because he treated them with respect. In fact, they worked damned hard to impress him. When the site was done, they all sat around the fire, sharing the last of the granola bars.

"This is cool," Justin said, and David nodded his agreement.

"It wasn't cool to take off without telling your parents," Gabe said firmly, stealing the words right out of her mouth.

Justin exchanged a guilty look with David but then said grumpily, "We just wanted to find the arrowheads before my birthday, and no one would take us."

"Doing what you did just proved that you weren't ready to make this journey," Gabe said. "The braves who started their trek were prepared for what they were going to encounter. They had been taught how to survive in the woods, to deal with the challenges that would face them. They were ready to prove themselves."

"We were ready," Justin said.

"Don't talk back," Alicia told him.

"It's okay, I've got this," Gabe said.

"All right," she said, a little surprised and curious to see how Gabe was going to deal with the kids.

"The braves had to exhibit five important traits in order to become warriors. Their journey to the rock wasn't so much about collecting the arrowheads along the way; it was about proving themselves worthy of the honor of being a warrior. You two showed courage when you got lost, wisdom when you followed the river, perseverance by trying to find your way home, and sacrifice when you shared your food with each other. But the one thing you didn't exhibit was patience. You didn't wait until someone could go with you on your journey. You scared your parents and half the town. That's not what men do."

"We're not men; we're only ten," Justin said.

Her son was never at a loss for words.

"You're not braves, either. You're kids," Gabe retorted. "And you owe your parents an apology."

"I'm sorry, Mom," Justin said immediately.

"I'm sorry, too," David said, rubbing his eyes with his hand. "I want my dad."

"You'll see him in the morning, honey," she said, putting her arm around David's shoulders.

Justin also scooted closer to his best friend. "It's going to be okay," he said. "I'll tell Keith it was my idea. Then he won't get so mad at you."

Her son might be headstrong and impulsive, but he was a good friend, and in spite of the bad choices he'd made, she was proud of him.

After Gabe's lecture, they talked of other things, and before long, the two tired boys were stretched out under the shelter, fast asleep.

Gabe moved around the fire to sit next to her. He put an arm around her shoulders as she leaned back against a fallen log. "You were amazing today," he said quietly.

"I was going to say the same thing to you. I couldn't have done this without you. I'm not sure I could have gotten into the raft if you weren't with me, and you pushed me when I needed to be pushed."

"I knew you could do it, Alicia. You have an amazing core of strength. Life may knock you down, but you always get back up."

"So do you," she said. "Apparently, we're both survivors."

"And warriors," he said with a smile. "You exhibited courage by facing your biggest fear, wisdom by getting prepared before you set off—"

"That was your idea," she cut in.

"You would have thought of it. I just beat you to the punch. And you showed perseverance through the white water, sacrifice by putting your life on the line for your kid, and patience by not giving up when it looked like we weren't going to find them. I now pronounce you a true warrior."

"Nice spin," she said with a smile. "The warrior's journey is a good metaphor for life."

"One worth following."

"I can't believe Mrs. Farr played on Justin's obsession and dropped the kids off alone in the woods. She's worked at the school for years. She's always been good with kids, but she used their trust in her to put them in danger." Anger ripped through her again. "What the hell is wrong with her?"

"Payback. You took her son. She took yours."

Alicia shook her head. "That's sick. How could she think she would get away with it, when the boys could identify her?"

"It doesn't sound like she was thinking. Grief can do strange things to people."

"I wonder if she set the fire, too." She paused. "Kelly told me earlier that her brother, Ian, was the one who cut my fuel line. Apparently, he owed money to some bookie, and the guy said that if he cut my line, his debt would be erased."

"Kelly ratted out her brother?" he said in surprise.

"Yes. Apparently, the fire scared her out of the cocoon of denial she's been living in. She finally acted, instead of letting everyone else around her act on her behalf. That's why she came to see me. I think we might actually be able to reclaim our friendship. I hope so; I've really missed her."

"I'm glad," he said with a smile. "The attacks should stop now. Once the police pick up Mrs. Farr, I suspect she'll reveal if it was her or one of her family or friends who set the fire."

"I hope it's over. Keith was so angry with me when he realized that it was my business that put David's life in danger. He'd been pleading with me to give it up before someone got hurt, but I was too stubborn, too determined to stand by principle."

"That's not a bad thing," Gabe commented.

"You'd be feeling differently if we hadn't found the kids."

"I'd be angry at whoever put them in danger but not at you."

"Thank you."

"I was very impressed with how you handled the river. You're very good at what you do."

"Oh, those rapids were not that big."

"Seriously?" he asked. "It gets better than that?"

She smiled at the expression on his face. "You liked it, didn't you?"

"It was a rush," he admitted. "I'd enjoy doing it again."

"I knew you would like it. You're a risk taker."

"In some areas," he said quietly.

A minute or two of silence passed between them.

"Gabe," she ventured. "When you said you loved me before, was it just something you said in the moment?"

He gazed back at her. "No. I do love you, Alicia. I fell for you the first minute I saw you, and I haven't found my feet since. You scare the hell out of me, making me want things that I told myself I would never have."

"You could have them," she said softly. "If you'd stop running away from me."

"I'm afraid I'll let you down."

"You won't."

"How can you be sure?"

She framed his face with her hands. "Because failure is not an option."

He smiled back. "Do you remember everything I say?"

"Only the important stuff. You *won't* let me down, Gabe. When you commit, you don't quit. The question is, are you ready to go all in?"

His long silence stretched her nerves to the breaking point. Was she pushing for too much too soon?

"All I really want," she said quickly, "is a chance. I know my life is different from yours, that you might not want to take on a wife, a kid, and a father-in-law, that you might not be happy to live in River Rock, but all of those things we can work out— if you want to work them out. I know you love the adrenaline rush of the Marines, but we can find some rapids—"

"Shh," he said, putting his hand over her mouth. "I didn't join the Marines for the thrill of fighting; I joined for a family. I reupped three years ago because Rob was going back, and I didn't want to leave him alone."

She was shocked. "You never said that before."

"I don't think I realized it until recently. But to be completely honest, that wasn't the whole reason. I didn't know how to walk away from something I knew to go after something that seemed impossible."

"It's not impossible."

"I hope not, because I want everything you just said." He

wrapped his arms around her. "I want you and Justin and your dad." She leaned in for his kiss, but he held her away. "What about Keith?"

"He knows we're not right for each other. We talked about it yesterday. He deserves someone who's madly in love with him, and that's not me."

"He's a good guy."

"He is, but he's not the right guy for me."

"Justin will be disappointed."

She gazed at her sleeping son. "I think Justin will be just fine." She turned back to him. "I love you, Gabe. And I hope you know that when I commit, I don't quit, either. If we get together, you're going to be stuck with me forever."

"I just hope that's long enough," he said, before sealing the promise with a passionate and tender kiss.

They sat by the fire, talking quietly about the future until they drifted asleep, wrapped in each other's arms.

They woke up early, the sun very low in the sky. They were debating whether to raft farther downstream or hike through the woods to the main road, when the search party found them. Keith led the pack, breaking into a run when he saw David.

Alicia put her arm around Justin's shoulders as she watched their reunion. She cared very much for both of them, but they couldn't be a real family without love, the kind of love she shared with Gabe.

Keith finally broke away from David and gave her a grateful smile. "Thank you, Alicia. I was so relieved when I got the message that you had found them. We were miles away from here. If you hadn't gone down the river, they might still be lost in these woods."

"I'm sorry this happened," she said.

"It wasn't your fault. I apologize for being so hard on you yesterday."

"I understood where you were coming from."

Keith let go of David and walked over to Gabe, extending his hand. "Thank you."

Gabe shook his hand. "Your son was very brave."

"We both were," Justin put in, never one to be out of the spotlight.

"And you're both in trouble," Keith said. "We'll talk about that when we get home."

The chief of police stepped forward, giving Alicia a smile. "Nice to see all of you."

"And you," she said. "We thought we might have a long trek back."

"We're not too far away. We found Mrs. Farr wandering around town, holding Brian's old teddy bear in her arms, telling whoever would listen that she had done a terrible thing," Ronnie said. "She's been arrested, and she's undergoing psychiatric evaluation."

The news didn't make Alicia feel any better. She was furious with Dina for endangering her son's life, but there was also a part of her that understood the mother's pain that Dina had gone through when she'd lost her son. She hoped Dina could get some help, but she still needed to pay for what she had done.

"Did she set the fire, too?" she asked.

"She said she did, but we're going to follow up and make

sure no one else was involved." He paused. "I'm sorry, Alicia, for everything you've been through. I didn't realize that things were going to get this bad."

"I didn't, either, Ronnie. I'm just glad it's over."

Their hike through the woods took about thirty minutes. The chief gave Alicia, Gabe, and Justin a ride home, while Keith and David headed home in another patrol car. At her house, Alicia was stunned to find a crowd waiting.

As they got out of the car, there were cheers and hugs from family, friends, and neighbors, many of whom had not been speaking to them for the last six months. Apparently, Justin and David's disappearance had put everything in perspective.

Kelly stood on the lawn with Alicia's father. When she saw Justin, she opened her arms, and Justin went flying into her embrace. She hugged him tight, giving Alicia a teary smile. "I'm so glad you found him. I was so worried. I'm never letting you two go again."

"I feel the same way," Alicia said.

"How come so many people are here?" Justin asked, clearly oblivious to the worry that his disappearance had brought to so many people.

"Go into the house, honey," Alicia said as Russell Farr stepped forward. Whatever he had to say, she didn't want Justin hearing it. "Dad?"

He nodded and grabbed Justin's hand. "You'd better tell me what you did, young man."

"We went looking for the arrowheads," Justin said with excitement as he disappeared into the house with his grandfather.

As Russell walked toward Alicia, the rest of the crowd fell

back—except for Gabe. He moved next to Alicia's side, and she was grateful for his presence.

"Alicia," Russell said, glancing over at Kelly.

Kelly gave him an encouraging nod, but he still looked like he had a mouth full of nails.

Finally, he said, "I'm sorry for what happened and for my mother's involvement. I had no idea she was in such bad shape." He paused. "Kelly told me that my anger fed my mother's pain, and she's right. I wasn't just pissed off at you and your father; I was furious with myself. It was my idea to take that trip, and I didn't save my brother. I couldn't live with the regret, so I took it out on you."

Alicia was shocked by the admission.

"We were all wrong," Kelly said loudly, looking around the crowd, "to blame you and your father for what was an accident. I spoke to one of Brian's friends, Marco. After some persuasion, he admitted to me that he and Brian and John drank shots of vodka on their lunch break that day. It was in their water bottles."

Alicia shook her head. Her instincts about Brian's behavior had been right. "I told them how dangerous the run was before we left. They knew there was no alcohol allowed. I never thought to check their water bottles."

"Why would you? They were grown men." Kelly took a deep breath. "We'll never know if the alcohol slowed Brian's reactions or if the current was just too strong. But what I know, and what I hope everyone else here knows, is that Brian wasn't a vengeful person. He loved rafting. He wanted to go on that trip. He was doing something that he enjoyed. When he died, he was living his life on his terms. And he would never want people seeking revenge on his behalf. He would hate that. And I hate it. I want it to stop." She looked at Russell.

"It stops now," he said.

The crowd applauded, and Russell walked away.

"Kelly, that was amazing," Alicia said, looking into the eyes of her best friend. She could see that Kelly was all the way back. There was no more fog in her gaze. No more fear.

"Ian is down at the police station, confessing to what he did. I'm on my way there now," Kelly told her.

"I don't want Ian to go to jail. Tell me what I need to do, and I'll do it."

"You need to let him take responsibility, and so do I."

"What about your mom?"

"She doesn't know anything yet. I'll tell her later." She put her arms around Alicia and gave her a tight hug. "I'm glad you're okay." She glanced over at Gabe, who had moved a few steps away. "Is he staying?"

"I really hope so," she said with a smile.

As Kelly left, Alicia was swarmed by family and friends. By the time they all were done telling her how sorry they were, she realized that Gabe had disappeared. She wanted to talk to him, but first, she needed to speak to her dad and make sure that Justin had whatever he needed. When she got into the house, both guys were asleep, Justin in his bed, her dad dozing in his armchair. She gave them both loving looks and went into her room to change clothes.

As she put on a fresh shirt, she noticed the white envelope on the dresser, and her heart started pounding faster.

Rob's letter. She'd never read it.

She opened the seal and pulled out a piece of paper.

Hey, Alicia. I hope you never read this letter, but if you do, I want to tell you a few things. I'm giving Gabe my house. I hope it doesn't hurt your feelings, but he needs somewhere to go. He's my best friend, and for three years, I've watched him try to pretend he doesn't care about you. I've seen you do the same thing. Did you two think I was stupid? I know you hooked up. I've been waiting for one of you to say something, but you're both damn stubborn.

She smiled through her tears.

So I made Gabe promise that if anything happened to me, he'd take the house, and he'd make sure you and Dad were okay. I'm worried about how things are going in town. And when I get home, I'm going to kick someone's ass about it. But if I don't make it back, then I'm relying on Gabe to do it.

She wiped her eyes with the back of her hand.

I told Gabe I was sending him to River Rock because you were going to need him. But the truth is, I'm sending him there because he needs you, Alicia. He's a good man, but he doesn't know how to let anyone love him. If anyone can get past his walls, it's you. And if you do, I guarantee that he'll stand by you for the rest of your life. So I'm hoping you two can work it out. You both need each other. And if you screw this up, I'm going to come back and haunt you.

Love you, Rob

Alicia sat for a moment, rereading some of it a second time. Then she put the letter back into the envelope, wiped her face with some tissues, and left the house.

She didn't bother to knock on Rob's door, just walked inside and barreled straight into Gabe, who appeared to be on his way out.

"I was just coming over to your house," he said. "I wanted to give you a minute to regroup."

"I'm fine," she said with a smile.

"That's good to hear," he said with love in his eyes. "Because I'm better than fine. And in case I haven't said it enough, I love you, and I'm staying here. You're never getting this house back."

"What are you going to do in this small town?"

He smiled. "Hell if I know. For the first time since I was eighteen years old, I don't have a plan."

"Sometimes plans are overrated."

"One thing I will do is love you, Alicia. I don't know if I'll be any good at it, but I'm going to try. I want to be the man you want me to be."

"You already are. You don't have to change. Just be you. That's who I fell in love with." She held up the letter. "I finally read this."

"What did Rob say?"

"That if we didn't get together, he would come back and haunt us."

Gabe grinned. "We can't have that."

"No, we can't," she said, before he kissed the breath out of her. "Wait," she said, gasping for air. "I want to say something else."

"What's that?"

"We don't have to stay here. We don't have to run my father's business."

"You love the river."

"I love you more," she said. "And I'll go wherever you want to go."

"We'll figure it out. Where's Justin?"

"Fast asleep. He's exhausted."

"So am I. Maybe we should go to bed," he suggested.

"If we do, you won't be getting any sleep for a while," she teased.

"I can live with that," he said as his mouth touched hers. Then he swept her up in his arms and carried her into the bedroom.

Epilogue

Two years later

Gabe stood on the front porch, looking down the wide expanse of lawn to the river that he had come to love. The boathouse and yard had been completely rebuilt, along with the dock. Rafting season would open in a couple of weeks, and they already had a full schedule booked. They'd hired four new guides who were very good at their jobs, and once in a while, he took on a run himself, loving the thrill of riding the white water. George and Alicia still took some fun runs, but Alicia spent most of her time selling her organic vegetables and herbs to local restaurants.

He'd found a love for building. Since settling in River Rock, he'd become a licensed contractor and was just finishing up the remodel next door. He'd turned Rob's one-story cabin into a two-story home with four bedrooms, two baths, and a big family room. He'd never imagined that he'd live in a house like that or that there would be enough people in his life to fill up the rooms—and to come to a birthday party.

But there were at least twenty people under the trees, enjoying a barbecue. George and Bill were at the grill, talking to neighbors and friends. Justin and David were throwing a football on the grass. Keith was there with a girlfriend, a new teacher at the elementary school. They'd all managed to stay friends for the sake of the kids, who were still as tight as ever.

The town had really come around since he'd first arrived in River Rock. Russell Farr had gotten married and moved away. Dina Farr was undergoing treatment in the prison ward of a mental institution in San Francisco. Her husband had moved there to be close to her. She'd apologized to Alicia through several letters, and both he and Alicia hoped that one day Dina could get her life back.

He turned his head as he heard Alicia calling, then headed over to the party.

"I need you," she said with a big smile.

He'd never get tired of hearing that. "What can I do?"

"Take your daughter," she said.

He swooped one-year-old Madeline Grace into his arms and stared into the blue eyes of his baby girl. She was such an angel; she made his heart ache with how much love he felt for her.

"And you can take your son," Alicia added. "I need to put candles on the cakes."

He moved Madeline to one arm so he could hold her twin, Andrew Robert. Andy had white-blond hair and looked a lot like Rob. He also had the same devilish personality. Even now, he was squirming to get down.

Gabe squatted so Andy could get down on the grass. His son was already walking. Maddie seemed more content to balance on his knees.

"Well, isn't this a picture?" Kelly teased, walking across the grass with her new husband, Jared. "You've got your hands full. Where's Alicia?"

"Putting candles on the cakes."

"As in two cakes?"

"She insists that the kids have their own cakes. Apparently, she always got stuck eating vanilla because it was Rob's favorite."

"Alicia will make sure that Maddie and Andy always feel special on their birthdays. Thank God we're not having twins," Kelly added to Jared.

"Yeah, one is enough," Jared said with a grin.

"One is never enough," Alicia interjected, returning with the candles. She hugged Kelly and gave her baby belly a loving pat. "I can't wait to meet your son. Two more weeks!"

"I'm hoping he comes while Ian is home for spring break."

"Ian is doing so well now," Alicia said. "He's graduating in June, right?"

"Yes, and then going to grad school to become a vet. He's finally moving in a good direction. No more gambling. No more bookies." She paused. "I can't believe Andy is walking."

"Maddie won't be far behind," Alicia proclaimed as they watched her crawl over to her brother.

"Then you'll really go crazy," Kelly declared.

"We love it," Alicia said, giving Gabe a warm smile. "Don't we, honey?"

"Absolutely," he said, getting to his feet. "Come over here and kiss me."

"You two should be careful with the kisses, or you'll end up with another set of twins," Jared joked.

Alicia gave Jared a smirking smile. "You and Kelly are all

over each other, too, so don't even start, Jared. I still can't believe she ended up with the guy who used to throw spit wads at her in second grade."

Jared grinned. "Will I never live that down? Gabe, you're lucky you didn't grow up around here. Some people have a long memory."

"I've already forgiven you for that," Kelly said with a smile. "Just don't teach our son that trick."

"I can't promise anything," Jared said. "Let's get something to drink. Do you two need anything?"

"I'm good," Alicia said.

"And I've got everything I need," Gabe said, meeting his wife's eyes. "More than I ever imagined. I have the perfect family."

Alicia kissed his lips. "And I have the perfect family man."